NON SANZ DROICT.

25d

William Shakespeare

The Tragedy of RICHARD the THIRD

EDITED BY MARK ECCLES

The Signet Classic Shakespeare
GENERAL EDITOR: SYLVAN BARNET

*Revised and Updated
Bibliography*

A SIGNET CLASSIC

NEW AMERICAN LIBRARY

NEW YORK AND SCARBOROUGH, ONTARIO

SIGNET, SIGNET CLASSIC, MENTOR, ONYX, PLUME, MERIDIAN AND
NAL BOOKS are published *in the United States* by
NAL PENGUIN INC.,
1633 Broadway, New York, New York 10019,
in Canada by The New American Library of Canada Limited,
81 Mack Avenue, Scarborough, Ontario M1L 1M8

First Printing, June, 1964

16   17   18   19   20   21   22   23   24

PRINTED IN THE UNITED STATES OF AMERICA

Contents

Shakespeare: Prefatory Remarks

Between the record of his baptism in Stratford on 26 April 1564 and the record of his burial in Stratford on 25 April 1616, some forty documents name Shakespeare, and many others name his parents, his children, and his grandchildren. More facts are known about William Shakespeare than about any other playwright of the period except Ben Jonson. The facts should, however, be distinguished from the legends. The latter, inevitably more engaging and better known, tell us that the Stratford boy killed a calf in high style, poached deer and rabbits, and was forced to flee to London, where he held horses outside a playhouse. These traditions are only traditions; they may be true, but no evidence supports them, and it is well to stick to the facts.

Mary Arden, the dramatist's mother, was the daughter of a substantial landowner; about 1557 she married John Shakespeare, who was a glove-maker and trader in various farm commodities. In 1557 John Shakespeare was a member of the Council (the governing body of Stratford), in 1558 a constable of the borough, in 1561 one of the two town chamberlains, in 1565 an alderman (entitling him to the appellation "Mr."), in 1568 high bailiff—the town's highest political office, equivalent to mayor. After 1577, for an unknown reason he drops out of local politics. The birthday of William Shakespeare, the eldest son of this locally prominent man, is unrecorded; but the Stratford parish register records that the infant was baptized on

26 April 1564. (It is quite possible that he was born on
23 April, but this date has probably been assigned by
tradition because it is the date on which, fifty-two years
later, he died.) The attendance records of the Stratford
grammar school of the period are not extant, but it is
reasonable to assume that the son of a local official attended the school and received substantial training in
Latin. The masters of the school from Shakespeare's seventh to fifteenth years held Oxford degrees; the Elizabethan curriculum excluded mathematics and the natural
sciences but taught a good deal of Latin rhetoric, logic,
and literature. On 27 November 1582 a marriage license
was issued to Shakespeare and Anne Hathaway, eight
years his senior. The couple had a child in May, 1583.
Perhaps the marriage was necessary, but perhaps the
couple had earlier engaged in a formal "troth plight"
which would render their children legitimate even if no
further ceremony were performed. In 1585 Anne Hathaway bore Shakespeare twins.

That Shakespeare was born is excellent; that he married
and had children is pleasant; but that we know nothing
about his departure from Stratford to London, or about
the beginning of his theatrical career, is lamentable and
must be admitted. We would gladly sacrifice details about
his children's baptism for details about his earliest days on
the stage. Perhaps the poaching episode is true (but it is
first reported almost a century after Shakespeare's death),
or perhaps he first left Stratford to be a schoolteacher, as
another tradition holds; perhaps he was moved by

> Such wind as scatters young men through the world,
> To seek their fortunes further than at home
> Where small experience grows.

In 1592, thanks to the cantankerousness of Robert
Greene, a rival playwright and a pamphleteer, we have
our first reference, a snarling one, to Shakespeare as an
actor and playwright. Greene warns those of his own educated friends who wrote for the theater against an actor
who has presumed to turn playwright:

There is an upstart crow, beautified with our feathers, that with his *tiger's heart wrapped in a player's hide* supposes he is as well able to bombast out a blank verse as the best of you, and being an absolute Johannes-factotum is in his own conceit the only Shake-scene in a country.

The reference to the player, as well as the allusion to Aesop's crow (who strutted in borrowed plumage, as an actor struts in fine words not his own), makes it clear that by this date Shakespeare had both acted and written. That Shakespeare is meant is indicated not only by "Shake-scene" but by the parody of a line from one of Shakespeare's plays, *3 Henry VI:* "O, tiger's heart wrapped in a woman's hide." If Shakespeare in 1592 was prominent enough to be attacked by an envious dramatist, he probably had served an apprenticeship in the theater for at least a few years.

In any case, by 1592 Shakespeare had acted and written, and there are a number of subsequent references to him as an actor: documents indicate that in 1598 he is a "principal comedian," in 1603 a "principal tragedian," in 1608 he is one of the "men players." The profession of actor was not for a gentleman, and it occasionally drew the scorn of university men who resented writing speeches for persons less educated than themselves, but it was respectable enough: players, if prosperous, were in effect members of the bourgeoisie, and there is nothing to suggest that Stratford considered William Shakespeare less than a solid citizen. When, in 1596, the Shakespeares were granted a coat of arms, the grant was made to Shakespeare's father, but probably William Shakespeare (who the next year bought the second-largest house in town) had arranged the matter on his own behalf. In subsequent transactions he is occasionally styled a gentleman.

Although in 1593 and 1594 Shakespeare published two narrative poems dedicated to the Earl of Southampton, *Venus and Adonis* and *The Rape of Lucrece,* and may well have written most or all of his sonnets in the middle nineties, Shakespeare's literary activity seems to have been

almost entirely devoted to the theater. (It may be significant that the two narrative poems were written in years
when the plague closed the theaters for several months.)
In 1594 he was a charter member of a theatrical company
called the Chamberlain's Men (which in 1603 changed its
name to the King's Men); until he retired to Stratford
(about 1611, apparently), he was with this remarkably
stable company. From 1599 the company acted primarily
at the Globe Theatre, in which Shakespeare held a one-
tenth interest. Other Elizabethan dramatists are known to
have acted, but no other is known also to have been en-
titled to a share in the profits of the playhouse.

Shakespeare's first eight published plays did not have
his name on them, but this is not remarkable; the most
popular play of the sixteenth century, Thomas Kyd's *The
Spanish Tragedy,* went through many editions without
naming Kyd, and Kyd's authorship is known only because
a book on the profession of acting happens to quote (and
attribute to Kyd) some lines on the interest of Roman
emperors in the drama. What is remarkable is that after
1598 Shakespeare's name commonly appears on printed
plays—some of which are not his. Another indication of
his popularity comes from Francis Meres, author of
Palladis Tamia: Wit's Treasury (1598): in this anthology
of snippets accompanied by an essay on literature, many
playwrights are mentioned, but Shakespeare's name oc-
curs more often than any other, and Shakespeare is the
only playwright whose plays are listed.

From his acting, playwriting, and share in a theater,
Shakespeare seems to have made considerable money. He
put it to work, making substantial investments in Stratford
real estate. When he made his will (less than a month before he died), he sought to leave his property intact to his
descendants. Of small bequests to relatives and to friends
(including three actors, Richard Burbage, John Heminges,
and Henry Condell), that to his wife of the second-best
bed has provoked the most comment; perhaps it was the
bed the couple had slept in, the best being reserved for
visitors. In any case, had Shakespeare not excepted it, the
bed would have gone (with the rest of his household pos-

sessions) to his daughter and her husband. On 25 April 1616 he was buried within the chancel of the church at Stratford. An unattractive monument to his memory, placed on a wall near the grave, says he died on 23 April. Over the grave itself are the lines, perhaps by Shakespeare, that (more than his literary fame) have kept his bones undisturbed in the crowded burial ground where old bones were often dislodged to make way for new:

> Good friend, for Jesus' sake forbear
> To dig the dust enclosèd here.
> Blessed be the man that spares these stones
> And cursed be he that moves my bones.

Thirty-seven plays, as well as some nondramatic poems, are held to constitute the Shakespeare canon. The dates of composition of most of the works are highly uncertain, but there is often evidence of a *terminus a quo* (starting point) and/or a *terminus ad quem* (terminal point) that provides a framework for intelligent guessing. For example, *Richard II* cannot be earlier than 1595, the publication date of some material to which it is indebted; *The Merchant of Venice* cannot be later than 1598, the year Francis Meres mentioned it. Sometimes arguments for a date hang on an alleged topical allusion, such as the lines about the unseasonable weather in *A Midsummer Night's Dream,* II.i.81–117, but such an allusion (if indeed it is an allusion) can be variously interpreted, and in any case there is always the possibility that a topical allusion was inserted during a revision, years after the composition of a play. Dates are often attributed on the basis of style, and although conjectures about style usually rest on other conjectures, sooner or later one must rely on one's literary sense. There is no real proof, for example, that *Othello* is not as early as *Romeo and Juliet,* but one feels *Othello* is later, and because the first record of its performance is 1604, one is glad enough to set its composition at that date and not push it back into Shakespeare's early years. The following chronology, then, is as much indebted to informed guesswork and sensitivity as it is to fact. The

dates, necessarily imprecise, indicate something like a
scholarly consensus.

PLAYS

1588–93	*The Comedy of Errors*
1588–94	*Love's Labor's Lost*
1590–91	*2 Henry VI*
1590–91	*3 Henry VI*
1591–92	*1 Henry VI*
1592–93	*Richard III*
1592–94	*Titus Andronicus*
1593–94	*The Taming of the Shrew*
1593–95	*The Two Gentlemen of Verona*
1594–96	*Romeo and Juliet*
1595	*Richard II*
1594–96	*A Midsummer Night's Dream*
1596–97	*King John*
1596–97	*The Merchant of Venice*
1597	*1 Henry IV*
1597–98	*2 Henry IV*
1598–1600	*Much Ado About Nothing*
1598–99	*Henry V*
1599	*Julius Caesar*
1599–1600	*As You Like It*
1599–1600	*Twelfth Night*
1600–01	*Hamlet*
1597–1601	*The Merry Wives of Windsor*
1601–02	*Troilus and Cressida*
1602–04	*All's Well That Ends Well*
1603–04	*Othello*
1604	*Measure for Measure*
1605–06	*King Lear*
1605–06	*Macbeth*
1606–07	*Antony and Cleopatra*
1605–08	*Timon of Athens*
1607–09	*Coriolanus*
1608–09	*Pericles*
1609–10	*Cymbeline*
1610	*The Winter's Tale*
1611–12	*The Tempest*

1612–13   *Henry VIII*

POEMS

1592   *Venus and Adonis*
1593–94   *The Rape of Lucrece*
1593–1600   *Sonnets*
1600–01   *The Phoenix and the Turtle*

Shakespeare's Theater

In Shakespeare's infancy, Elizabethan actors performed wherever they could—in great halls, at court, in the courtyards of inns. The innyards must have made rather unsatisfactory theaters: on some days they were unavailable because carters bringing goods to London used them as depots; when available, they had to be rented from the innkeeper; perhaps most important, London inns were subject to the Common Council of London, which was not well disposed toward theatricals. In 1574 the Common Council required that plays and playing places in London be licensed. It asserted that

> sundry great disorders and inconveniences have been found to ensue to this city by the inordinate haunting of great multitudes of people, specially youth, to plays, interludes, and shows, namely occasion of frays and quarrels, evil practices of incontinency in great inns having chambers and secret places adjoining to their open stages and galleries,

and ordered that innkeepers who wished licenses to hold performances put up a bond and make contributions to the poor.

The requirement that plays and innyard theaters be licensed, along with the other drawbacks of playing at inns, probably drove James Burbage (a carpenter-turned-actor) to rent in 1576 a plot of land northeast of the city walls and to build here—on property outside the jurisdiction of the city—England's first permanent construction designed for plays. He called it simply the Theatre. About all that is known of its construction is that it was wood. It soon had imitators, the most famous being the Globe (1599), built across the Thames (again outside the city's jurisdiction), out of timbers of the Theatre, which had been dismantled when Burbage's lease ran out.

There are three important sources of information about the structure of Elizabethan playhouses—drawings, a contract, and stage directions in plays. Of drawings, only the so-called De Witt drawing (c. 1596) of the Swan—really a friend's copy of De Witt's drawing—is of much significance. It shows a building of three tiers, with a stage jutting from a wall into the yard or center of the building. The tiers are roofed, and part of the stage is covered by a roof that projects from the rear and is supported at its front on two posts, but the groundlings, who paid a penny to stand in front of the stage, were exposed to the sky. (Performances in such a playhouse were held only in the daytime; artificial illumination was not used.) At the rear of the stage are two doors; above the stage is a gallery. The second major source of information, the contract for the Fortune, specifies that although the Globe is to be the model, the Fortune is to be square, eighty feet outside and fifty-five inside. The stage is to be forty-three feet broad, and is to extend into the middle of the yard (i.e., it is twenty-seven and a half feet deep). For patrons willing to pay more than the general admission charged of the groundlings, there were to be three galleries provided with seats. From the third chief source, stage directions, one learns that entrance to the stage was by doors, presumably spaced widely apart at the rear ("Enter one citizen at one door, and another at the other"), and that in addition to the platform stage there was occasionally some sort of curtained booth or alcove allowing for "discovery" scenes, and some sort of playing space "aloft" or "above" to represent (for example) the top of a city's walls or a room above the street. Doubtless each theater had its own peculiarities, but perhaps we can talk about a "typical" Elizabethan theater if we realize that no theater need exactly have fit the description, just as no father is the typical father with 3.7 children. This hypothetical theater is wooden, round or polygonal (in *Henry V* Shakespeare calls it a "wooden *O*"), capable of holding some eight hundred spectators standing in the yard around the projecting elevated stage and some fifteen hundred additional spectators seated in the three roofed galleries. The stage, protected by a "shadow" or "heavens" or roof, is entered by two doors; behind the doors is the "tiring house" (attiring house, i.e., dressing room), and above the doors is some sort of gallery that may sometimes hold spectators but that can be used (for example) as the bedroom from which Romeo—according to a stage direction in one text —"goeth down." Some evidence suggests that a throne can be lowered onto the platform stage, perhaps from the "shadow"; certainly characters can descend from the stage through a trap or traps into the cellar or "hell." Sometimes this space beneath the platform accommodates a sound-effects man or musician (in *Antony and Cleopatra* "music of the hautboys is under the stage") or an actor (in *Hamlet* the "Ghost cries under the stage"). Most characters simply walk on and off, but because there is no curtain in front of the platform, corpses will have to be carried off (Hamlet must lug Polonius' guts into the neighbor room), or will have to fall at the rear, where the curtain on the alcove or booth can be drawn to conceal them.

Such may have been the so-called "public theater." Another kind of theater, called the "private theater" because its much greater admission charge limited its audience to the wealthy or the prodigal, must be briefly mentioned. The private theater was basically a large room, entirely roofed and therefore artificially illuminated, with a stage at one end. In 1576 one such theater was established in Blackfriars, a Dominican priory in London that had been suppressed in 1538 and confiscated by the Crown and thus was not under the city's jurisdiction. All the actors in the Blackfriars theater were boys about eight to thirteen years old (in the public theaters similar boys played female parts; a boy Lady Macbeth played to a man Macbeth). This private theater had a precarious existence, and ceased operations in 1584. In 1596 James Burbage, who had already made theatrical history by building the Theatre, began to construct a second Blackfriars theater. He died in 1597, and for several years this second Blackfriars theater was used by a troupe of boys, but in 1608 two of Burbage's sons and five other actors (including Shakespeare) became joint operators of the theater, using it in the winter when the open-air Globe was unsuitable. Perhaps such a smaller theater, roofed, artificially illuminated, and with a tradition of a courtly audience, exerted an influence on Shakespeare's late plays.

Performances in the private theaters may well have had intermissions during which music was played, but in the public theaters the action was probably uninterrupted, flowing from scene to scene almost without a break. Actors would enter, speak, exit, and others would immediately enter and establish (if necessary) the new locale by a few properties and by words and gestures. Here are some samples of Shakespeare's scene painting:

> This is Illyria, lady.

> Well, this is the Forest of Arden.

> This castle hath a pleasant seat; the air
> Nimbly and sweetly recommends itself
> Unto our gentle senses.

On the other hand, it is a mistake to conceive of the Elizabethan stage as bare. Although Shakespeare's Chorus in *Henry V* calls the stage an "unworthy scaffold" and urges the spectators to "eke out our performance with your mind," there was considerable spectacle. The last act of *Macbeth,* for example, has five stage directions calling for "drum and colors," and another sort of appeal to the eye is indicated by the stage direction "Enter Macduff, with Macbeth's head." Some scenery and properties may have been substantial; doubtless a throne was used, and in one play of the period we encounter this direction: "Hector takes up a great piece of rock and casts at Ajax, who tears up a young tree by the roots and assails Hector."

The matter is of some importance, and will be glanced at again in the next section.

The Texts of Shakespeare

Though eighteen of his plays were published during his lifetime, Shakespeare seems never to have supervised their publication. There is nothing unusual here; when a playwright sold a play to a theatrical company he surrendered his ownership of it. Normally a company would not publish the play, because to publish it meant to allow competitors to acquire the piece. Some plays, however, did get published: apparently treacherous actors sometimes pieced together a play for a publisher, sometimes a company in need of money sold a play, and sometimes a company allowed a play to be published that no longer drew audiences. That Shakespeare did not concern himself with publication, then, is scarcely remarkable; of his contemporaries only Ben Jonson carefully supervised the publication of his own plays. In 1623, seven years after Shakespeare's death, John Heminges and Henry Condell (two senior members of Shakespeare's company, who had performed with him for about twenty years) collected his plays—published and unpublished—into a large volume, commonly called the First Folio. (A folio is a volume consisting of sheets that have been folded once, each sheet thus making two leaves, or four pages. The eighteen plays published during Shakespeare's lifetime had been issued one play per volume in small books called quartos. Each sheet in a quarto has been folded twice, making four leaves, or eight pages.) The First Folio contains thirty-six plays; a thirty-seventh, *Pericles,* though not in the Folio, is regarded as canonical. Heminges and Condell suggest in an address "To the great variety of readers" that the republished plays are presented in better form than in the quartos: "Before you were abused with diverse stolen and surreptitious copies, maimed and deformed by the frauds and stealths of injurious impostors that exposed them; even those, are now offered to your view cured and perfect of their limbs, and all the rest absolute in their numbers, as he [i.e., Shakespeare] conceived them."

Whoever was assigned to prepare the texts for publication in the First Folio seems to have taken his job seriously and yet not to have performed it with uniform care. The sources of the texts seem to have been, in general, good unpublished copies or the best published copies. The first play in the collection, *The Tempest,* is divided into acts and scenes, has unusually full stage directions and descriptions of spectacle, and concludes with a list of the characters, but the editor was not able (or willing) to present all of the succeeding texts so fully dressed. Later texts occasionally show signs of carelessness: in one scene of *Much Ado About Nothing* the names of actors, instead of characters, appear as speech prefixes, as they had in the quarto, which the Folio reprints; proofreading throughout the Folio is spotty and apparently was done without reference to the printer's copy; the pagination of *Hamlet* jumps from 156 to 257.

A modern editor of Shakespeare must first select his copy; no problem if the play exists only in the Folio, but a considerable problem if the relationship between a quarto and the Folio—or an early quarto and a later one—is unclear. When an editor has chosen what seems to him to be the most authoritative text or texts for his copy, he has not done with making decisions. First of all, he must reckon with Elizabethan spelling. If he is not producing a facsimile, he probably modernizes it, but ought he to preserve the old forms of words that apparently were pronounced quite unlike their modern forms—"lanthorn," "alablaster"? If he preserves these forms, is he really preserving Shakespeare's forms or perhaps those of a compositor in the printing house? What is one to do when one finds "lanthorn" and "lantern" in adjacent lines? (The editors of this series in general, but not invariably, assume that words should be spelled in their modern form.) Elizabethan punctuation, too, presents problems. For example in the First Folio, the only text for the play, Macbeth rejects his wife's idea that he can wash the blood from his hand:

> no: this my Hand will rather
> The multitudinous Seas incarnardine,
> Making the Greene one, Red.

Obviously an editor will remove the superfluous capitals, and he will probably alter the spelling to "incarnadine," but will he leave the comma before "red," letting Macbeth speak of the sea as "the green one," or will he (like most modern editors) remove the comma and thus have Macbeth say that his hand will make the ocean *uniformly* red?

An editor will sometimes have to change more than spelling or punctuation. Macbeth says to his wife:

> I dare do all that may become a man,
> Who dares no more, is none.

For two centuries editors have agreed that the second line is unsatisfactory, and have emended "no" to "do": "Who dares do more is none." But when in the same play Ross says that fearful persons

> floate vpon a wilde and violent Sea
> Each way, and moue,

need "move" be emended to "none," as it often is, on the hunch that the compositor misread the manuscript? The editors of the Signet Classic Shakespeare have restrained themselves from making abundant emendations. In their minds they hear Dr. Johnson on the dangers of emending: "I have adopted the Roman sentiment, that it is more honorable to save a citizen than to kill an enemy." Some departures (in addition to spelling, punctuation, and lineation) from the copy text have of course been made, but the original readings are listed in a note following the play, so that the reader can evaluate them for himself.

The editors of the Signet Classic Shakespeare, following tradition, have added line numbers and in many cases act and scene divisions as well as indications of locale at the beginning of scenes. The Folio divided most of the plays into acts and some into scenes. Early eighteenth-century editors increased the divisions. These divisions, which provide a convenient way of referring to passages in the plays, have been retained, but when not in the text chosen as the basis for the Signet Classic text they are enclosed in square brackets [ ] to indicate that they are editorial additions. Similarly, although no play of Shakespeare's published during his lifetime was equipped with indications of locale at the heads of scene divisions, locales have here been added in square brackets for the convenience of the reader, who lacks the information afforded to spectators by costumes, properties, and gestures. The spectator can tell at a glance he is in the throne room, but without an editorial indication the reader may be puzzled for a while. It should be mentioned, incidentally, that there are a few authentic stage directions—perhaps Shakespeare's, perhaps a prompter's—that suggest locales: for example, "Enter Brutus in his orchard," and "They go up into the Senate house." It is hoped that the bracketed additions provide the reader with the sort of help provided in these two authentic directions, but it is equally hoped that the reader will remember that the stage was not loaded with scenery.

No editor during the course of his work can fail to recollect some words Heminges and Condell prefixed to the Folio:

> It had been a thing, we confess, worthy to have been wished, that the author himself had lived to have set forth and overseen his own writings. But since it hath been ordained otherwise, and he by death departed from that right, we pray you do not envy his friends the office of their care and pain to have collected and published them.

Nor can an editor, after he has done his best, forget Heminges and Condell's final words: "And so we leave you to other of his friends, whom if you need can be your guides. If you need them not, you can lead yourselves, and others. And such readers we wish him."

SYLVAN BARNET
Tufts University

Introduction

Richard III is above all a play for the stage. It was Shakespeare's first great success, a sudden leap up from his three plays on the reign of Henry VI. Richard Burbage made his reputation by playing Richard III; so did David Garrick when he conquered London in the eighteenth century. *Richard III* was the first Shakespeare play acted professionally in America, in 1750; it was a favorite of Lincoln, who knew by heart "Now is the winter of our discontent"; and the Shakespeare Festival of Canada opened with a brilliant production. Sir Laurence Olivier has brought Richard to life again on the stage and on the screen.

When Shakespeare wrote this play, about 1592 or 1593, his audiences were eager for plays on English history. Such plays were like mirrors in which they could see what had happened to England in past crises and what might happen to themselves in the near future after the death of Queen Elizabeth. Would their next ruler be one who could unite his people, like Henry V or Henry VII, or one who would bring on civil war, like Henry VI or Richard III? The most popular plays on English history had dramatized wars and struggles for power: *The Famous Victories of Henry V*, *The Troublesome Reign of King John,* and the one great historical tragedy before Shakespeare's, Marlowe's *The Troublesome Reign and Lamentable Death of Edward II, King of England, with the Tragical Fall of Proud Mortimer*. Shakespeare emphasized as leading ideas of his English history plays the danger of division and the necessity of union: "United we stand, divided we fall."

Richard III is a tragedy of crimes punished by divine justice. Both branches of the royal Plantagenets, Lancaster and York, had committed cruel murders. Queen Margaret, the "she-wolf of France," had beheaded Richard, Duke of York; in revenge York's sons murdered her son, Prince Edward, and her husband, Henry VI. The murderers of Clarence tell him that he deserves God's vengeance for stabbing Prince Edward and for breaking his oath to God to fight for King Henry. Richard III must pay with his life for causing the deaths of his brother, his nephews, his wife, and his best friends. The demands for vengeance made by Queen Margaret are fulfilled; for, as Holinshed expressed the traditional religious view of history, "such is God's justice, to leave no unrepentant wickedness unpunished." God used Richard as a scourge to punish the sins of others; the "high All-Seer" then raised up Richmond to cancel Richard, "One that hath ever been God's enemy."

Yet it is one of Shakespeare's paradoxes that God's enemy is so much more fascinating than the puppet Richmond, who speaks with no voice of his own. Richard is alive; he is himself alone; he is what part of ourselves would like to be, free from the censor conscience. He can win women; he can win power; he can enjoy using his power to destroy, to do whatever he wants to do. We know he will not get away with it in the end; but meanwhile, what fun he is having! His gay soliloquies make us share his enjoyment:

> Was ever woman in this humor wooed?
> Was ever woman in this humor won?
> I'll have her, but I will not keep her long.
>
> (I.ii.227–29)

Richard is the actor making up his part as he goes along, and making sure that it is the leading part.

How did Shakespeare create an acting role which has held so many audiences spellbound? For one thing, he made Richard a devil masked as a man: able to put on in turn the masks of the loyal brother, the impassioned lover, the kindly uncle, the self-sacrificing king. The masks are both tragic and comic; they hide death, and they mock at human folly. We pity Richard's victims, but we feel superior to them; we, of course, would never be taken in. For another thing, Richard is the underdog who fights his way to the top, one man against the world, with everything against him. The climb to power is a treacherous one, dangerous to Richard, deadly to anyone who blocks his path; he climbs over their bodies till he stands, though not for long, where he had determined to stand. This triumph of will is exciting theater; at the same time it is sharply ironic—so many years to rise, to fall in one day.

Richard dominates the play; he appears in fourteen out of twenty-five scenes, and his shadow hangs over the rest. It is the longest of Shakespeare's history plays, and longer than any other of Shakespeare's except *Hamlet*. Richard himself speaks nearly a third of the lines, and five of his ten soliloquies come in the first three scenes, so that we see him at once take the center of the stage. His opening speech is masterly. Winter is now summer, the killing is over, it is time to live and love, but not for Richard; his keenest pleasures are to come, and the first will be to destroy his brother. Shakespeare had shown Richard's will to power in *Henry VI, Part 3*, I.ii:

> How sweet a thing it is to wear a crown;
> Within whose circuit is Elysium,
> And all that poets feign of bliss and joy.

In III.ii of the same play Richard had planned his strategy for winning the crown:

> Why, I can smile, and murder whiles I smile,
> And cry "Content" to that which grieves my heart,
> And wet my cheeks with artificial tears,
> And frame my face to all occasions. . . .
> I can add colors to the chameleon,
> Change shapes with Proteus for advantages,
> And set the murderous Machiavel to school.
> Can I do this, and cannot get a crown?

And in V.vi, after stabbing King Henry in the Tower, he had promised that Clarence would be next:

> I have no brother, I am like no brother;
> And this word "love," which graybeards call divine,
> Be resident in men like one another
> And not in me: I am myself alone.

In the first scene of *Richard III* he is in high spirits as he speaks with and without the mask: "your imprisonment shall not be long," to Clarence, and then, to himself, "I do love thee so/That I will shortly send thy soul to heaven." Richard Crookback has a crooked but original sense of humor.

Why did Shakespeare invent the famous scene of Richard's wooing of Lady Anne? The soliloquy which ends the scene provides, I think, the key to Shakespeare's purpose. Richard took up the challenge of a task that seemed impossible; if he could succeed against such odds, for him nothing would be impossible:

> What! I that killed her husband and his father
> To take her in her heart's extremest hate . . .
> And yet to win her, all the world to nothing!
>
> (I.ii.230–31, 237)

He chose a time which presented the greatest obstacles, so that he could overcome them: a time when she was calling for vengeance upon him as the murderer of King Henry and of her husband. He provoked her to attack him with words and then gave her a chance to act, to kill him with his own sword. His will proved stronger than hers. Her change is sudden, but Shakespeare means it to be. Theatrically, he achieves the shock of surprise; dramatically, he convinces us that Richard will find hardly any difficulty too great for him to master.

Shakespeare created most of the first act from his own imagination; and such history as he used he rearranged for dramatic effect. He read in Holinshed that Richard, in 1471, murdered Henry VI, whose body was brought to

St. Paul's and then buried at Chertsey; Shakespeare imagined the scene between Richard and Anne. In 1478 Edward IV had Clarence condemned to death by parliament and drowned in wine at the Tower; Shakespeare made Richard plot his brother's death, and he invented the whole vivid scene of Clarence's dream and murder. Queen Margaret had left England to live in France; Shakespeare brought her into the third scene to prophesy retribution for the house of York and especially for Richard. Margaret, Clarence, Edward IV, and Hastings were omitted from the acting version by Colley Cibber which held the stage from 1700 to 1877, a travesty of the play which contained more Cibber than Shakespeare. All are essential to Shakespeare's drama. Margaret, for example, invokes the justice of God to punish the crimes of her enemies. Recalling the bloody past, she calls for the future to pay blood for blood. As York's dread curse had prevailed with heaven to make her suffer the loss of her husband, her son, and her kingdom, so she prays that her rival Elizabeth may "Die neither mother, wife, nor England's Queen." Richard deserves to suffer the worst plagues of all: the worm of conscience, suspicion and betrayal, and the terror of tormenting dreams. Shakespeare makes Margaret no ghost crying for revenge, but a bitter, passionate woman. Yet he gives her a major function in the play: to thunder with the power of a prophetess, sent to warn that no sinner can escape his doom.

The first doom fell upon Clarence. Nothing in his life became him like the dream of his death, for while he slept, his conscience was awake. If he escaped the Tower, he feared he would find himself in hell, facing the father-in-law he had betrayed and the King's son he had stabbed to death. His repentance was genuine, but it came too late to save his life; when he warned his murderers of God's vengeance, they reminded him that he himself was a murderer. Shakespeare packs the scene with tragic irony: Clarence supposing that Richard caused his death in the dream by chance, not by design, and assuring the murderers that Richard would reward them for saving his life. The reluctant Second Murderer might still have saved him by listening to the dregs of conscience; he tried, perhaps, to warn him by crying "Look behind you, my lord!" and immediately afterward he wished he could wash his hands of the murder. Shakespeare ends the first act with Richard one step closer to the crown.

After Act I Shakespeare dramatizes the history of only two years, from the death of Edward IV in 1483 to the battle of Bosworth Field in 1485. Again and again he heightens the dramatic effect of events already full of drama. He brings Richard to the deathbed of Edward in II.i to play-act the lover of peace and then to explode the news of Clarence's death and blame "the guilty kindred of the Queen," when he alone is guilty. No sooner does Richard mount the throne in IV.ii than Shakespeare shows him trying to incite Buckingham to murder the Princes, with the result that he drives his strongest supporter into rebellion. Above all, in V.iii Shakespeare changes Richard's dream of "images like terrible devils," as Holinshed calls them, into a vision of the souls of all whom he has murdered, crying out "Despair and die!" Here Shakespeare makes Richard look into himself with fear and horror and see how he has cut himself off from mankind:

> I shall despair. There is no creature loves me;
> And if I die, no soul will pity me.   (V.iii.201–02)

Though no one pities Richard, Shakespeare builds up recurring scenes of pity for those who suffer during this reign of terror. In II.ii he shows three generations— mother, wife, and children—left desolate by the loss of Edward and of Clarence. In IV.i the old Duchess of York longs for peace in the grave; Anne, who has had no rest with Richard, wishes that her crown were red-hot steel; and Queen Elizabeth, thinking only of her children, seeks pity for them from the stones of the Tower. The murderers of the two boys tell their death's sad story (IV.iii); and the next scene rises to a chorus of grief in the laments of their mother, of their grandmother, and of Queen Margaret. Each of these scenes intensifies emotion by a three-fold pattern, as though the sorrow were too great to be expressed by only one person, and even Tyrrel shares the remorse of Dighton and Forrest. The killing of the Princes is a massacre of the innocents, and their mother is like Rachel weeping for her children.

Shakespeare secures a more complex response in scenes which present characters of mixed good and evil, persons who suffer for their sins and yet who call forth pity for their suffering. Hastings and Buckingham, together with Clarence and the shadowy Rivers, Grey, and Vaughan, are neither ruthless tyrants nor innocent children. Hastings is shown hoping for revenge upon his enemies, the Queen's kinsmen (I.i), hiding his hate under a vow of love for Rivers and Dorset (II.i), and then rejoicing at the execution of Rivers and the rest (III.ii). When he is condemned to die the same day (III.iv), he repents his too triumphant joy that his enemies were butchered and admits that Margaret's curse, for standing by when her son was murdered, has lighted on his head. On the other hand, he dies for loyalty to the true king, for refusing to help Richard usurp the throne. Shakespeare brings out the drama of his sudden fall when he least expects it, and the irony of his overconfident belief that Richard loves him well and that the boar will use him kindly. His last words, "They smile at me who shortly shall be dead," foretell a parallel fall for Buckingham, who mocked at Hastings and yet still trusts Richard. Blinded by infatuation, Buckingham has already disregarded Margaret's warning to beware of Richard (I.iii). He digs a pit for himself when he prays in II.i that if ever he harms Queen Elizabeth or her family God may punish him with hate where he expects most love, and yet becomes Richard's right-hand man to plot against her and her sons. Hesitating only at murder, he gains a crown for Richard and death for himself, and in V.i he acknowledges the justice of his death. As with Hastings, he is both sinning and sinned against, and his tragic recognition of his errors leads in the end to pity for his fall.

The blank verse in *Richard III* marches to a strong, emphatic rhythm. The pause at the end of the line, or sometimes of two lines (as in I.i.1–4, 10–13), lets the

actor dwell on the meaning with clarity and force. Shakespeare, who constructs his sonnets with three quatrains
and a couplet, likes to build dramatic monologues also in
groups of four lines. Richard's first speech is composed in
quatrains, expanded twice to five lines and once to six.
The second scene begins and ends with monologues which
contain many quatrains, as well as groups of three or five
lines. The dialogues show more variety, but Shakespeare
makes striking use of stichomythia, which sets single line
against single line, in Richard's duels of words with Anne
in I.ii, York in III.i, and Queen Elizabeth in IV.iv. The
verse of *Richard III* is far from subtle, but its careful
design contributes to its power.

Shakespeare heightens the dramatic effect of speech by
an extraordinary range of rhetoric. The opening scene is
rich in antitheses, between war and peace, the lover and
the villain, true Edward and treacherous Richard and
simple, plain Clarence. Anne expresses the intensity of her
grief by figures of repetition and parallelism: "Set down,
set down," "bloodless . . . blood," "O cursèd . . . Cursèd,"
"If ever he have child . . . If ever he have wife." Queen
Margaret gives force to her prophetic curse in I.iii.187 ff.
by pouring forth questions and exclamations, by reiter-
ating key words like "curse," "heaven," and "death," and
by emphasizing parallel constructions: "Edward thy son,
that now is Prince of Wales,/For Edward our son, that
was Prince of Wales," or "Thyself a queen, for me that
was a queen." All these and more appear in IV.iv: paradoxical antithesis in "Dead life, blind sight, poor mortal
living ghost," repeated questions like "Where is thy husband now? Where be thy brothers?" and emphatic paral-
lels, as in line 20–21, 40–46, and 98–104. The conscious
eloquence of the orations in V.iii contrasts with the more
intense rhetoric which expresses fear and despair in Richard's soliloquy. *Richard III* shows Shakespeare rejoicing
in his mastery over language, though he has not yet learned
the art of concealing his art.

The play is not merely a melodrama, although it tends
towards melodrama in its exaggeration of Richard's villainy. It is the tragedy of a man, of a family, and of a

nation. The tragedy is ironic in that Richard, by destroying others, brings destruction upon himself. Right does not triumph without probability, as in melodrama, but as a probable result of human actions. Richard rises steadily until he orders the murder of his nephews (IV.ii); from that moment he turns friends into enemies, till "He hath no friends but what are friends for fear" (V.ii). But he does not have the inner conflict of Macbeth, who inspires pity as well as fear. Retributive justice strikes down not only Richard but the whole family of Plantagenet. The sons of York pay for the murder of Henry VI and his son by their own deaths and the murder of Edward's sons. Finally, Shakespeare shows how the people of England suffered from tyranny and civil war, when "The brother blindly shed the brother's blood." He ends the play with a heartfelt prayer that his country, united, may now live in peace.

MARK ECCLES
University of Wisconsin

The Tragedy of Richard the Third

King Edward IV
Edward, Prince of Wales, afterwards King Edward V} sons of
Richard, Duke of York   } the King
George, Duke of Clarence
Richard, Duke of Gloucester, afterwards King } brothers of
   Richard III   } the King
A young son of Clarence (Edward)
Henry, Earl of Richmond, afterwards King Henry VII
Cardinal Bourchier, Archbishop of Canterbury
Thomas Rotherham, Archbishop of York
John Morton, Bishop of Ely
Duke of Buckingham
Duke of Norfolk
Earl of Surrey, his son
Anthony Woodville, Earl Rivers, brother of Queen Elizabeth
Marquis of Dorset and Lord Grey, sons of Queen Elizabeth
Earl of Oxford
Lord Stanley, called also Earl of Derby
Lord Hastings

Lord Woodville	Sir Richard Ratcliffe
Lord Scales	Sir James Tyrrel
Lord Lovell	Sir James Blunt
Sir Robert Brakenbury,	Sir Walter Herbert
Lieutenant of the Tower	Sir William Brandon
Sir Thomas Vaughan	William Catesby

Lord Mayor of London
Christopher Urswick, a chaplain
Tressel and Barkley, gentlemen attending on Lady Anne
Queen Elizabeth, wife of King Edward IV
Queen Margaret, widow of King Henry VI
Duchess of York, mother of King Edward IV, Clarence, and
   Gloucester
Lady Anne, widow of Edward Prince of Wales, son of King
   Henry VI; afterwards married to Richard
A young daughter of Clarence (Margaret)
Ghosts of Richard's victims, Lords and other Attendants, Bishops,
   Priest, Sheriff, Keeper, Two Murderers, Pursuivant, Scrivener,
   Page, Citizens, Messengers, Soldiers, &c.

Scene: England]

The Tragedy of Richard the Third

ACT I

Scene I. [*London. A street.*]

Enter Richard, Duke of Gloucester, solus.°¹

Richard. Now is the winter of our discontent
Made glorious summer by this sun° of York;
And all the clouds that loured upon our house
In the deep bosom of the ocean buried.
Now are our brows bound with victorious wreaths,   5
Our bruisèd arms hung up for monuments,°
Our stern alarums° changed to merry meetings,
Our dreadful marches to delightful measures.°
Grim-visaged War hath smoothed his wrinkled
front,°
And now, instead of mounting barbèd° steeds   10
To fright the souls of fearful adversaries,
He capers nimbly in a lady's chamber
To the lascivious pleasing of a lute.
But I, that am not shaped for sportive tricks
Nor made to court an amorous looking glass;   15

¹ The degree sign (°) indicates a footnote, which is keyed to the
text by line number. Text references are printed in *italic* type; the an-
notation follows in roman type.
I.i. s.d. *solus* alone   2 *sun* (1) emblem of King Edward (2) son
6 *monuments* memorials   7 *alarums* calls to arms   8 *measures*
dances   9 *front* forehead   10 *barbèd* armored

I, that am rudely stamped, and want° love's
    majesty
To strut before a wanton ambling nymph;
I, that am curtailed of this fair proportion,
Cheated of feature° by dissembling Nature,
20 Deformed, unfinished, sent before my time
Into this breathing world scarce half made up,
And that so lamely and unfashionable
That dogs bark at me as I halt° by them;
Why, I, in this weak piping time° of peace,
25 Have no delight to pass away the time,
Unless to spy my shadow in the sun
And descant° on mine own deformity.
And therefore, since I cannot prove a lover
To entertain° these fair well-spoken days,
30 I am determinèd to prove a villain
And hate the idle pleasures of these days.
Plots have I laid, inductions° dangerous,
By drunken prophecies, libels, and dreams,
To set my brother Clarence and the King
35 In deadly hate the one against the other;
And if King Edward be as true and just
As I am subtle, false, and treacherous,
This day should Clarence closely be mewed up•
About a prophecy which says that G
40 Of Edward's heirs the murderer shall be.
Dive, thoughts, down to my soul. Here Clarence
    comes.

    Enter Clarence, guarded, and Brakenbury,
        [Lieutenant of the Tower].

Brother, good day. What means this armèd guard
That waits upon your Grace?

Clarence.   His Majesty,
Tend'ring° my person's safety, hath appointed
45 This conduct° to convey me to the Tower.

16 *want* lack   19 *feature* good shape   23 *halt* limp   24 *piping time*
i.e., time when shepherds play their pipes   27 *descant* comment
29 *entertain* while away   32 *inductions* first steps   38 *mewed up*
caged in prison   44 *Tend'ring* taking care of   45 *conduct* escort

Richard. Upon what cause?

Clarence.   Because my name is George.

Richard. Alack, my lord, that fault is none of yours;
  He should for that commit your godfathers.
  O, belike° his Majesty hath some intent
  That you should be new christ'ned in the Tower.   *50*
  But what's the matter, Clarence? May I know?

Clarence. Yea, Richard, when I know; for I protest
  As yet I do not. But, as I can learn,
  He harkens after prophecies and dreams,
  And from the crossrow° plucks the letter *G,*   *55*
  And says a wizard told him that by *G*
  His issue disinherited should be;
  And, for° my name of George begins with *G,*
  It follows in his thought that I am he.
  These (as I learn) and suchlike toys° as these   *60*
  Hath moved his Highness to commit me now.

Richard. Why, this it is when men are ruled by
    women.
  'Tis not the King that sends you to the Tower.
  My Lady Grey his wife, Clarence, 'tis she
  That tempers° him to this extremity.°   *65*
  Was it not she, and that good man of worship,°
  Anthony Woodeville° her brother there,
  That made him send Lord Hastings to the Tower,
  From whence this present day he is deliverèd?
  We are not safe, Clarence, we are not safe.   *70*

Clarence. By heaven, I think there is no man secure
  But the Queen's kindred, and night-walking
    heralds°
  That trudge betwixt the King and Mistress Shore.°

---

49 *belike* probably   55 *crossrow* alphabet   58 *for* because   60 *toys*
trifles   65 *tempers* persuades   65 *extremity* extreme severity   66
good man of worship (play on "goodman," common man, raised to
"worship," honor, as Earl Rivers   67 *Woodeville* (trisyllabic, play
on "would evil")   72 *heralds* king's messengers (ironic)   73 *Mistress Shore* Jane Shore, wife of a London citizen; Edward IV's mistress

Heard you not what an humble suppliant
75   Lord Hastings was to her for his delivery?

Richard. Humbly complaining to her deity
Got my Lord Chamberlain his liberty.
I'll tell you what, I think it is our way,
If we will keep in favor with the King,
80   To be her men and wear her livery.
The jealous o'erworn widow° and herself,
Since that our brother dubbed them gentlewomen,
Are mighty gossips° in our monarchy.

Brakenbury. I beseech your Graces both to pardon me.
85   His Majesty hath straitly° given in charge
That no man shall have private conference,
Of what degree° soever, with your brother.

Richard. Even so? And° please your worship, Braken-
bury,
You may partake of anything we say.
90   We speak no treason, man; we say the King
Is wise and virtuous, and his noble queen
Well struck° in years, fair, and not jealous;
We say that Shore's wife hath a pretty foot,
A cherry lip, a bonny eye, a passing pleasing
tongue;
95   And that the Queen's kindred are made gentlefolks.
How say you, sir? Can you deny all this?

Brakenbury. With this, my lord, myself have nought
to do.

Richard. Naught° to do with Mistress Shore! I tell
thee, fellow,
He that doth naught with her, excepting one,
100   Were best to do it secretly alone.

Brakenbury. What one, my lord?

Richard. Her husband, knave. Wouldst thou betray
me?

---

81 *widow* Queen Elizabeth, widow of Sir John Grey   83 *gossips*
chattering women, busybodies   85 *straitly* strictly   87 *degree* rank
88 *And* if   92 *struck* advanced   98 *Naught* evil

Brakenbury. I beseech your Grace to pardon me, and
    withal°
Forbear your conference with the noble Duke.

Clarence. We know thy charge, Brakenbury, and will
    obey.   105

Richard. We are the Queen's abjects,° and must obey.
Brother, farewell. I will unto the King;
And whatsoe'er you will employ me in,
Were it to call King Edward's widow sister,
I will perform it to enfranchise° you.   110
Meantime, this deep disgrace in brotherhood
Touches me deeper than you can imagine.

Clarence. I know it pleaseth neither of us well.

Richard. Well, your imprisonment shall not be long;
I will deliver you, or else lie for° you.   115
Meantime, have patience.

Clarence.   I must perforce. Farewell.
        Exit Clarence, [with Brakenbury and Guard].

Richard. Go tread the path that thou shalt ne'er
    return.
Simple plain Clarence, I do love thee so
That I will shortly send thy soul to heaven,
If heaven will take the present at our hands.   120
But who comes here? The new-deliverèd Hastings!

                Enter Lord Hastings.

Hastings. Good time of day unto my gracious lord.

Richard. As much unto my good Lord Chamberlain.
Well are you welcome to the open air.
How hath your lordship brooked° imprisonment?   125

Hastings. With patience, noble lord, as prisoners must.
But I shall live, my lord, to give them thanks
That were the cause of my imprisonment.

---

103 *withal* moreover   106 *abjects* abject slaves   110 *enfranchise* set
free   115 *lie for* (1) go to prison instead of (2) tell lies about
125 *brooked* endured

Richard. No doubt, no doubt; and so shall Clarence
    too,
130   For they that were your enemies are his
    And have prevailed as much on him as you.

Hastings. More pity that the eagles should be mewed
    Whiles kites° and buzzards prey at liberty.

Richard. What news abroad?

135 *Hastings.* No news so bad abroad as this at home:
    The King is sickly, weak, and melancholy,
    And his physicians fear° him mightily.

Richard. Now, by Saint John, that news is bad in-
    deed.
    O, he hath kept an evil diet° long
140   And overmuch consumed his royal person.
    'Tis very grievous to be thought upon.
    What, is he in his bed?

Hastings. He is.

Richard. Go you before, and I will follow you.
                        Exit Hastings.
145   He cannot live, I hope, and must not die
    Till George be packed with post horse° up to
      heaven.
    I'll in to urge his hatred more to Clarence
    With lies well steeled° with weighty arguments;
    And, if I fail not in my deep intent,
150   Clarence hath not another day to live.
    Which done, God take King Edward to his mercy
    And leave the world for me to bustle in!
    For then I'll marry Warwick's youngest daughter.°
    What though I killed her husband and her father?°
155   The readiest way to make the wench amends
    Is to become her husband and her father.
    The which will I, not all so much for love

133 *kites* birds of the hawk family   137 *fear* fear for   139 *diet*
way of living   146 *packed with post horse* sent off in a hurry
148 *steeled* reinforced   153 *Warwick's youngest daughter* Lady
Anne   154 *father* father-in-law (Henry VI)

As for another secret close intent
By marrying her which I must reach unto.
But yet I run before my horse to market.   *160*
Clarence still breathes, Edward still lives and reigns;
When they are gone, then must I count my gains.
                                                    Exit.

Scene II. [*A street.*]

*Enter the corse° of Henry the Sixth, with Hal-
berds° to guard it, Lady Anne being the mourner.*

Anne. Set down, set down your honorable load—
    If honor may be shrouded in a hearse—
    Whilst I awhile obsequiously° lament
    Th' untimely fall of virtuous Lancaster.
            [*The Bearers set down the hearse.*]
    Poor key-cold figure of a holy king,   *5*
    Pale ashes of the house of Lancaster,
    Thou bloodless remnant of that royal blood,
    Be it lawful that I invocate thy ghost
    To hear the lamentations of poor Anne,
    Wife to thy Edward, to thy slaught'red son,   *10*
    Stabbed by the selfsame hand that made these
        wounds!
    Lo, in these windows that let forth thy life
    I pour the helpless° balm of my poor eyes.
    O, cursèd be the hand that made these holes!
    Cursèd the heart that had the heart to do it!   *15*
    Cursèd the blood that let this blood from hence!
    More direful hap betide° that hated wretch
    That makes us wretched by the death of thee
    Than I can wish to wolves, to spiders, toads,

I.ii.s.d. *corse* corpse   s.d. *Halberds* guards armed with long poleaxes
3 *obsequiously* like a mourner at a funeral   13 *helpless* unavailing   17 *hap betide* fortune happen to

20 Or any creeping venomed thing that lives!
If ever he have child, abortive be it,
Prodigious,° and untimely brought to light,
Whose ugly and unnatural aspect
May fright the hopeful mother at the view,
25 And that be heir to his unhappiness!°
If ever he have wife, let her be made
More miserable by the life of him
Than I am made by my young lord and thee!
Come, now towards Chertsey with your holy load,
30 Taken from Paul's° to be interrèd there;
                    [*The Bearers take up the hearse.*]
And still as° you are weary of this weight,
Rest you, whiles I lament King Henry's corse.

Enter Richard, Duke of Gloucester.

Richard. Stay, you that bear the corse, and set it
down.

Anne. What black magician conjures up this fiend
35 To stop devoted charitable deeds?

Richard. Villains, set down the corse, or, by Saint
Paul,
I'll make a corse of him that disobeys.

Gentleman. My lord, stand back and let the coffin
pass.

Richard. Unmannered dog, stand° thou when I command!
40 Advance thy halberd higher than my breast,
Or, by Saint Paul, I'll strike thee to my foot
And spurn° upon thee, beggar, for thy boldness.
                    [*The Bearers set down the hearse.*]

Anne. What, do you tremble? Are you all afraid?
Alas, I blame you not, for you are mortal,
45 And mortal eyes cannot endure the devil.
Avaunt,° thou dreadful minister of hell!

22 *Prodigious* monstrous   25 *unhappiness* wickedness   30 *Paul's*
St. Paul's Cathedral   31 *still as* whenever   39 *stand* halt   42 *spurn*
trample   46 *Avaunt* begone

Thou hadst but power over his mortal body,
His soul thou canst not have; therefore, begone.

Richard. Sweet saint, for charity, be not so curst.°

Anne. Foul devil, for God's sake hence, and trouble
   us not,   50
For thou hast made the happy earth thy hell,
Filled it with cursing cries and deep exclaims.
If thou delight to view thy heinous deeds,
Behold this pattern° of thy butcheries.
O gentlemen, see, see dead Henry's wounds   55
Open their congealed mouths and bleed afresh!
Blush, blush, thou lump of foul deformity,
For 'tis thy presence that exhales° this blood
From cold and empty veins where no blood dwells.
Thy deed inhuman and unnatural   60
Provokes this deluge most unnatural.
O God, which this blood mad'st, revenge his death!
O earth, which this blood drink'st, revenge his
   death!
Either heav'n, with lightning strike the murd'rer
   dead,
Or earth, gape open wide and eat him quick,°   65
As thou dost swallow up this good king's blood
Which his hell-governed arm hath butcherèd!

Richard. Lady, you know no rules of charity,
Which renders good for bad, blessings for curses.

Anne. Villain, thou know'st nor law of God nor man.   70
No beast so fierce but knows some touch of pity.

Richard. But I know none, and therefore am no beast.

Anne. O wonderful, when devils tell the truth!

Richard. More wonderful, when angels are so angry.
Vouchsafe, divine perfection of a woman,   75
Of these supposèd crimes to give me leave
By circumstance° but to acquit myself.

49 *curst* sharp-tongued   54 *pattern* example   58 *exhales* causes to
flow   65 *quick* alive   77 *By circumstance* in detail

Anne. Vouchsafe, diffused° infection of a man,
    Of these known evils but to give me leave
80 By circumstance to accuse thy cursèd self.

Richard. Fairer than tongue can name thee, let me have
    Some patient leisure to excuse myself.

Anne. Fouler than heart can think thee, thou canst make
    No excuse current° but to hang thyself.

85 *Richard.* By such despair I should accuse myself.

Anne. And by despairing shalt thou stand excusèd
    For doing worthy vengeance on thyself
    That didst unworthy slaughter upon others.

Richard. Say that I slew them not?

Anne.   Then say they were not slain.
90   But dead they are, and, devilish slave, by thee.

Richard. I did not kill your husband.

Anne.   Why, then he is alive.

Richard. Nay, he is dead, and slain by Edward's hands.

Anne. In thy foul throat thou li'st! Queen Margaret saw
    Thy murd'rous falchion° smoking in his blood;
95   The which thou once didst bend against her breast,
    But that thy brothers beat aside the point.

Richard. I was provokèd by her sland'rous tongue,
    That laid their guilt upon my guiltless shoulders.

Anne. Thou wast provokèd by thy bloody mind,
100 That never dream'st on aught but butcheries.
    Didst thou not kill this king?

Richard.   I grant ye.

---

78 *diffused* shapeless   84 *current* genuine   94 *falchion* curved sword

Anne. Dost grant me, hedgehog? Then God grant me
    too
  Thou mayst be damnèd for that wicked deed!
  O, he was gentle, mild, and virtuous!

Richard. The better for the King of heaven that hath
    him.   105

Anne. He is in heaven, where thou shalt never come.

Richard. Let him thank me that holp° to send him
    thither;
  For he was fitter for that place than earth.

Anne. And thou unfit for any place but hell.

Richard. Yes, one place else, if you will hear me name
    it.   110

Anne. Some dungeon.

Richard.   Your bedchamber.

Anne. Ill rest betide the chamber where thou liest!

Richard. So will it, madam, till I lie with you.

Anne. I hope so.

Richard.   I know so. But, gentle Lady Anne,
  To leave this keen encounter of our wits   115
  And fall something into a slower method,
  Is not the causer of the timeless° deaths
  Of these Plantagenets, Henry and Edward,
  As blameful as the executioner?

Anne. Thou wast the cause and most accursed effect.°   120

Richard. Your beauty was the cause of that effect;
  Your beauty, that did haunt me in my sleep
  To undertake the death of all the world,
  So I might live one hour in your sweet bosom.

Anne. If I thought that, I tell thee, homicide,   125

107 *holp* helped   117 *timeless* untimely   120 *effect* effective agent

These nails should rend that beauty from my
cheeks.

Richard. These eyes could not endure that beauty's
wrack.°
You should not blemish it if I stood by.
As all the world is cheerèd by the sun,
130   So I by that; it is my day, my life.

Anne. Black night o'ershade thy day, and death thy
life!

Richard. Curse not thyself, fair creature; thou art both.

Anne. I would I were, to be revenged on thee.

Richard. It is a quarrel most unnatural
135   To be revenged on him that loveth thee.

Anne. It is a quarrel just and reasonable
To be revenged on him that killed my husband.

Richard. He that bereft thee, lady, of thy husband,
Did it to help thee to a better husband.

140 *Anne.* His better doth not breathe upon the earth.

Richard. He lives that loves thee better than he could.

Anne. Name him.

Richard.   Plantagenet.

Anne.   Why, that was he.

Richard. The selfsame name, but one of better nature.

Anne. Where is he?

Richard.   Here.   [*She*] *spits at him.*
                    Why dost thou spit at me?

145 *Anne.* Would it were mortal poison for thy sake!

Richard. Never came poison from so sweet a place.

Anne. Never hung poison on a fouler toad.
Out of my sight! Thou dost infect mine eyes.

127 *wrack* destruction

Richard. Thine eyes, sweet lady, have infected mine.

Ann. Would they were basilisks° to strike thee dead!   150

Richard. I would they were, that I might die at once;°
For now they kill me with a living death.
Those eyes of thine from mine have drawn salt
  tears,
Shamed their aspect° with store of childish drops,
These eyes which never shed remorseful° tear,   155
No, when my father York and Edward wept
To hear the piteous moan that Rutland° made
When black-faced° Clifford shook his sword at him,
Nor when thy warlike father, like a child,
Told the sad story of my father's death   160
And twenty times made pause to sob and weep,
That all the standers-by had wet their cheeks
Like trees bedashed with rain. In that sad time
My manly eyes did scorn an humble tear;
And what these sorrows could not thence exhale   165
Thy beauty hath, and made them blind with weep-
  ing.
I never sued to friend nor enemy;
My tongue could never learn sweet smoothing°
  word;
But now thy beauty is proposed my fee,
My proud heart sues, and prompts my tongue to
  speak.
                                                      170
                        She looks scornfully at him.
Teach not thy lip such scorn, for it was made
For kissing, lady, not for such contempt.
If thy revengeful heart cannot forgive,
Lo, here I lend thee this sharp-pointed sword;
Which if thou please to hide in this true breast   175
And let the soul forth that adoreth thee,
I lay it naked to the deadly stroke

150 *basilisks* fabulous monsters believed to kill by a look   151 *at once* once and for all   154 *aspect* appearance   155 *remorseful* pitying   157 *Rutland* a young brother of Richard (see *3 Henry VI*, I.iii)   158 *black-faced* cruel-looking   168 *smoothing* flattering

And humbly beg the death upon my knee.

He lays his breast open.
She offers at [it] with his sword.

Nay, do not pause, for I did kill King Henry,
180   But 'twas thy beauty that provokèd me.
Nay, now dispatch; 'twas I that stabbed young Edward,
But 'twas thy heavenly face that set me on.

She falls° the sword.

Take up the sword again, or take up me.

Anne. Arise, dissembler; though I wish thy death,
185   I will not be thy executioner.

Richard. Then bid me kill myself, and I will do it.

Anne. I have already.

Richard.   That was in thy rage.
Speak it again, and even with the word
This hand, which for thy love did kill thy love,
190   Shall for thy love kill a far truer love.
To both their deaths shalt thou be accessary.°

Anne. I would I knew thy heart.

Richard. 'Tis figured° in my tongue.

Anne. I fear me both are false.

195   *Richard.* Then never was man true.

Anne. Well, well, put up your sword.

Richard. Say, then, my peace is made.

Anne. That shalt thou know hereafter.

Richard. But shall I live in hope?

200   *Anne.* All men, I hope, live so.

Richard. Vouchsafe° to wear this ring.

Anne. To take is not to give.

[*Richard puts the ring on her finger.*]

---

182 s.d. *falls* lets fall   191 *accessary* sharing in guilt   193 *figured*
pictured   201 *Vouchsafe* consent

Richard. Look how° my ring encompasseth thy finger,
    Even so thy breast encloseth my poor heart.
    Wear both of them, for both of them are thine.   205
    And if thy poor devoted servant may
    But beg one favor at thy gracious hand,
    Thou dost confirm his happiness forever.

Anne. What is it?

Richard. That it may please you leave these sad de-
    signs   210
    To him that hath most cause to be a mourner,
    And presently° repair to Crosby House,
    Where, after I have solemnly interred
    At Chertsey monast'ry this noble king
    And wet his grave with my repentant tears,   215
    I will with all expedient° duty see you.
    For divers unknown° reasons, I beseech you,
    Grant me this boon.

Anne. With all my heart; and much it joys me too
    To see you are become so penitent.   220
    Tressel and Barkley, go along with me.

Richard. Bid me farewell.

Anne.   'Tis more than you deserve;
    But since you teach me how to flatter you,
    Imagine I have said farewell already.
                     Exit two with Anne.

Richard. Sirs, take up the corse.

Gentleman.   Towards Chertsey, noble lord?   225

Richard. No, to Whitefriars; there attend° my coming.
          Exit [Bearers and Gentlemen with] corse.
    Was ever woman in this humor° wooed?
    Was ever woman in this humor won?
    I'll have her, but I will not keep her long.
    What! I that killed her husband and his father   230
    To take her in her heart's extremest hate,

203 *Look how* just as   212 *presently* immediately   216 *expedient*
speedy   217 *unknown* secret   226 *attend* await   227 *humor* mood

With curses in her mouth, tears in her eyes,
The bleeding witness of my hatred by,
Having God, her conscience, and these bars against
    me,
235 And I no friends to back my suit at all
But the plain devil and dissembling looks,
And yet to win her, all the world to nothing!
Ha!
Hath she forgot already that brave prince,
240 Edward her lord, whom I, some three months since,
Stabbed in my angry mood at Tewkesbury?°
A sweeter and a lovelier gentleman,
Framed in the prodigality° of nature,
Young, valiant, wise, and, no doubt, right royal,
245 The spacious world cannot again afford.°
And will she yet abase her eyes on me,
That cropped the golden prime° of this sweet
    prince
And made her widow to a woeful bed?
On me, whose all not equals Edward's moi'ty?°
250 On me, that halts and am misshapen thus?
My dukedom to a beggarly denier,°
I do mistake my person all this while.
Upon my life, she finds, although I cannot,
Myself to be a marv'lous proper° man.
255 I'll be at charges for° a looking glass
And entertain° a score or two of tailors
To study fashions to adorn my body.
Since I am crept in favor with myself,
I will maintain it with some little cost.
260 But first I'll turn yon fellow in° his grave,
And then return lamenting to my love.
Shine out, fair sun, till I have bought a glass
That I may see my shadow as I pass.   *Exit.*

241 *Tewkesbury* scene of a Yorkist victory   243 *prodigality* lavish-
ness   245 *afford* supply   247 *prime* springtime   249 *moi'ty* half
251 *denier* French coin worth a tenth of an English penny
254 *marv'lous proper* wonderfully handsome   255 *at charges for*
at the expense of   256 *entertain* engage   260 *in* into

Scene III. [*The palace.*]

Enter Queen [Elizabeth,] Lord Rivers, [Dorset,]
and Lord Grey.

Rivers. Have patience, madam; there's no doubt his Majesty
Will soon recover his accustomed health.

Grey. In that you brook° it ill, it makes him worse.
Therefore for God's sake entertain good comfort
And cheer his Grace with quick and merry eyes.   5

Queen Elizabeth. If he were dead, what would betide on° me?

Grey. No other harm but loss of such a lord.

Queen Elizabeth. The loss of such a lord includes all harms.

Grey. The heavens have blessed you with a goodly son
To be your comforter when he is gone.   10

Queen Elizabeth. Ah, he is young, and his minority
Is put unto the trust of Richard Gloucester,
A man that loves not me, nor none of you.

Rivers. Is it concluded he shall be Protector?

Queen Elizabeth. It is determined, not concluded° yet;   15
But so it must be if the King miscarry.°

Enter Buckingham and [Stanley, Earl of] Derby.

Grey. Here come the lords of Buckingham and Derby.

Buckingham. Good time of day unto your royal Grace!

I.iii.3 *brook* endure   6 *betide on* happen to   15 *determined, not concluded* decided, not finally decreed   16 *miscarry* die

Stanley. God make your Majesty joyful as you have
    been!

Queen Elizabeth. The Countess Richmond,° good my
20   Lord of Derby,
    To your good prayer will scarcely say "Amen."
    Yet, Derby, notwithstanding she's your wife
    And loves not me, be you, good lord, assured
    I hate not you for her proud arrogance.

25 *Stanley.* I do beseech you, either not believe
    The envious slanders of her false accusers,
    Or, if she be accused on true report,
    Bear with her weakness, which I think proceeds
    From wayward sickness and no grounded malice.

Queen Elizabeth. Saw you the King today, my Lord
30   of Derby?

Stanley. But now° the Duke of Buckingham and I
    Are come from visiting his Majesty.

Queen Elizabeth. What likelihood of his amendment,
    lords?

Buckingham. Madam, good hope; his Grace speaks
    cheerfully.

Queen Elizabeth. God grant him health! Did you con-
35   fer with him?

Buckingham. Ay, madam; he desires to make atone-
    ment°
    Between the Duke of Gloucester and your brothers,
    And between them and my Lord Chamberlain,°
    And sent to warn° them to his royal presence.

Queen Elizabeth. Would all were well! But that will
40   never be.
    I fear our happiness is at the height.

---

20 *Countess Richmond* Margaret Tudor, mother of the Earl of Richmond (later Henry VII) and wife of Lord Stanley   31 *But now* just
now   36 *atonement* reconciliation   38 *Lord Chamberlain* Hastings
39 *warn* summon

Enter Richard [and Hastings].

Richard. They do me wrong, and I will not endure it!
  Who is it that complains unto the King
  That I, forsooth, am stern, and love them not?
  By holy Paul, they love his Grace but lightly   *45*
  That fill his ears with such dissentious rumors.
  Because I cannot flatter and look fair,
  Smile in men's faces, smooth, deceive, and cog,°
  Duck with French nods and apish courtesy,
  I must be held a rancorous enemy.   *50*
  Cannot a plain man live and think no harm
  But thus his simple truth must be abused
  With silken, sly, insinuating Jacks?°

Grey. To who in all this presence speaks your Grace?

Richard. To thee, that hast nor honesty nor grace.°   *55*
  When have I injured thee? When done thee wrong?
  Or thee? Or thee? Or any of your faction?
  A plague upon you all! His royal Grace—
  Whom God preserve better than you would wish!—
  Cannot be quiet scarce a breathing while°   *60*
  But you must trouble him with lewd° complaints.

Queen Elizabeth. Brother of Gloucester, you mistake
    the matter.
  The King on his own royal disposition,
  And not provoked by any suitor else,
  Aiming, belike, at your interior hatred   *65*
  That in your outward action shows itself
  Against my children, brothers, and myself,
  Makes° him to send that he may learn the ground.

Richard. I cannot tell; the world is grown so bad
  That wrens make prey where eagles dare not perch.   *70*
  Since every Jack became a gentleman,
  There's many a gentle° person made a Jack.

---

48 *cog* fawn   53 *Jacks* knaves   55 *grace* virtue   60 *breathing while*
time to take a breath   61 *lewd* wicked   68 *Makes* (the subject has
shifted from *The King* to *your interior hatred*)   72 *gentle* wellborn

Queen Elizabeth. Come, come, we know your mean-
　　ing, brother Gloucester.
　　You envy my advancement and my friends'.
75　　God grant we never may have need of you!

Richard. Meantime, God grants that I have need of
　　you.
　　Our brother is imprisoned by your means,
　　Myself disgraced, and the nobility
　　Held in contempt, while great promotions
80　　Are daily given to ennoble those
　　That scarce, some two days since, were worth a
　　noble.°

Queen Elizabeth. By him that raised me to this care-
　　ful° height
　　From that contented hap° which I enjoyed,
　　I never did incense his Majesty
85　　Against the Duke of Clarence, but have been
　　An earnest advocate to plead for him.
　　My lord, you do me shameful injury
　　Falsely to draw me in° these vile suspects.°

Richard. You may deny that you were not the mean
90　　Of my Lord Hastings' late imprisonment.

Rivers. She may, my lord, for—

Richard. She may, Lord Rivers! Why, who knows not
　　so?
　　She may do more, sir, than denying that:
　　She may help you to many fair preferments,°
95　　And then deny her aiding hand therein
　　And lay those honors on your high desert.
　　What may she not? She may, ay, marry,° may she!

Rivers. What, marry, may she?

Richard. What, marry, may she! Marry with a king,
100　　A bachelor and a handsome stripling too.

81 *noble* coin worth a third of a pound 82 *careful* care-filled
83 *hap* fortune 88 *in* into 88 *suspects* suspicions 94 *preferments*
promotions 97 *marry* indeed (from "By the Virgin Mary")

Iwis° your grandam had a worser match.

Queen Elizabeth. My Lord of Gloucester, I have too
    long borne
Your blunt upbraidings and your bitter scoffs.
By heaven, I will acquaint his Majesty
Of those gross taunts that oft I have endured.   *105*
I had rather be a country servant maid
Than a great queen with this condition,
To be so baited,° scorned, and stormèd at.

       Enter old Queen Margaret, [behind].

Small joy have I in being England's Queen.

Queen Margaret. [*Aside*] And less'ned be that small,
    God I beseech him!   *110*
Thy honor, state, and seat is due to me.

Richard. What! Threat you me with telling of the
    King?
Tell him and spare not. Look what° I have said
I will avouch in presence of the King.
I dare adventure to be sent to th' Tow'r.   *115*
'Tis time to speak; my pains° are quite forgot.

Queen Margaret. [*Aside*] Out, devil! I do remember
    them too well.
Thou kill'dst my husband Henry in the Tower
And Edward, my poor son, at Tewkesbury.

Richard. Ere you were queen, ay, or your husband
    king,   *120*
I was a packhorse in his great affairs,
A weeder-out of his proud adversaries,
A liberal rewarder of his friends;
To royalize his blood I spent mine own.

Queen Margaret. [*Aside*] Ay, and much better blood
    than his or thine.   *125*

Richard. In all which time you and your husband Grey

101 *Iwis* certainly   108 *baited* tormented   113 *Look what* whatever   116 *pains* efforts

Were factious for the house of Lancaster;
And, Rivers, so were you. Was not your husband
In Margaret's battle° at Saint Albans slain?
130   Let me put in your minds, if you forget,
What you have been ere this, and what you are;
Withal, what I have been, and what I am.

Queen Margaret. [*Aside*] A murd'rous villain, and so
        still thou art.

Richard. Poor Clarence did forsake his father° War-
        wick;
135   Ay, and forswore himself—which Jesu pardon!—

Queen Margaret. [*Aside*] Which God revenge!

Richard. To fight on Edward's party for the crown;
And for his meed,° poor lord, he is mewèd up.
I would to God my heart were flint like Edward's,
140   Or Edward's soft and pitiful like mine.
I am too childish-foolish for this world.

Queen Margaret. [*Aside*] Hie thee to hell for shame
        and leave this world,
Thou cacodemon!° There thy kingdom is.

Rivers. My Lord of Gloucester, in those busy days
145   Which here you urge to prove us enemies,
We followed then our lord, our sovereign king.
So should we you, if you should be our king.

Richard. If I should be! I had rather be a peddler.
Far be it from my heart, the thought thereof!

150   *Queen Elizabeth.* As little joy, my lord, as you suppose
You should enjoy were you this country's king,
As little joy you may suppose in me
That I enjoy, being the queen thereof.

Queen Margaret. [*Aside*] A little joy enjoys the queen
        thereof;
155   For I am she, and altogether joyless.
I can no longer hold me patient. [*Comes forward.*]

---

129 *battle* army   134 *father* father-in-law   138 *meed* reward   143
cacodemon evil spirit

Hear me, you wrangling pirates, that fall out
In sharing that which you have pilled° from me!
Which of you trembles not that looks on me?
If not, that I am queen, you bow like subjects,   160
Yet that,° by you deposed, you quake like rebels.
Ah, gentle° villain, do not turn away!

Richard. Foul wrinkled witch, what mak'st thou° in
    my sight?

Queen Margaret. But repetition of what thou hast
    marred;
That will I make before I let thee go.   165

Richard. Wert thou not banishèd on pain of death?

Queen Margaret. I was; but I do find more pain in
    banishment
Than death can yield me here by my abode.
A husband and a son thou ow'st to me;
And thou a kingdom; all of you allegiance.   170
This sorrow that I have, by right is yours,
And all the pleasures you usurp are mine.

Richard. The curse my noble father laid on thee
When thou didst crown his warlike brows with
    paper
And with thy scorns drew'st rivers from his eyes   175
And then to dry them gav'st the Duke a clout°
Steeped in the faultless blood of pretty Rutland,
His curses then from bitterness of soul
Denounced against thee are all fall'n upon thee;
And God, not we, hath plagued thy bloody deed.   180

Queen Elizabeth. So just is God to right the innocent.

Hastings. O, 'twas the foulest deed to slay that babe
And the most merciless that e'er was heard of!

Rivers. Tyrants themselves wept when it was reported.

Dorset. No man but prophesied revenge for it.   185

158 *pilled* plundered   160–61 *that . . . that* because . . . because
162 *gentle* (1) wellborn (2) kindly (ironic)   163 *mak'st thou* are
you doing   176 *clout* piece of cloth

Buckingham. Northumberland, then present, wept to
    see it.

Queen Margaret. What! Were you snarling all before I
    came,
    Ready to catch each other by the throat,
    And turn you all your hatred now on me?
    Did York's dread curse prevail so much with
190   heaven
    That Henry's death, my lovely Edward's death,
    Their kingdom's loss, my woeful banishment,
    Should all but answer° for that peevish° brat?
    Can curses pierce the clouds and enter heaven?
    Why then, give way, dull clouds, to my quick°
195   curses!
    Though not by war, by surfeit die your king,
    As ours by murder, to make him a king!
    Edward thy son, that now is Prince of Wales,
    For Edward our son, that was Prince of Wales,
200   Die in his youth by like untimely violence!
    Thyself a queen, for me that was a queen,
    Outlive thy glory like my wretched self!
    Long mayst thou live to wail thy children's death
    And see another, as I see thee now,
205   Decked in thy rights as thou art stalled° in mine!
    Long die thy happy days before thy death,
    And, after many length'ned hours of grief,
    Die neither mother, wife, nor England's Queen!
    Rivers and Dorset, you were standers-by,
210   And so wast thou, Lord Hastings, when my son
    Was stabbed with bloody daggers. God I pray him
    That none of you may live his natural age,
    But by some unlooked accident cut off!

Richard. Have done thy charm,° thou hateful withered
    hag!

Queen Margaret. And leave out thee? Stay, dog, for
215   thou shalt hear me.

---

193 *but answer* only pay back   193 *peevish* foolish   195 *quick* full
of life   205 *stalled* installed   214 *charm* spell, curse

If heaven have any grievous plague in store
Exceeding those that I can wish upon thee,
O let them keep it till thy sins be ripe
And then hurl down their indignation
On thee, the troubler of the poor world's peace!　　220
The worm of conscience still begnaw thy soul!
Thy friends suspect for traitors while thou liv'st,
And take deep traitors for thy dearest friends!
No sleep close up that deadly eye of thine,
Unless it be while some tormenting dream　　225
Affrights thee with a hell of ugly devils!
Thou elvish-marked,° abortive, rooting hog!°
Thou that wast sealed° in thy nativity
The slave of nature and the son of hell!
Thou slander of thy heavy° mother's womb!　　230
Thou loathèd issue of thy father's loins!
Thou rag of honor! Thou detested—

Richard. Margaret.

Queen Margaret. Richard!

Richard.　　　　　　　　　Ha?

Queen Margaret.　　　　　　　I call thee not.

Richard. I cry thee mercy° then, for I did think
That thou hadst called me all these bitter names.　　235

Queen Margaret. Why, so I did, but looked for no
reply.
O, let me make the period° to my curse!

Richard. 'Tis done by me, and ends in "Margaret."

Queen Elizabeth. Thus have you breathed your curse
against yourself.

Queen Margaret. Poor painted° queen, vain flourish°
of my fortune,　　240
Why strew'st thou sugar on that bottled° spider

227 *elvish-marked* disfigured by evil fairies　227 *hog* (the boar
was Richard's emblem)　228 *sealed* marked　230 *heavy* sorrowful
234 *cry thee mercy* beg your pardon　237 *period* end　240 *painted*
unreal　240 *vain flourish* useless decoration　241 *bottled* swollen

Whose deadly web ensnareth thee about?
Fool, fool, thou whet'st a knife to kill thyself.
The day will come that thou shalt wish for me
To help thee curse this poisonous bunch-backed
245   toad.

Hastings. False-boding woman, end thy frantic curse,
Lest to thy harm thou move our patience.

Queen Margaret. Foul shame upon you! You have all
moved mine.

Rivers. Were you well served, you would be taught
250   your duty.

Queen Margaret. To serve me well, you all should do
me duty,
Teach me to be your queen and you my subjects.
O, serve me well and teach yourselves that duty!

Dorset. Dispute not with her; she is lunatic.

Queen Margaret. Peace, Master Marquis, you are
malapert.°
255   Your fire-new stamp° of honor is scarce current.
O that your young nobility could judge
What 'twere to lose it and be miserable!
They that stand high have many blasts to shake
them,
And if they fall, they dash themselves to pieces.

Richard. Good counsel, marry! Learn it, learn it, Mar-
260   quis.

Dorset. It touches you, my lord, as much as me.

Richard. Ay, and much more; but I was born so high.
Our aerie° buildeth in the cedar's top
And dallies with the wind and scorns the sun.

Queen Margaret. And turns the sun to shade, alas!
265   alas!
Witness my son, now in the shade of death,

---

254 *malapert* impudent   255 *fire-new stamp* newly coined title
263 *aerie* brood of eagles

Whose bright outshining beams thy cloudy wrath
Hath in eternal darkness folded up.
Your aerie buildeth in our aerie's nest.
O God, that seest it, do not suffer it!   270
As it is won with blood, lost be it so!

Buckingham. Peace, peace, for shame, if not for
   charity.

Queen Margaret. Urge neither charity nor shame to
   me.
Uncharitably with me have you dealt,
And shamefully my hopes by you are butchered.   275
My charity is outrage, life my shame,
And in that shame still live my sorrow's rage!

Buckingham. Have done, have done.

Queen Margaret. O princely Buckingham, I'll kiss thy
   hand
In sign of league and amity with thee.   280
Now fair befall thee and thy noble house!
Thy garments are not spotted with our blood,
Nor thou within the compass of my curse.

Buckingham. Nor no one here; for curses never pass
The lips of those that breathe them in the air.   285

Queen Margaret. I will not think but they ascend the
   sky
And there awake God's gentle-sleeping peace.
O Buckingham, take heed of yonder dog!
Look when° he fawns he bites; and when he bites,
His venom tooth will rankle to the death.   290
Have not to do with him, beware of him.
Sin, death, and hell have set their marks on him
And all their ministers attend on him.

Richard. What doth she say, my Lord of Buckingham?

Buckingham. Nothing that I respect,° my gracious
   lord.   295

289 *Look when* whenever   295 *respect* pay heed to

Queen Margaret. What, dost thou scorn me for my
    gentle counsel
    And soothe the devil that I warn thee from?
    O, but remember this another day,
    When he shall split thy very heart with sorrow,
300   And say poor Margaret was a prophetess.
    Live each of you the subjects to his hate,
    And he to yours, and all of you to God's!   *Exit.*

Buckingham. My hair doth stand on end to hear her
    curses.

Rivers. And so doth mine. I muse° why she's at
    liberty.

305 *Richard.* I cannot blame her. By God's holy mother,
    She hath had too much wrong, and I repent
    My part thereof that I have done to her.

Queen Elizabeth. I never did her any to my knowl-
    edge.

Richard. Yet you have all the vantage of her wrong:
310   I was too hot to do somebody good
    That is too cold in thinking of it now.
    Marry, as for Clarence, he is well repaid;
    He is franked up° to fatting for his pains.
    God pardon them that are the cause thereof!

315 *Rivers.* A virtuous and a Christianlike conclusion,
    To pray for them that have done scathe° to us.

Richard. So do I ever—[*speaks to himself*] being well
    advised;
    For had I cursed now, I had cursed myself.

Enter Catesby.

Catesby. Madam, his Majesty doth call for you;
320   And for your Grace; and yours, my gracious lord.

Queen Elizabeth. Catesby, I come. Lords, will you go
    with me?

---

304 *muse* wonder   313 *franked up* shut up (like an animal to be
slaughtered)   316 *scathe* harm

Rivers. We wait upon your Grace.
                    Exeunt all but [*Richard of*] *Gloucester.*

Richard. I do the wrong, and first begin to brawl.
  The secret mischiefs that I set abroach°
  I lay unto the grievous charge of others.   325
  Clarence, who I indeed have cast in darkness,
  I do beweep to many simple gulls,°
  Namely to Derby, Hastings, Buckingham,
  And tell them 'tis the Queen and her allies°
  That stir the King against the Duke my brother.   330
  Now they believe it, and withal whet me
  To be revenged on Rivers, Dorset, Grey.
  But then I sigh, and with a piece of Scripture
  Tell them that God bids us do good for evil;
  And thus I clothe my naked villainy   335
  With odd old ends stol'n forth of holy writ,
  And seem a saint when most I play the devil.

                    Enter two Murderers.

  But soft! Here come my executioners.
  How now, my hardy, stout-resolvèd mates!
  Are you now going to dispatch this thing?   340

First Murderer. We are, my lord, and come to have
    the warrant
  That we may be admitted where he is.

Richard. Well thought upon; I have it here about me.
                    [*Gives the warrant.*]
  When you have done, repair to Crosby Place.
  But, sirs, be sudden in the execution,   345
  Withal obdurate, do not hear him plead;
  For Clarence is well-spoken, and perhaps
  May move your hearts to pity if you mark him.

First Murderer. Tut, tut, my lord, we will not stand
    to prate.
  Talkers are no good doers; be assured   350
  We go to use our hands and not our tongues.

324 *set abroach* originate   327 *gulls* dupes   329 *allies* kindred

Richard. Your eyes drop millstones when fools' eyes
    fall° tears.
  I like you, lads; about your business straight.°
  Go, go, dispatch.

First Murderer.   We will, my noble lord.   *Exeunt.*

Scene IV. [*The Tower.*]

Enter Clarence and Keeper.

Keeper. Why looks your Grace so heavily° today?

Clarence. O, I have passed a miserable night,
  So full of fearful dreams, of ugly sights,
  That, as I am a Christian faithful man,
5 I would not spend another such a night
  Though 'twere to buy a world of happy days,
  So full of dismal terror was the time.

Keeper. What was your dream, my lord? I pray you
  tell me.

Clarence. Methoughts° that I had broken from the
  Tower
10 And was embarked to cross to Burgundy,
  And in my company my brother Gloucester,
  Who from my cabin tempted me to walk
  Upon the hatches. Thence we looked toward Eng-
    land
  And cited up a thousand heavy times,
15 During the wars of York and Lancaster,
  That had befall'n us. As we paced along
  Upon the giddy footing of the hatches,
  Methought that Gloucester stumbled, and in falling
  Struck me (that thought to stay° him) overboard

352 *fall* let fall   353 *straight* at once I.iv.1 *heavily* sadly   9 *Methoughts* it seemed to me   19 *stay* support

Into the tumbling billows of the main.°   20
O Lord, methought what pain it was to drown!
What dreadful noise of water in mine ears!
What sights of ugly death within mine eyes!
Methoughts I saw a thousand fearful wracks;
A thousand men that fishes gnawed upon;   25
Wedges of gold, great anchors, heaps of pearl,
Inestimable stones, unvaluèd° jewels,
All scatt'red in the bottom of the sea.
Some lay in dead men's skulls, and in the holes
Where eyes did once inhabit there were crept,   30
As 'twere in scorn of eyes, reflecting gems
That wooed the slimy bottom of the deep
And mocked the dead bones that lay scatt'red by.

Keeper. Had you such leisure in the time of death
To gaze upon these secrets of the deep?   35

Clarence. Methought I had; and often did I strive
To yield the ghost, but still the envious flood
Stopped in my soul and would not let it forth
To find the empty, vast, and wand'ring air,
But smothered it within my panting bulk,°   40
Who almost burst to belch it in the sea.

Keeper. Awaked you not in this sore agony?

Clarence. No, no, my dream was lengthened after life.
O, then began the tempest to my soul!
I passed, methought, the melancholy flood,   45
With that sour ferryman° which poets write of,
Unto the kingdom of perpetual night.
The first that there did greet my stranger soul
Was my great father-in-law, renownèd Warwick,
Who spake aloud, "What scourge for perjury   50
Can this dark monarchy afford false Clarence?"
And so he vanished. Then came wand'ring by
A shadow like an angel, with bright hair
Dabbled in blood, and he shrieked out aloud,

20 *main* ocean   27 *unvaluèd* priceless   40 *bulk* body   46 *ferryman*
Charon, who ferried the dead across the Styx

"Clarence is come, false, fleeting,° perjured Clar-
55   ence,
That stabbed me in the field by Tewkesbury.
Seize on him, Furies, take him unto torment!"
With that, methought, a legion of foul fiends
Environed me and howlèd in mine ears
60   Such hideous cries that with the very noise
I, trembling, waked, and for a season after
Could not believe but that I was in hell,
Such terrible impression made my dream.

Keeper. No marvel, lord, though it affrighted you.
65   I am afraid, methinks, to hear you tell it.

Clarence. Ah, keeper, keeper, I have done these things
That now give evidence against my soul
For Edward's sake, and see how he requites me!
O God! If my deep pray'rs cannot appease thee,
70   But thou wilt be avenged on my misdeeds,
Yet execute thy wrath in me alone.
O, spare my guiltless wife and my poor children!
Keeper, I prithee sit by me awhile.
My soul is heavy, and I fain would sleep.

Keeper. I will, my lord. God give your Grace good
75   rest!   [*Clarence sleeps.*]

Enter Brakenbury, the Lieutenant.

Brakenbury. Sorrow breaks seasons and reposing
      hours,
Makes the night morning and the noontide night.
Princes have but their titles for their glories,
An outward honor for an inward toil,
80   And for unfelt imaginations°
They often feel a world of restless cares;
So that between their titles and low name
There's nothing differs but the outward fame.

Enter two Murderers.

First Murderer. Ho! Who's here?

55 *fleeting* fickle   80 *unfelt imaginations* pleasures imagined but not
felt

Brakenbury. What wouldst thou, fellow? And how
   cam'st thou hither?   85

First Murderer. I would speak with Clarence, and I
   came hither on my legs.

Brakenbury. What, so brief?

Second Murderer. 'Tis better, sir, than to be tedious.
   Let him see our commission, and talk no more.   90
                   [Brakenbury] reads [it].

Brakenbury. I am in this commanded to deliver
   The noble Duke of Clarence to your hands.
   I will not reason what is meant hereby,
   Because I will be guiltless from the meaning.
   There lies the Duke asleep, and there the keys.   95
   I'll to the King and signify to him
   That thus I have resigned to you my charge.

First Murderer. You may, sir, 'tis a point of wisdom.
   Fare you well.
            Exit [Brakenbury with Keeper].

Second Murderer. What, shall we stab him as he   100
   sleeps?

First Murderer. No, he'll say 'twas done cowardly
   when he wakes.

Second Murderer. Why, he shall never wake until the
   great Judgment Day.   105

First Murderer. Why, then he'll say we stabbed him
   sleeping.

Second Murderer. The urging of that word "judgment"
   hath bred a kind of remorse in me.

First Murderer. What, art thou afraid?   110

Second Murderer. Not to kill him, having a warrant;
   but to be damned for killing him, from the which
   no warrant can defend me.

First Murderer. I thought thou hadst been resolute.

115 *Second Murderer.* So I am—to let him live.

First Murderer. I'll back to the Duke of Gloucester and tell him so.

Second Murderer. Nay, I prithee stay a little. I hope this passionate humor° of mine will change; it was
120 wont to hold me but while one tells° twenty.

First Murderer. How dost thou feel thyself now?

Second Murderer. Faith, some certain dregs of conscience are yet within me.

First Murderer. Remember our reward when the
125 deed's done.

Second Murderer. Zounds,° he dies! I had forgot the reward.

First Murderer. Where's thy conscience now?

Second Murderer. O, in the Duke of Gloucester's
130 purse.

First Murderer. When he opens his purse to give us our reward, thy conscience flies out.

Second Murderer. 'Tis no matter, let it go. There's few or none will entertain it.

135 *First Murderer.* What if it come to thee again?

Second Murderer. I'll not meddle with it; it makes a man a coward. A man cannot steal, but it accuseth him; a man cannot swear, but it checks him; a man cannot lie with his neighbor's wife, but it detects
140 him. 'Tis a blushing shamefaced spirit that mutinies in a man's bosom. It fills a man full of obstacles. It made me once restore a purse of gold that, by chance, I found. It beggars any man that keeps it. It is turned out of towns and cities for a dangerous
145 thing, and every man that means to live well endeavors to trust to himself and live without it.

---

119 *passionate humor* compassionate mood   120 *tells* counts   126
Zounds (an oath, from "By God's wounds")

First Murderer. Zounds, 'tis even now at my elbow, persuading me not to kill the Duke.

Second Murderer. Take the devil in thy mind, and believe him° not. He would insinuate with thee but   150
to make thee sigh.

First Murderer. I am strong-framed; he cannot prevail with me.

Second Murderer. Spoke like a tall° man that respects thy reputation. Come, shall we fall to work?   155

First Murderer. Take him on the costard° with the hilts of thy sword, and then throw him into the malmsey butt° in the next room.

Second Murderer. O excellent device! And make a sop° of him.   160

First Murderer. Soft, he wakes.

Second Murderer. Strike!

First Murderer. No, we'll reason° with him.

Clarence. Where art thou, keeper? Give me a cup of wine.

Second Murderer. You shall have wine enough, my lord, anon.   165

Clarence. In God's name, what art thou?

First Murderer. A man, as you are.

Clarence. But not as I am, royal.

First Murderer. Nor you as we are, loyal.

Clarence. Thy voice is thunder, but thy looks are humble.   170

First Murderer. My voice is now the King's, my looks mine own.

150 *him* i.e., conscience   154 *tall* brave   156 *costard* head   158 *malmsey butt* cask of malmsey, a Greek wine   160 *sop* piece of bread soaked in wine   163 *reason* talk

Clarence. How darkly and how deadly dost thou
   speak!
   Your eyes do menace me. Why look you pale?
   Who sent you hither? Wherefore do you come?

175 *Second Murderer.* To, to, to—

Clarence. To murder me?

Both. Ay, ay.

Clarence. You scarcely have the hearts to tell me so,
   And therefore cannot have the hearts to do it.
180 Wherein, my friends, have I offended you?

First Murderer. Offended us you have not, but the
   King.

Clarence. I shall be reconciled to him again.

Second Murderer. Never, my lord; therefore prepare
   to die.

Clarence. Are you drawn forth among a world of men
185 To slay the innocent? What is my offense?
   Where is the evidence that doth accuse me?
   What lawful quest° have given their verdict up
   Unto the frowning judge? Or who pronounced
   The bitter sentence of poor Clarence' death?
190 Before I be convict by course of law,
   To threaten me with death is most unlawful.
   I charge you, as you hope to have redemption
   By Christ's dear blood shed for our grievous sins,
   That you depart, and lay no hands on me.
195 The deed you undertake is damnable.°

First Murderer. What we will do, we do upon command.

Second Murderer. And he that hath commanded is our
   king.

Clarence. Erroneous vassals! The great King of kings
   Hath in the table of his law commanded
200 That thou shalt do no murder. Will you then

187 *quest* jury   195 *damnable* i.e., one which will damn your souls

Spurn at his edict and fulfill a man's?
Take heed; for he holds vengeance in his hand
To hurl upon their heads that break his law.

Second Murderer. And that same vengeance doth he
    hurl on thee
For false forswearing and for murder too.   205
Thou didst receive the sacrament to fight
In quarrel of the house of Lancaster.

First Murderer. And like a traitor to the name of God
Didst break that vow, and with thy treacherous
    blade
Unrip'st the bowels of thy sov'reign's son.   210

Second Murderer. Whom thou wast sworn to cherish
    and defend.

First Murderer. How canst thou urge God's dreadful
    law to us
When thou hast broke it in such dear° degree?

Clarence. Alas! For whose sake did I that ill deed?
For Edward, for my brother, for his sake.   215
He sends you not to murder me for this,
For in that sin he is as deep as I.
If God will be avengèd for the deed,
O, know you yet he doth it publicly.
Take not the quarrel from his pow'rful arm.   220
He needs no indirect or lawless course
To cut off those that have offended him.

First Murderer. Who made thee then a bloody min-
    ister
When gallant-springing brave Plantagenet,
That princely novice,° was struck dead by thee?   225

Clarence. My brother's love, the devil, and my rage.

First Murderer. Thy brother's love, our duty, and thy
    faults
Provoke us hither now to slaughter thee.

Clarence. If you do love my brother, hate not me.

213 *dear* high   225 *princely novice* young prince

230   I am his brother, and I love him well.
       If you are hired for meed,° go back again,
       And I will send you to my brother Gloucester,
       Who shall reward you better for my life
       Than Edward will for tidings of my death.

Second Murderer. You are deceived; your brother
235   Gloucester hates you.

Clarence. O, no, he loves me and he holds me dear.
       Go you to him from me.

First Murderer.   Ay, so we will.

Clarence. Tell him, when that our princely father York
       Blessed his three sons with his victorious arm
240   And charged us from his soul to love each other,
       He little thought of this divided friendship.
       Bid Gloucester think on this, and he will weep.

First Murderer. Ay, millstones, as he lessoned° us to
       weep.

Clarence. O, do not slander him, for he is kind.

First Murderer. Right as° snow in harvest. Come, you
245   deceive yourself.
       'Tis he that sends us to destroy you here.

Clarence. It cannot be, for he bewept my fortune
       And hugged me in his arms and swore with sobs
       That he would labor° my delivery.

250 *First Murderer.* Why so he doth, when he delivers you
       From this earth's thralldom to the joys of heaven.

Second Murderer. Make peace with God, for you must
       die, my lord.

Clarence. Have you that holy feeling in your souls
       To counsel me to make my peace with God,
255   And are you yet to your own souls so blind
       That you will war with God by murd'ring me?

---

231 *meed* reward   243 *lessoned* taught   245 *Right as* just like
249 *labor* work for

O, sirs, consider, they that set you on
To do this deed will hate you for the deed.

Second Murderer. What shall we do?

Clarence.   Relent, and save your souls.

First Murderer. Relent! No. 'Tis cowardly and woman-
  ish.   260

Clarence. Not to relent is beastly, savage, devilish.
  [*To Second Murderer*] My friend, I spy some pity
  in thy looks.
  O, if thine eye be not a flatterer,
  Come thou on my side and entreat for me.
  A begging prince what beggar pities not?   265
  Which of you, if you were a prince's son,
  Being pent from liberty as I am now,
  If two such murderers as yourselves came to you,
  Would not entreat for life? As you would beg,
  Were you in my distress—   270

Second Murderer. Look behind you, my lord!

First Murderer. Take that! And that! (*Stabs him.*) If
  all this will not do,
  I'll drown you in the malmsey butt within.
                              Exit [*with the body*].

Second Murderer. A bloody deed and desperately
  dispatched!
  How fain, like Pilate, would I wash my hands   275
  Of this most grievous murder!

                Enter First Murderer.

First Murderer. How now? What mean'st thou that
  thou help'st me not?
  By heaven, the Duke shall know how slack you
  have been.

Second Murderer. I would he knew that I had saved
  his brother!
  Take thou the fee, and tell him what I say,   280
  For I repent me that the Duke is slain.   *Exit.*

First Murderer. So do not I. Go, coward as thou art.
　　　　Well, I'll go hide the body in some hole
　　　　Till that the Duke give order for his burial;
285　　And when I have my meed, I will away,
　　　　For this will out, and then I must not stay.　　*Exit.*

ACT II

Scene I. [*The palace.*]

Flourish.° Enter the King, sick, the Queen, Lord
Marquis Dorset, [Grey,] Rivers, Hastings,
Catesby, Buckingham, Woodville, [and Scales].

King Edward. Why, so. Now have I done a good day's
    work.
  You peers, continue this united league.
  I every day expect an embassage
  From my Redeemer to redeem me hence;
  And more in peace my soul shall part to heaven,   *5*
  Since I have made my friends at peace on earth.
  Rivers and Hastings, take each other's hand;
  Dissemble° not your hatred, swear your love.

Rivers. By heaven, my soul is purged from grudging
    hate,
  And with my hand I seal my true heart's love.   *10*

Hastings. So thrive I as I truly swear the like!

King Edward. Take heed you dally° not before your
    king,
  Lest he that is the supreme King of kings

II.i.s.d. *Flourish* fanfare of trumpets   8 *Dissemble* disguise by false
pretense   12 *dally* trifle

Confound your hidden falsehood and award
15 Either of you to be the other's end.

Hastings. So prosper I as I swear perfect love!

Rivers. And I as I love Hastings with my heart!

King Edward. Madam, yourself is not exempt from
     this;
   Nor you, son Dorset; Buckingham, nor you;
20 You have been factious one against the other.
   Wife, love Lord Hastings, let him kiss your hand,
   And what you do, do it unfeignedly.

Queen Elizabeth. There, Hastings. I will never more
     remember
   Our former hatred, so thrive I and mine!

King Edward. Dorset, embrace him; Hastings, love
25   Lord Marquis.

Dorset. This interchange of love, I here protest,
   Upon my part shall be inviolable.

Hastings. And so swear I.

King Edward. Now, princely Buckingham, seal thou
     this league
30 With thy embracements to my wife's allies,
   And make me happy in your unity.

Buckingham. [*To the Queen*] Whenever Buckingham
     doth turn his hate
   Upon your Grace, but° with all duteous love
   Doth cherish you and yours, God punish me
35 With hate in those where I expect most love!
   When I have most need to employ a friend,
   And most assurèd that he is a friend,
   Deep, hollow, treacherous, and full of guile
   Be he unto me! This do I beg of God,
40 When I am cold in zeal to you or yours. *Embrace.*

King Edward. A pleasing cordial, princely Bucking-
     ham,

33 *but* (the meaning calls for "and not")

Is this thy vow unto my sickly heart.
There wanteth now our brother Gloucester here
To make the blessèd period° of this peace.

Buckingham. And in good time,   45
Here comes Sir Richard Ratcliffe and the Duke.

Enter Ratcliffe and [Richard, Duke of] Gloucester.

Richard. Good morrow to my sovereign king and
    queen;
And, princely peers, a happy time of day!

King Edward. Happy indeed, as we have spent the
    day.
Gloucester, we have done deeds of charity,   50
Made peace of enmity, fair love of hate,
Between these swelling wrong-incensèd peers.

Richard. A blessèd labor, my most sovereign lord.
Among this princely heap° if any here
By false intelligence or wrong surmise   55
Hold me a foe;
If I unwittingly, or in my rage,
Have aught committed that is hardly borne°
By any in this presence, I desire
To reconcile me to his friendly peace.   60
'Tis death to me to be at enmity;
I hate it, and desire all good men's love.
First, madam, I entreat true peace of you,
Which I will purchase with my duteous service;
Of you, my noble cousin Buckingham,   65
If ever any grudge were lodged between us;
Of you and you, Lord Rivers and of Dorset,
That all without desert° have frowned on me;
Of you, Lord Woodville, and, Lord Scales,° of you;
Dukes, earls, lords, gentlemen; indeed, of all.   70
I do not know that Englishman alive
With whom my soul is any jot at odds

44 *period* conclusion   54 *heap* company, group   58 *hardly borne*
resented   68 *all without desert* wholly without my deserving it
69 *Lord Woodville, and, Lord Scales* (historically, these are both
other titles of Anthony Woodville, Earl Rivers)

More than the infant that is born tonight.
I thank my God for my humility.

Queen Elizabeth. A holy day shall this be kept here-
75   after.
I would to God all strifes were well compounded.°
My sovereign lord, I do beseech your Highness
To take our brother Clarence to your Grace.

Richard. Why, madam, have I off'red love for this,
80   To be so flouted in this royal presence?
Who knows not that the gentle Duke is dead?

                               They all start.

You do him injury to scorn his corse.

King Edward. Who knows not he is dead! Who knows
he is?

Queen Elizabeth. All-seeing heaven, what a world is
this!

85 *Buckingham.* Look I so pale, Lord Dorset, as the rest?

Dorset. Ay, my good lord; and no man in the presence
But his red color hath forsook his cheeks.

King Edward. Is Clarence dead? The order was reversed.

Richard. But he, poor man, by your first order died,
90   And that a wingèd Mercury did bear;
Some tardy cripple bare the countermand,
That came too lag° to see him burièd.
God grant that some, less noble and less loyal,
Nearer in bloody thoughts, and° not in blood,
95   Deserve not worse than wretched Clarence did,
And yet go current from° suspicion!

      Enter [Lord Stanley,] Earl of Derby.

Stanley. A boon, my sovereign, for my service done!

King Edward. I prithee peace. My soul is full of
sorrow.

76 *compounded* settled   92 *lag* late   94 *and* if   96 *go current from*
are taken at face value without

Stanley. I will not rise unless your Highness hear me.

King Edward. Then say at once what is it thou requests.   *100*

Stanley. The forfeit, sovereign, of my servant's life,°
  Who slew today a riotous gentleman
  Lately attendant on the Duke of Norfolk.

King Edward. Have I a tongue to doom my brother's
  death,
  And shall that tongue give pardon to a slave?   *105*
  My brother killed no man, his fault was thought,
  And yet his punishment was bitter death.
  Who sued to me for him? Who, in my wrath,
  Kneeled at my feet and bid me be advised?°
  Who spoke of brotherhood? Who spoke of love?   *110*
  Who told me how the poor soul did forsake
  The mighty Warwick and did fight for me?
  Who told me, in the field at Tewkesbury
  When Oxford had me down, he rescuèd me
  And said, "Dear brother, live, and be a king"?   *115*
  Who told me, when we both lay in the field
  Frozen almost to death, how he did lap° me
  Even in his garments, and did give himself
  All thin and naked, to the numb-cold night?
  All this from my remembrance brutish wrath   *120*
  Sinfully plucked, and not a man of you
  Had so much grace to put it in my mind.
  But when your carters or your waiting vassals
  Have done a drunken slaughter and defaced
  The precious image of our dear Redeemer,   *125*
  You straight are on your knees for "Pardon,
    pardon!"
  And I, unjustly too, must grant it you.
                                    [*Stanley rises.*]
  But for my brother not a man would speak,
  Nor I, ungracious, speak unto myself
  For him, poor soul. The proudest of you all   *130*
  Have been beholding to him in his life;

101 *forfeit . . . life* i.e., forfeited life   109 *be advised* consider carefully   117 *lap* wrap

Yet none of you would once beg for his life.
O God, I fear thy justice will take hold
On me and you, and mine and yours, for this!
Come, Hastings, help me to my closet.° Ah, poor
135   Clarence!   *Exeunt some with King and Queen.*

Richard. This is the fruits of rashness. Marked you not
How that the guilty kindred of the Queen
Looked pale when they did hear of Clarence'
      death?
O, they did urge it still unto the King!
140   God will revenge it. Come, lords, will you go
To comfort Edward with our company?

Buckingham. We wait upon your Grace.   *Exeunt.*

Scene II. [*The palace.*]

*Enter the old Duchess of York, with the two Children
of Clarence.*

Boy. Good grandam, tell us, is our father dead?

Duchess of York. No, boy.

Daughter. Why do you weep so oft, and beat your
      breast,
And cry, "O Clarence, my unhappy son"?

5   *Boy.* Why do you look on us, and shake your head,
And call us orphans, wretches, castaways,
If that our noble father were alive?

Duchess of York. My pretty cousins,° you mistake me
      both.
I do lament the sickness of the King,
10   As loath to lose him, not your father's death.
It were lost sorrow to wail one that's lost.

135 *closet* private room   II.ii.8 *cousins* relatives

Boy. Then you conclude, my grandam, he is dead.
  The King mine uncle is too blame° for it.
  God will revenge it, whom I will importune
  With earnest prayers all to that effect.   15

Daughter. And so will I.

Duchess of York. Peace, children, peace! The King
    doth love you well.
  Incapable° and shallow innocents,
  You cannot guess who caused your father's death.

Boy. Grandam, we can; for my good uncle Gloucester   20
  Told me the King, provoked to it by the Queen,
  Devised impeachments° to imprison him;
  And when my uncle told me so, he wept,
  And pitied me, and kindly kissed my cheek;
  Bade me rely on him as on my father,   25
  And he would love me dearly as a child.

Duchess of York. Ah, that deceit should steal such
    gentle shape°
  And with a virtuous visor° hide deep vice!
  He is my son, ay, and therein my shame;
  Yet from my dugs he drew not this deceit.   30

Boy. Think you my uncle did dissemble, grandam?

Duchess of York. Ay, boy.

Boy. I cannot think it. Hark! What noise is this?

  *Enter the Queen, [Elizabeth,] with her hair about
      her ears, Rivers and Dorset after her.*

Queen Elizabeth. Ah, who shall hinder me to wail and
    weep,
  To chide my fortune, and torment myself?   35
  I'll join with black despair against my soul
  And to myself become an enemy.

Duchess of York. What means this scene of rude im-
    patience?

13 *too blame* too blameworthy   18 *Incapable* unable to understand
22 *impeachments* accusations   27 *shape* disguise   28 *visor* mask

Queen Elizabeth. To make an act of tragic violence.
40   Edward, my lord, thy son, our king, is dead!
        Why grow the branches when the root is gone?
        Why wither not the leaves that want their sap?
        If you will live, lament; if die, be brief,
        That our swift-wingèd souls may catch the King's,
45   Or like obedient subjects follow him
        To his new kingdom of ne'er-changing night.

Duchess of York. Ah, so much interest° have I in thy
            sorrow
        As I had title° in thy noble husband!
        I have bewept a worthy husband's death,
50   And lived with looking on his images;°
        But now two mirrors of his princely semblance°
        Are cracked in pieces by malignant death,
        And I for comfort have but one false glass
        That grieves me when I see my shame in him.
55   Thou art a widow, yet thou art a mother
      · And hast the comfort of thy children left;
        But death hath snatched my husband from mine
            arms
        And plucked two crutches from my feeble hands,
        Clarence and Edward. O, what° cause have I,
60   Thine being but a moi'ty of my moan,°
        To overgo thy woes and drown thy cries!

Boy. Ah, aunt, you wept not for our father's death.
        How can we aid you with our kindred tears?

Daughter. Our fatherless distress was left unmoaned;
65   Your widow-dolor likewise be unwept!

Queen Elizabeth. Give me no help in lamentation;
        I am not barren to bring forth complaints.
        All springs reduce° their currents to mine eyes,
        That I, being governed by the watery moon,
70   May send forth plenteous tears to drown the world.
        Ah for my husband, for my dear lord Edward!

---

47 *interest* share   48 *title* legal right   50 *images* i.e., children
51 *semblance* appearance   59 *what* how much   60 *moi'ty of my
moan* half of my grief   68 *reduce* bring

Children. Ah for our father, for our dear lord Clarence!

Duchess of York. Alas for both, both mine, Edward and Clarence!

Queen Elizabeth. What stay° had I but Edward? And he's gone.

Children. What stay had we but Clarence? And he's gone.   75

Duchess of York. What stays had I but they? And they are gone.

Queen Elizabeth. Was never widow had so dear a loss.

Children. Were never orphans had so dear a loss.

Duchess of York. Was never mother had so dear a loss.
 Alas, I am the mother of these griefs!   80
 Their woes are parceled,° mine is general.
 She for an Edward weeps, and so do I;
 I for a Clarence weep, so doth not she.
 These babes for Clarence weep, and so do I;
 I for an Edward weep, so do not they.   85
 Alas, you three on me, threefold distressed,
 Pour all your tears! I am your sorrow's nurse,
 And I will pamper it with lamentation.

Dorset. Comfort, dear mother; God is much displeased
 That you take with unthankfulness his doing.   90
 In common worldly things 'tis called ungrateful
 With dull unwillingness to repay a debt
 Which with a bounteous hand was kindly lent;
 Much more to be thus opposite with° heaven
 For° it requires the royal debt it lent you.   95

Rivers. Madam, bethink you like a careful mother
 Of the young prince your son. Send straight for him;

74 *stay* support 81 *parceled* particular 94 *opposite with* opposed to 95 *For* because

Let him be crowned; in him your comfort lives.
Drown desperate sorrow in dead Edward's grave
100 And plant your joys in living Edward's throne.

Enter Richard, Buckingham, [Stanley, Earl of]
Derby, Hastings, and Ratcliffe.

Richard. Sister, have comfort. All of us have cause
To wail the dimming of our shining star;
But none can help our harms by wailing them.
Madam, my mother, I do cry you mercy;
105 I did not see your Grace. Humbly on my knee
I crave your blessing.

Duchess of York. God bless thee, and put meekness
in thy breast,
Love, charity, obedience, and true duty!

Richard. Amen! [*Aside*] And make me die a good old
man!
110 That is the butt-end of a mother's blessing;
I marvel that her Grace did leave it out.

Buckingham. You cloudy princes and heart-sorrowing
peers
That bear this heavy mutual load of moan,
Now cheer each other in each other's love.
115 Though we have spent our harvest of this king,
We are to reap the harvest of his son.
The broken rancor of your high-swol'n hates,
But lately splintered,° knit, and joined together,
Must gently be preserved, cherished, and kept.°
120 Me seemeth° good that with some little train
Forthwith from Ludlow the young prince be fet°
Hither to London, to be crowned our king.

Rivers. Why with some little train, my Lord of Buckingham?

Buckingham. Marry, my lord, lest by a multitude

---

118 *splintered* set in splints   119 *Must . . . kept* (the subject has
shifted from *rancor* to its opposite)   120 *Me seemeth* it seems to
me   121 *fet* fetched

The new-healed wound of malice should break out,   *125*
Which would be so much the more dangerous
By how much the estate is green° and yet un-
    governed.
Where every horse bears his commanding rein
And may direct his course as please himself,
As well the fear of harm as harm apparent,°   *130*
In my opinion, ought to be prevented.

Richard. I hope the King made peace with all of us;
And the compact is firm and true in me.

Rivers. And so in me; and so (I think) in all.
Yet, since it is but green, it should be put   *135*
To no apparent likelihood of breach,
Which haply° by much company might be urged.
Therefore I say with noble Buckingham
That it is meet° so few should fetch the Prince.

Hastings. And so say I.   *140*

Richard. Then be it so; and go we to determine
Who they shall be that straight shall post to Lud-
    low.
Madam, and you, my sister, will you go
To give your censures° in this business?

Queen and Duchess of York. With all our hearts.   *145*
        Exeunt. Manet° Buckingham and Richard.

Buckingham. My lord, whoever journeys to the
    Prince,
For God sake let not us two stay at home;
For by the way I'll sort occasion,°
As index° to the story we late talked of,
To part the Queen's proud kindred from the Prince.   *150*

Richard. My other self, my counsel's consistory,°

127 *estate is green* regime is new   130 *apparent* seen clearly
137 *haply* perhaps   139 *meet* fitting   144 *censures* judgments   145
s.d. *Manet* (Latin for "remains." The third person plural is *manent*,
but the Elizabethans commonly used the third person singular—like
"exit"—for the plural)   148 *sort occasion* contrive opportunity
149 *index* preface   151 *consistory* council chamber

My oracle, my prophet, my dear cousin,
I, as a child, will go by thy direction.
Toward Ludlow then, for we'll not stay behind.

Exeunt.

Scene III. [*A street.*]

*Enter one Citizen at one door and another at the
other.*

First Citizen. Good morrow, neighbor. Whither away
    so fast?

Second Citizen. I promise you, I scarcely know myself.
    Hear you the news abroad?

First Citizen.   Yes, that the King is dead.

Second Citizen. Ill news, by'r Lady; seldom comes the
    better.°
5   I fear, I fear 'twill prove a giddy world.

Enter another Citizen.

Third Citizen. Neighbors, Godspeed!

First Citizen.   Give you good morrow, sir.

Third Citizen. Doth the news hold of good King Ed-
    ward's death?

Second Citizen. Ay, sir, it is too true, God help the
    while!

Third Citizen. Then, masters, look to see a troublous
    world.

First Citizen. No, no; by God's good grace his son
10   shall reign.

II.iii.4 *seldom comes the better* change for the better is rare (a
proverb)

Third Citizen. Woe to that land that's governed by a
  child!

Second Citizen. In him there is a hope of government,
  Which in his nonage counsel° under him,
  And, in his full and ripened years, himself,
  No doubt shall then and till then govern well.   15

First Citizen. So stood the state when Henry the Sixth
  Was crowned in Paris but at nine months old.

Third Citizen. Stood the state so? No, no, good
  friends, God wot!°
  For then this land was famously enriched
  With politic grave counsel; then the King   20
  Had virtuous uncles to protect his Grace.

First Citizen. Why, so hath this, both by his father and
  mother.

Third Citizen. Better it were they all came by his
  father,
  Or by his father there were none at all;
  For emulation° who shall now be nearest   25
  Will touch us all too near, if God prevent not.
  O, full of danger is the Duke of Gloucester,
  And the Queen's sons and brothers haught° and
  proud!
  And were they to be ruled,° and not to rule,
  This sickly land might solace° as before.   30

First Citizen. Come, come, we fear the worst. All will
  be well.

Third Citizen. When clouds are seen, wise men put on
  their cloaks;
  When great leaves fall, then winter is at hand;
  When the sun sets, who doth not look for night?
  Untimely storms makes men expect a dearth.°   35
  All may be well; but if God sort° it so,

12–13 *In him . . . counsel* there is hope of good rule in him, during
whose minority advisers 18 *wot* knows 25 *emulation* rivalry
28 *haught* haughty 29 *were they to be ruled* if they could be controlled 30 *solace* take comfort 35 *dearth* famine 36 *sort* arrange

'Tis more than we deserve or I expect.

Second Citizen. Truly, the hearts of men are full of
    fear.
    You cannot reason,° almost, with a man
40   That looks not heavily and full of dread.

Third Citizen. Before the days of change, still is it so.
    By a divine instinct men's minds mistrust
    Ensuing danger, as by proof° we see
    The water swell before a boist'rous storm.
45   But leave it all to God. Whither away?

Second Citizen. Marry, we were sent for to the justices.

Third Citizen. And so was I. I'll bear you company.
                     Exeunt.

Scene IV. [*The palace.*]

Enter [*the*] *Archbishop* [*of York*], [*the*] *young*
[*Duke of*] *York, the Queen,* [*Elizabeth,*] *and*
the Duchess [*of York*].

Archbishop. Last night, I hear, they lay at Stony
    Stratford;
    And at Northampton they do rest tonight;
    Tomorrow or next day they will be here.

Duchess of York. I long with all my heart to see the
    Prince.
5   I hope he is much grown since last I saw him.

Queen Elizabeth. But I hear no; they say my son of
    York
    Has almost overta'en him in his growth.

York. Ay, mother, but I would not have it so.

39 *reason* talk   43 *proof* experience

Duchess of York. Why, my good cousin? It is good to
  grow.

York. Grandam, one night as we did sit at supper,   *10*
  My uncle Rivers talked how I did grow
  More than my brother. "Ay," quoth my uncle
    Gloucester,
  "Small herbs have grace,° great weeds do grow
    apace."°
  And since, methinks, I would not grow so fast,
  Because sweet flow'rs are slow and weeds make
    haste.   *15*

Duchess of York. Good faith, good faith, the saying
    did not hold
  In him that did object° the same to thee.
  He was the wretched'st thing when he was young,
  So long a-growing and so leisurely,
  That, if his rule were true, he should be gracious.°   *20*

Archbishop. And so no doubt he is, my gracious
    madam.

Duchess of York. I hope he is; but yet let mothers
    doubt.

York. Now, by my troth, if I had been rememb'red,°
  I could have given my uncle's grace a flout°
  To touch his growth nearer than he touched mine.   *25*

Duchess of York. How, my young York? I prithee let
    me hear it.

York. Marry, they say, my uncle grew so fast
  That he could gnaw a crust at two hours old.
  'Twas full two years ere I could get a tooth.
  Grandam, this would have been a biting jest.   *30*

Duchess of York. I prithee, pretty York, who told thee
    this?

York. Grandam, his nurse.

II.iv.13 *grace* virtue   13 *apace* quickly   17 *object* bring as a
reproach   20 *gracious* virtuous   23 *been rememb'red* thought
24 *flout* taunt

Duchess of York. His nurse! Why, she was dead ere
    thou wast born.

York. If 'twere not she, I cannot tell who told me.

Queen Elizabeth. A parlous° boy! Go to, you are too
35   shrewd.°

Duchess of York. Good madam, be not angry with the
    child.

Queen Elizabeth. Pitchers have ears.°

Enter a Messenger.

Archbishop. Here comes a messenger. What news?

Messenger. Such news, my lord, as grieves me to re-
    port.

Queen Elizabeth. How doth the Prince?

40 *Messenger.*   Well, madam, and in health.

Duchess of York. What is thy news?

Messenger. Lord Rivers and Lord Grey are sent to
    Pomfret,
And with them Sir Thomas Vaughan, prisoners.

Duchess of York. Who hath committed them?

Messenger.   The mighty dukes,
Gloucester and Buckingham.

45 *Archbishop.*   For what offense?

Messenger. The sum of all I can I have disclosed.
Why or for what the nobles were committed
Is all unknown to me, my gracious lord.

Queen Elizabeth. Ay me! I see the ruin of my house.
50   The tiger now hath seized the gentle hind;°
Insulting tyranny begins to jut°
Upon the innocent and aweless° throne.
Welcome destruction, blood, and massacre!

---

35 *parlous* terribly quick-witted   35 *shrewd* sharp-tongued   37
Pitchers have ears (a proverb: small pitchers have great ears)
50 *hind* doe   51 *jut* encroach   52 *aweless* inspiring no awe

 I see, as in a map, the end of all.

Duchess of York. Accursèd and unquiet wrangling
  days,   55
 How many of you have mine eyes beheld!
 My husband lost his life to get the crown,
 And often up and down my sons were tossed
 For me to joy and weep their gain and loss;
 And being seated, and domestic broils°   60
 Clean overblown, themselves, the conquerors,
 Make war upon themselves, brother to brother,
 Blood to blood, self against self. O preposterous°
 And frantic outrage, end thy damnèd spleen,°
 Or let me die, to look on death no more!   65

Queen Elizabeth. Come, come, my boy; we will to
  sanctuary.°
 Madam, farewell.

Duchess of York. Stay, I will go with you.

Queen Elizabeth. You have no cause.

Archbishop.   [*To the Queen*] My gracious lady, go,
 And thither bear your treasure and your goods.
 For my part, I'll resign unto your Grace   70
 The seal I keep; and so betide to me
 As well I tender° you and all of yours!
 Go, I'll conduct you to the sanctuary.   *Exeunt.*

---

60 *domestic broils* civil wars   63 *preposterous* inverting natural
order   64 *spleen* malice   66 *sanctuary* refuge on church property
72 *tender* care for

ACT III

Scene I. [*A street.*]

The trumpets sound. Enter [the] young Prince,
the Dukes of Gloucester and Buckingham,
Lord Cardinal, [Catesby,] with others.

Buckingham. Welcome, sweet Prince, to London, to
your chamber.°

Richard. Welcome, dear cousin, my thoughts' sovereign.
The weary way hath made you melancholy.

Prince Edward. No, uncle, but our crosses° on the
way
5   Have made it tedious, wearisome, and heavy.
I want° more uncles here to welcome me.

Richard. Sweet Prince, the untainted virtue of your
years
Hath not yet dived into the world's deceit;
Nor more can you distinguish of a man
10   Than of his outward show, which, God he knows,
Seldom or never jumpeth° with the heart.
Those uncles which you want were dangerous;

III.i.1 *chamber* capital   **4** *crosses* vexations   **6** *want* (1) lack (2)
wish for   **11** *jumpeth* agrees

Your Grace attended to their sug'red words
But looked not on the poison of their hearts.
God keep you from them, and from such false
    friends!   *15*

Prince Edward. God keep me from false friends!
    But they were none.

Richard. My lord, the Mayor of London comes to
    greet you.

Enter Lord Mayor [and Citizens].

Lord Mayor. God bless your Grace with health and
    happy days!

Prince Edward. I thank you, good my lord, and thank
    you all.   [*Mayor and Citizens stand aside.*]
I thought my mother and my brother York   *20*
Would long ere this have met us on the way.
Fie, what a slug° is Hastings that he comes not
To tell us whether they will come or no!

Enter Lord Hastings.

Buckingham. And in good time here comes the sweat-
    ing lord.

Prince Edward. Welcome, my lord. What, will our
    mother come?   *25*

Hastings. On what occasion° God he knows, not I,
The Queen your mother and your brother York
Have taken sanctuary. The tender Prince
Would fain have come with me to meet your Grace,
But by his mother was perforce° withheld.   *30*

Buckingham. Fie, what an indirect and peevish°
    course
Is this of hers! Lord Cardinal, will your Grace
Persuade the Queen to send the Duke of York
Unto his princely brother presently?°

22 *slug* sluggard   26 *On what occasion* for what cause   30 *perforce*
by force   31 *indirect and peevish* devious and obstinate   34 *presently* at once

35 If she deny, Lord Hastings, go with him
    And from her jealous° arms pluck him perforce.

Cardinal. My Lord of Buckingham, if my weak or-
    atory
    Can from his mother win the Duke of York,
    Anon expect him here; but if she be obdurate
40 To mild entreaties, God in heaven forbid
    We should infringe the holy privilege
    Of blessèd sanctuary! Not for all this land
    Would I be guilty of so deep a sin.

Buckingham. You are too senseless-obstinate, my lord,
45 Too ceremonious° and traditional.
    Weigh it but with the grossness° of this age,
    You break not sanctuary in seizing him.
    The benefit thereof is always granted
    To those whose dealings have deserved the place
50 And those who have the wit to claim the place.
    This prince hath neither claimed it nor deserved it,
    And therefore, in mine opinion, cannot have it.
    Then, taking him from thence that is not there,
    You break no privilege nor charter there.
55 Oft have I heard of sanctuary men,
    But sanctuary children ne'er till now.

Cardinal. My lord, you shall o'errule my mind for
    once.
    Come on, Lord Hastings, will you go with me?

Hastings. I go, my lord.

Prince Edward. Good lords, make all the speedy haste
60   you may.   *Exit Cardinal and Hastings.*
    Say, uncle Gloucester, if our brother come,
    Where shall we sojourn till our coronation?

Richard. Where it seems best unto your royal self.
    If I may counsel you, some day or two
65 Your Highness shall repose you at the Tower;
    Then where you please, and shall be thought most
        fit

36 *jealous* suspicious   45 *ceremonious* punctilious   46 *grossness*
coarseness

For your best health and recreation.

Prince Edward. I do not like the Tower, of any place.°
Did Julius Caesar build that place, my lord?

Buckingham. He did, my gracious lord, begin that
place,   70
Which since succeeding ages have re-edified.°

Prince Edward. Is it upon record, or else reported
Successively from age to age, he built it?

Buckingham. Upon record, my gracious lord.

Prince Edward. But say, my lord, it were not reg-
ist'red,   75
Methinks the truth should live from age to age,
As 'twere retailed° to all posterity,
Even to the general all-ending day.

Richard. [*Aside*] So wise so young, they say do ne'er
live long.

Prince Edward. What say you, uncle?   80

Richard. I say, without characters° fame lives long.
[*Aside*] Thus, like the formal° Vice,° Iniquity,
I moralize° two meanings in one word.

Prince Edward. That Julius Caesar was a famous man.
With what° his valor did enrich his wit,   85
His wit set down to make his valor live.
Death makes no conquest of this conqueror,
For now he lives in fame, though not in life.
I'll tell you what, my cousin Buckingham—

Buckingham. What, my gracious lord?   90

Prince Edward. And if I live until I be a man,
I'll win our ancient right in France again
Or die a soldier as I lived a king.

---

68 *of any place* of all places   71 *re-edified* rebuilt   77 *retailed*
reported   81 *characters* written letters   82 *formal* careful to ob-
serve forms (i.e., hypocritical)   82 *Vice* mischief-maker in a morality play   83 *moralize* interpret   85 *With what* that with which

Richard. [*Aside*] Short summers lightly have a forward spring.°

Enter [*the*] *young* [*Duke of*] *York, Hastings, and
Cardinal.*

Buckingham. Now in good time here comes the Duke
95   of York.

Prince Edward. Richard of York, how fares our loving
brother?

York. Well, my dread° lord—so must I call you now.

Prince Edward. Ay, brother, to our grief, as it is yours.
Too late° he died that might have kept that title,
100   Which by his death hath lost much majesty.

Richard. How fares our cousin, noble Lord of York?

York. I thank you, gentle uncle. O, my lord,
You said that idle° weeds are fast in growth.
The Prince my brother hath outgrown me far.

Richard. He hath, my lord.

105   *York.*   And therefore is he idle?

Richard. O my fair cousin, I must not say so.

York. Then he is more beholding to you than I.

Richard. He may command me as my sovereign,
But you have power in me as in a kinsman.

110   *York.* I pray you, uncle, give me this dagger.

Richard. My dagger, little cousin? With all my heart.

Prince Edward. A beggar, brother?

York. Of my kind uncle, that I know will give,
And being but a toy,° which is no grief to give.

115   *Richard.* A greater gift than that I'll give my cousin.

94 *Short . . . spring* i.e., the short-lived are usually (*lightly*) preco-
cious   97 *dread* revered   99 *late* recently   103 *idle* useless   114 *toy*
trifle

York. A greater gift? O, that's the sword to it.

Richard. Ay, gentle cousin, were it light enough.

York. O, then I see you will part but with light° gifts!
In weightier things you'll say a beggar nay.

Richard. It is too heavy for your Grace to wear.   120

York. I weigh° it lightly, were it heavier.

Richard. What, would you have my weapon, little
lord?

York. I would, that I might thank you as you call me.

Richard. How?

York. Little.   125

Prince Edward. My Lord of York will still be cross°
in talk.
Uncle, your Grace knows how to bear with him.

York. You mean, to bear me, not to bear with me.
Uncle, my brother mocks both you and me;
Because that I am little, like an ape,   130
He thinks that you should bear me on your
shoulders.°

Buckingham. [*Aside*] With what a sharp, provided°
wit he reasons!
To mitigate the scorn he gives his uncle
He prettily and aptly taunts himself.
So cunning and so young is wonderful.   135

Richard. My lord, will't please you pass along?
Myself and my good cousin Buckingham
Will to your mother, to entreat of her
To meet you at the Tower and welcome you.

York. What, will you go unto the Tower, my lord?   140

---

118 *light* slight   121 *weigh* value   126 *still be cross* always be contrary   131 *bear me on your shoulders* i.e., carry me on your hunch-
back   132 *provided* ready

Prince Edward. My Lord Protector needs will have it
   so.

York. I shall not sleep in quiet at the Tower.

Richard. Why, what should you fear?

York. Marry, my uncle Clarence' angry ghost.
145   My grandam told me he was murd'red there.

Prince Edward. I fear no uncles dead.

Richard. Nor none that live, I hope.

Prince Edward. And if they live, I hope I need not
      fear.
   But come, my lord; with a heavy heart,
150   Thinking on them, go I unto the Tower.
   A sennet.° Exeunt Prince [*Edward*], *York, Hastings,*
                  [*Cardinal, and others*]. *Manet Richard,*
                        Buckingham, and Catesby.

Buckingham. Think you, my lord, this little prating
      York
   Was not incensèd° by his subtle mother
   To taunt and scorn you thus opprobriously?

Richard. No doubt, no doubt. O, 'tis a parlous boy,
155   Bold, quick, ingenious, forward, capable:
   He is all the mother's, from the top to toe.

Buckingham. Well, let them rest. Come hither,
      Catesby.
   Thou art sworn as deeply to effect° what we in-
      tend
   As closely to conceal what we impart.
160   Thou knowest our reasons urged upon the way.
   What thinkest thou? Is it not an easy matter
   To make William Lord Hastings of our mind
   For the installment° of this noble duke
   In the seat royal of this famous isle?

165 *Catesby.* He for his father's sake so loves the Prince

---

150 s.d. *sennet* trumpet signal   152 *incensèd* stirred up   158 *effect*
carry out   163 *installment* installation as a king

That he will not be won to aught against him.

Buckingham. What thinkest thou then of Stanley?
    What will he?

Catesby. He will do all in all as Hastings doth.

Buckingham. Well then, no more but this: go, gentle
    Catesby,
And, as it were far off, sound thou Lord Hastings   *170*
How he doth stand affected° to our purpose,
And summon him tomorrow to the Tower
To sit° about the coronation.
If thou dost find him tractable to us,
Encourage him, and tell him all our reasons.   *175*
If he be leaden, icy-cold, unwilling,
Be thou so too, and so break off the talk,
And give us notice of his inclination;
For we tomorrow hold divided councils,°
Wherein thyself shalt highly be employed.   *180*

Richard. Commend me to Lord William. Tell him,
    Catesby,
His ancient knot° of dangerous adversaries
Tomorrow are let blood at Pomfret Castle,
And bid my lord, for joy of this good news,
Give Mistress Shore one gentle kiss the more.   *185*

Buckingham. Good Catesby, go effect this business
    soundly.

Catesby. My good lords both, with all the heed I can.

Richard. Shall we hear from you, Catesby, ere we
    sleep?

Catesby. You shall, my lord.

Richard. At Crosby House, there shall you find us
    both.   *190*

                      Exit Catesby.

---

171 *affected* inclined   173 *sit* meet with the council   179 *divided
councils* i.e., meetings of the council in two separate groups   182
ancient knot long-standing clique

Buckingham. Now, my lord, what shall we do if we
    perceive
    Lord Hastings will not yield to our complots?°

Richard. Chop off his head. Something we will deter-
    mine.
    And look when° I am king, claim thou of me
195 The earldom of Hereford and all the movables°
    Whereof the King my brother was possessed.

Buckingham. I'll claim that promise at your Grace's
    hand.

Richard. And look° to have it yielded with all kind-
    ness.
    Come, let us sup betimes,° that afterwards
200 We may digest° our complots in some form.
                                             Exeunt.

Scene II. [*Before Lord Hastings' house.*]

Enter a Messenger to the door of Hastings.

Messenger. My lord! My lord!

Hastings. [*Within*] Who knocks?

Messenger. One from the Lord Stanley.

Hastings. [*Within*] What is't o'clock?

5 *Messenger.* Upon the stroke of four.

                Enter Lord Hastings.

Hastings. Cannot my Lord Stanley sleep these tedious
    nights?

Messenger. So it appears by that I have to say:

192 *complots* plots   194 *look when* whenever   195 *movables* goods
198 *look* expect   199 *betimes* early   200 *digest* arrange

First, he commends him to your noble self.

Hastings. What then?

Messenger. Then certifies your lordship that this night   10
He dreamt the boar had rasèd off his helm.°
Besides, he says there are two councils kept,
And that may be determined at the one
Which may make you and him to rue at th' other.
Therefore he sends to know your lordship's
    pleasure,   15
If you will presently take horse with him
And with all speed post with him toward the
    north
To shun the danger that his soul divines.

Hastings. Go, fellow, go return unto thy lord;
Bid him not fear the separated council.   20
His honor and myself are at the one,
And at the other is my good friend Catesby;
Where nothing can proceed that toucheth us
Whereof I shall not have intelligence.
Tell him his fears are shallow, without instance;°   25
And for his dreams, I wonder he's so simple
To trust the mock'ry of unquiet slumbers.
To fly the boar before the boar pursues
Were to incense the boar to follow us
And make pursuit where he did mean no chase.   30
Go bid thy master rise and come to me,
And we will both together to the Tower,
Where he shall see the boar will use us kindly.

Messenger. I'll go, my lord, and tell him what you
    say.   *Exit.*

Enter Catesby.

Catesby. Many good morrows to my noble lord!   35

Hastings. Good morrow, Catesby; you are early stir-
    ring.
What news, what news, in this our tott'ring state?

111.ii.11 *the boar . . . helm* i.e., Richard had cut off his head   25
instance cause

Catesby. It is a reeling world indeed, my lord,
And I believe will never stand upright
40   Till Richard wear the garland of the realm.

Hastings. How! Wear the garland! Dost thou mean
the crown?

Catesby. Ay, my good lord.

Hastings. I'll have this crown of mine cut from my
shoulders
Before I'll see the crown so foul misplaced.
45   But canst thou guess that he doth aim at it?

Catesby. Ay, on my life, and hopes to find you
forward
Upon his party° for the gain thereof;
And thereupon he sends you this good news,
That this same very day your enemies,
50   The kindred of the Queen, must die at Pomfret.

Hastings. Indeed I am no mourner for that news,
Because they have been still my adversaries;
But that I'll give my voice on Richard's side
To bar my master's heirs in true descent,
55   God knows I will not do it, to the death!

Catesby. God keep your lordship in that gracious°
mind!

Hastings. But I shall laugh at this a twelvemonth
hence,
That they which brought me in my master's hate,
I live to look upon their tragedy.
60   Well, Catesby, ere a fortnight make me older,
I'll send some packing° that yet think not on't.

Catesby. 'Tis a vile thing to die, my gracious lord,
When men are unprepared and look not for it.

Hastings. O monstrous, monstrous! And so falls it out
65   With Rivers, Vaughan, Grey; and so 'twill do
With some men else that think themselves as safe

47 *party* side   56 *gracious* virtuous   61 *send some packing* get rid
of some

As thou and I, who, as thou know'st, are dear
To princely Richard and to Buckingham.

Catesby. The Princes both make high account of
you—
[*Aside*] For they account his head upon the Bridge.°   *70*

Hastings. I know they do, and I have well deserved it.

Enter Lord Stanley.

Come on, come on! Where is your boarspear, man?
Fear you the boar, and go so unprovided?

Stanley. My lord, good morrow; good morrow,
Catesby.
You may jest on, but, by the holy rood,°   *75*
I do not like these several° councils, I.

Hastings. My lord, I hold my life as dear as yours,°
And never in my days, I do protest,
Was it so precious to me as 'tis now.
Think you, but that I know our state° secure,   *80*
I would be so triumphant as I am?

Stanley. The lords at Pomfret, when they rode from
London,
Were jocund and supposed their states were sure,
And they indeed had no cause to mistrust;
But yet you see how soon the day o'ercast.   *85*
This sudden stab of rancor I misdoubt.°
Pray God, I say, I prove a needless coward!
What, shall we toward the Tower? The day is
spent.°

Hastings. Come, come, have with you. Wot° you what,
my lord?
Today the lords you talk of are beheaded.   *90*

Stanley. They, for their truth,° might better wear
their heads

---

70 *the Bridge* London Bridge (where traitors' heads were displayed)
75 *rood* cross   76 *several* separate   77 *as yours* i.e., as you do
yours   80 *state* position   86 *misdoubt* have misgivings about
88 *spent* wasted   89 *Wot* know   91 *truth* loyalty

Than some that have accused them wear their hats.
But come, my lord, let's away.

Enter a Pursuivant.°

Hastings. Go on before. I'll talk with this good fellow.
    Exit Lord Stanley, and Catesby.
95   How now, sirrah?° How goes the world with thee?

Pursuivant. The better that your lordship please to
    ask.

Hastings. I tell thee, man, 'tis better with me now
Than when thou met'st me last where now we meet.
Then was I going prisoner to the Tower
100   By the suggestion° of the Queen's allies;
But now I tell thee—keep it to thyself—
This day those enemies are put to death,
And I in better state than e'er I was.

Pursuivant. God hold it, to your honor's good con-
    tent!

105 *Hastings.* Gramercy,° fellow; there, drink that for me.
    Throws him his purse.

Pursuivant. I thank your honor.   *Exit Pursuivant.*

Enter a Priest.

Priest. Well met, my lord; I am glad to see your honor.

Hastings. I thank thee, good Sir° John, with all my
    heart.
I am in your debt for your last exercise;°
110   Come the next Sabbath, and I will content° you.
    He whispers in his ear.

Enter Buckingham.

Buckingham. What, talking with a priest, Lord Cham-
    berlain?
Your friends at Pomfret, they do need the priest;

93 s.d. *Pursuivant* royal messenger with power to execute warrants
95 *sirrah* (common form of address to an inferior)   100 *suggestion*
instigation   105 *Gramercy* much thanks   108 *Sir* (used for a
priest, as well as for a knight)   109 *exercise* sermon   110 *content*
reward

Your honor hath no shriving° work in hand.

Hastings. Good faith, and when I met this holy man
The men you talk of came into my mind.   115
What, go you toward the Tower?

Buckingham. I do, my lord, but long I cannot stay
there.
I shall return before your lordship thence.

Hastings. Nay, like enough, for I stay dinner there.

Buckingham. [*Aside*] And supper too, although thou
know'st it not.   120
Come, will you go?

Hastings.   I'll wait upon your lordship.
                                                Exeunt.

Scene III. [*Pomfret Castle.*]

*Enter Sir Richard Ratcliffe, with Halberds,
carrying the Nobles, [Rivers, Grey, and
Vaughan,] to death at Pomfret.*

Rivers. Sir Richard Ratcliffe, let me tell thee this:
Today shalt thou behold a subject die
For truth, for duty, and for loyalty.

Grey. God bless the Prince from all the pack of you!
A knot you are of damnèd bloodsuckers.   5

Vaughan. You live that shall cry woe for this hereafter.

Ratcliffe. Dispatch; the limit of your lives is out.

Rivers. O Pomfret, Pomfret! O thou bloody prison,
Fatal and ominous to noble peers!
Within the guilty closure° of thy walls   10

113 *shriving* confessing   III.iii.10 *closure* circuit

Richard the Second here was hacked to death;
And, for more slander° to thy dismal seat,
We give to thee our guiltless blood to drink.

Grey. Now Margaret's curse is fall'n upon our heads,
15   When she exclaimed on Hastings, you, and I,
For standing by when Richard stabbed her son.

Rivers. Then cursed she Richard, then cursed she
Buckingham,
Then cursed she Hastings. O, remember, God,
To hear her prayer for them, as now for us!
20   And for my sister and her princely sons,
Be satisfied, dear God, with our true blood,
Which, as thou know'st, unjustly must be spilt.

Ratcliffe. Make haste; the hour of death is expiate.°

Rivers. Come, Grey, come, Vaughan, let us here
embrace.
25   Farewell, until we meet again in heaven.   *Exeunt.*

Scene IV. [*The Tower.*]

Enter   Buckingham,   [Lord   Stanley,   Earl   of]
Derby, Hastings, Bishop of Ely, Norfolk, Rat-
cliffe, Lovell, with others, at a table.

Hastings. Now, noble peers, the cause why we are
met
Is to determine of the coronation.
In God's name, speak, when is the royal day?

Buckingham. Is all things ready for the royal time?

5   *Stanley.* It is, and wants but nomination.°

12 *slander* disgrace   23 *expiate* come for suffering   III.iv.5 *nom-*
ination naming

Bishop of Ely. Tomorrow then I judge a happy day.

Buckingham. Who knows the Lord Protector's mind
    herein?
  Who is most inward° with the noble Duke?

Bishop of Ely. Your Grace, we think, should soonest
    know his mind.

Buckingham. We know each other's faces; for our
    hearts,   10
  He knows no more of mine than I of yours;
  Or I of his, my lord, than you of mine.
  Lord Hastings, you and he are near in love.

Hastings. I thank his Grace, I know he loves me well;
  But for his purpose in the coronation   15
  I have not sounded him, nor he delivered
  His gracious pleasure any way therein.
  But you, my honorable lords, may name the time,
  And in the Duke's behalf I'll give my voice,
  Which I presume he'll take in gentle part.   20

     Enter [Richard, Duke of] Gloucester.

Bishop of Ely. In happy time here comes the Duke
    himself.

Richard. My noble lords and cousins all, good
    morrow.
  I have been long a sleeper, but I trust
  My absence doth neglect° no great design
  Which by my presence might have been concluded.   25

Buckingham. Had you not come upon your cue, my
    lord,
  William Lord Hastings had pronounced your part,
  I mean your voice for crowning of the King.

Richard. Than my Lord Hastings no man might be
    bolder.
  His lordship knows me well and loves me well.   30
  My Lord of Ely, when I was last in Holborn
  I saw good strawberries in your garden there.

8 *inward* intimate   24 *neglect* cause neglect of

I do beseech you send for some of them.

Bishop of Ely. Marry, and will, my lord, with all my
heart.   *Exit Bishop.*

35 *Richard.* Cousin of Buckingham, a word with you.
                                    [*Takes him aside.*]
Catesby hath sounded Hastings in our business
And finds the testy gentleman so hot
That he will lose his head ere give consent
His master's child, as worshipfully° he terms it,
40 Shall lose the royalty of England's throne.

Buckingham. Withdraw yourself awhile. I'll go with
you.   *Exeunt [Richard and Buckingham].*

Stanley. We have not yet set down this day of triumph.
Tomorrow, in my judgment, is too sudden;
For I myself am not so well provided
45 As else I would be, were the day prolonged.°

Enter the Bishop of Ely.

Bishop of Ely. Where is my lord the Duke of
Gloucester?
I have sent for these strawberries.

Hastings. His Grace looks cheerfully and smooth this
morning;
There's some conceit° or other likes° him well
50 When that he bids good morrow with such spirit.
I think there's never a man in Christendom
Can lesser hide his love or hate than he,
For by his face straight shall you know his heart.

Stanley. What of his heart perceive you in his face
55 By any livelihood° he showed today?

Hastings. Marry, that with no man here he is offended;
For were he, he had shown it in his looks.

---

39 *worshipfully* respectfully   45 *prolonged* postponed   49 *conceit*
idea   49 *likes* pleases   55 *livelihood* liveliness

Enter Richard and Buckingham.

Richard. I pray you all, tell me what they deserve
  That do conspire my death with devilish plots
  Of damnèd witchcraft, and that have prevailed   60
  Upon my body with their hellish charms.

Hastings. The tender love I bear your Grace, my lord,
  Makes me most forward in this princely presence
  To doom th' offenders, whosoe'er they be.
  I say, my lord, they have deservèd death.   65

Richard. Then be your eyes the witness of their evil.
  Look how I am bewitched. Behold, mine arm
  Is like a blasted sapling withered up;
  And this is Edward's wife, that monstrous witch,
  Consorted with that harlot strumpet Shore,   70
  That by their witchcraft thus have markèd me.

Hastings. If they have done this deed, my noble lord—

Richard. If! Thou protector of this damnèd strumpet,
  Talk'st thou to me of if's? Thou art a traitor.
  Off with his head! Now by Saint Paul I swear   75
  I will not dine until I see the same.
  Lovell and Ratcliffe, look that it be done.
  The rest that love me, rise and follow me.

            Exeunt. Manet Lovell and Ratcliffe, with
                            the Lord Hastings.

Hastings. Woe, woe for England, not a whit for me!
  For I, too fond,° might have prevented this.   80
  Stanley did dream the boar did rase our helms,
  And I did scorn it and disdain to fly.
  Three times today my footcloth horse° did stumble,
  And started when he looked upon the Tower,
  As loath to bear me to the slaughterhouse.   85
  O, now I need the priest that spake to me!
  I now repent I told the pursuivant,
  As too triumphing, how mine enemies
  Today at Pomfret bloodily were butchered,

80 *fond* foolish   83 *footcloth horse* richly decorated horse

90   And I myself secure in grace and favor.
        O Margaret, Margaret, now thy heavy curse
        Is lighted on poor Hastings' wretched head!

        Ratcliffe. Come, come, dispatch; the Duke would be
            at dinner.
        Make a short shrift;° he longs to see your head.

95 *Hastings.* O momentary grace° of mortal men,
        Which we more hunt for than the grace of God!
        Who builds his hope in air of your good looks
        Lives like a drunken sailor on a mast,
        Ready with every nod to tumble down
100   Into the fatal bowels of the deep.

        Lovell. Come, come, dispatch; 'tis bootless° to ex-
            claim.

        Hastings. O bloody Richard! Miserable England!
        I prophesy the fearful'st time to thee
        That ever wretched age hath looked upon.
105   Come, lead me to the block; bear him my head.
        They smile at me who shortly shall be dead.
                                        Exeunt.

                [Scene V. *The Tower walls.*]

        *Enter Richard, [Duke of Gloucester,] and Buck-
        ingham, in rotten° armor, marvelous ill-favored.°*

        Richard. Come, cousin, canst thou quake and change
            thy color,
        Murder thy breath in middle of a word,
        And then again begin, and stop again,
        As if thou wert distraught and mad with terror?

---

94 *shrift* confession   95 *grace* favor   101 *bootless* useless   III.
v.s.d. *rotten* worn-out   s.d. *ill-favored* bad-looking

Buckingham. Tut, I can counterfeit the deep tra-
    gedian,   *5*
  Speak and look back, and pry on every side,
  Tremble and start at wagging of a straw,
  Intending° deep suspicion. Ghastly looks
  Are at my service, like enforcèd smiles;
  And both are ready in their offices°   *10*
  At any time to grace my stratagems.
  But what, is Catesby gone?

Richard. He is; and see, he brings the Mayor along.

                    Enter the Mayor and Catesby.

Buckingham. Lord Mayor—

Richard. Look to the drawbridge there!   *15*

Buckingham. Hark! A drum.

Richard. Catesby, o'erlook° the walls.

Buckingham. Lord Mayor, the reason we have sent—

Richard. Look back, defend thee! Here are enemies.

Buckingham. God and our innocency defend and
    guard us!   *20*

    Enter Lovell and Ratcliffe, with Hastings' head.

Richard. Be patient, they are friends, Ratcliffe and
    Lovell.

Lovell. Here is the head of that ignoble traitor,
  The dangerous and unsuspected Hastings.

Richard. So dear I loved the man that I must weep:
  I took him for the plainest harmless creature   *25*
  That breathed upon the earth a Christian;
  Made him my book,° wherein my soul recorded
  The history of all her secret thoughts.
  So smooth he daubed° his vice with show of virtue
  That, his apparent open guilt omitted,   *30*

8 *Intending* pretending   10 *offices* functions   17 *o'erlook* watch
over   27 *book* notebook   29 *daubed* whitewashed

I mean his conversation° with Shore's wife,
He lived from all attainder of suspects.°

Buckingham. Well, well, he was the covert'st° shelt'red
    traitor
    That ever lived.
35   Would you imagine, or almost believe,
    Were't not that by great preservation
    We live to tell it, that the subtle traitor
    This day had plotted, in the council house,
    To murder me and my good Lord of Gloucester?

40   *Mayor.* Had he done so?

Richard. What! Think you we are Turks or infidels?
    Or that we would, against the form of law,
    Proceed thus rashly in the villain's death
    But that the extreme peril of the case,
45   The peace of England, and our persons' safety
    Enforced us to this execution?

Mayor. Now fair befall you! He deserved his death,
    And your good Graces both have well proceeded
    To warn false traitors from the like attempts.

50   *Buckingham.* I never looked for better at his hands
    After he once fell in with Mistress Shore.
    Yet had we not determined he should die
    Until your lordship came to see his end,
    Which now the loving haste of these our friends,
55   Something against our meanings, have prevented;°
    Because, my lord, I would have had you heard
    The traitor speak, and timorously confess
    The manner and the purpose of his treasons,
    That you might well have signified the same
60   Unto the citizens, who haply may
    Misconster° us in him and wail his death.

Mayor. But, my good lord, your Grace's words shall
    serve
    As well as I had seen and heard him speak;

31 *conversation* intercourse   32 *from . . . suspects* free from all
stain of suspicions   33 *covert'st* most secret   55 *prevented* fore-
stalled   61 *Misconster* misjudge

And do not doubt, right noble princes both,
But I'll acquaint our duteous citizens   *65*
With all your just proceedings in this case.

Richard. And to that end we wished your lordship
    here,
T' avoid the censures of the carping world.

Buckingham. Which,° since you come too late of° our
    intent,
Yet witness what you hear we did intend.   *70*
And so, my good Lord Mayor, we bid farewell.
                    Exit Mayor.

Richard. Go after, after, cousin Buckingham.
The Mayor towards Guildhall° hies him in all
    post.°
There, at your meetest° vantage of the time,
Infer° the bastardy of Edward's children.   *75*
Tell them how Edward put to death a citizen
Only for saying he would make his son
Heir to the Crown, meaning indeed his house,
Which by the sign thereof was termèd so.
Moreover, urge his hateful luxury°   *80*
And bestial appetite in change of lust,
Which stretched unto their servants, daughters,
    wives,
Even where his raging eye or savage heart,
Without control, lusted to make a prey.
Nay, for a need, thus far come near my person: *85*
Tell them, when that my mother went with child
Of that insatiate Edward, noble York
My princely father then had wars in France,
And by true computation of the time
Found that the issue was not his begot;   *90*
Which well appearèd in his lineaments,
Being nothing like the noble Duke my father.
Yet touch this sparingly, as 'twere far off,
Because, my lord, you know my mother lives.

69 *Which* as to which   69 *of* for   73 *Guildhall* the city hall of London   73 *post* haste   74 *meetest* fittest   75 *Infer* bring forward as an
argument   80 *luxury* lechery

95   *Buckingham.* Doubt not, my lord, I'll play the orator
        As if the golden fee for which I plead
        Were for myself; and so, my lord, adieu.

        Richard. If you thrive well, bring them to Baynard's
            Castle,
        Where you shall find me well accompanied
100   With reverend fathers and well-learnèd bishops.

        Buckingham. I go; and towards three or four o'clock
        Look for the news that the Guildhall affords.
                        Exit Buckingham.

        Richard. Go, Lovell, with all speed to Doctor Shaw.
        [*To Catesby*] Go thou to Friar Penker. Bid them
            both
105   Meet me within this hour at Baynard's Castle.
                Exeunt [Lovell, Catesby, and Ratcliffe].
        Now will I go to take some privy order°
        To draw the brats of Clarence out of sight,
        And to give order that no manner° person
        Have any time recourse unto the Princes.   *Exit.*

                [Scene VI. *A street.*]

        Enter a Scrivener [with a paper in his hand].

        Scrivener. Here is the indictment of the good Lord
            Hastings,
        Which in a set° hand fairly is engrossed°
        That it may be today read o'er in Paul's.°
        And mark how well the sequel hangs together:
5   Eleven hours I have spent to write it over,
        For yesternight by Catesby was it sent me;
        The precedent° was full as long a-doing;

---

106 *privy order* secret arrangement   108 *no manner* no sort of
III.vi.2 *set* formal   2 *fairly is engrossed* is written clearly   3 *Paul's*
St. Paul's   7 *precedent* original draft

And yet within these five hours Hastings lived,
Untainted,° unexamined, free, at liberty.
Here's a good world the while! Who is so gross°   *10*
That cannot see this palpable device?°
Yet who so bold but says he sees it not?
Bad is the world, and all will come to nought
When such ill dealing must be seen in thought.°

                                           Exit.

[Scene VII. *Baynard's Castle.*]

*Enter Richard, [Duke of Gloucester,] and Buck-
        ingham at several° doors.*

Richard. How now, how now? What say the citizens?

Buckingham. Now, by the holy Mother of our Lord,
    The citizens are mum, say not a word.

Richard. Touched you the bastardy of Edward's
    children?

Buckingham. I did, with his contract with Lady Lucy°   *5*
    And his contract by deputy° in France;
    Th' unsatiate greediness of his desire
    And his enforcement of the city wives;
    His tyranny for trifles; his own bastardy,
    As being got,° your father then in France,   *10*
    And his resemblance,° being not like the Duke.
    Withal I did infer your lineaments,
    Being the right idea° of your father
    Both in your form and nobleness of mind;
    Laid open all your victories in Scotland,   *15*

9 *Untainted* not accused   10 *gross* dull   11 *palpable device* ob-
vious trick   14 *in thought* i.e., in silence   III.vii. s.d. *several* separate   5 *Lady Lucy* Elizabeth Lucy (whose betrothal to Edward
was never proved)   6 *by deputy* (Edward had sent Warwick to arrange a French marriage)   10 *got* begotten   11 *resemblance* appearance   13 *right idea* exact image

Your discipline in war, wisdom in peace,
Your bounty, virtue, fair humility;
Indeed, left nothing fitting for your purpose
Untouched or slightly handlèd in discourse;
20 And when my oratory drew toward end,
I bid them that did love their country's good
Cry, "God save Richard, England's royal king!"

Richard. And did they so?

Buckingham. No, so God help me, they spake not a
        word,
25 But like dumb statues° or breathing stones
Stared each on other and looked deadly pale.
Which when I saw, I reprehended them
And asked the Mayor what meant this willful
        silence.
His answer was, the people were not usèd
30 To be spoke to but by the Recorder.°
Then he was urged to tell my tale again:
"Thus saith the Duke, thus hath the Duke in-
        ferred";
But nothing spoke in warrant from himself.
When he had done, some followers of mine own
35 At lower end of the hall hurled up their caps,
And some ten voices cried, "God save King
        Richard!"
And thus I took the vantage of those few:
"Thanks, gentle citizens and friends," quoth I.
"This general applause and cheerful shout
40 Argues your wisdom and your love to Richard";
And even here brake off and came away.

Richard. What tongueless blocks were they! Would
        they not speak?
Will not the Mayor then and his brethren come?

Buckingham. The Mayor is here at hand. Intend°
        some fear;
45 Be not you spoke with but by mighty suit;°

25 *statues* (pronounced "stat-u-es")   30 *Recorder* chief legal official
of the city   44 *Intend* pretend   45 *suit* petition

And look you get a prayer book in your hand
And stand between two churchmen, good my lord,
For on that ground° I'll make a holy descant;°
And be not easily won to our requests.
Play the maid's part: still answer nay,° and take it.   *50*

Richard. I go; and if you plead as well for them
As I can say nay to thee for myself,
No doubt we bring it to a happy issue.

Buckingham. Go, go up to the leads.° The Lord
Mayor knocks.   [*Exit Richard.*]

          Enter the Mayor, and Citizens.

Welcome, my lord. I dance attendance here.   *55*
I think the Duke will not be spoke withal.°

                Enter Catesby.

Now, Catesby, what says your lord to my request?

Catesby. He doth entreat your Grace, my noble lord,
To visit him tomorrow or next day.
He is within, with two right reverend fathers,   *60*
Divinely bent to meditation,
And in no worldly suits would he be moved
To draw him from his holy exercise.°

Buckingham. Return, good Catesby, to the gracious
Duke.
Tell him, myself, the Mayor and Aldermen,   *65*
In deep designs, in matter of great moment,
No less importing than our general good,
Are come to have some conference with his Grace.

Catesby. I'll signify so much unto him straight.   *Exit.*

Buckingham. Ah ha, my lord, this prince is not an
Edward!   *70*
He is not lulling° on a lewd love-bed,

---

48 *ground* (1) melody (2) basis   48 *descant* (1) musical variation
(2) argument   50 *still answer nay* always say no (a proverb)   54
leads flat roof covered with lead   56 *withal* with   63 *exercise* act
of devotion   71 *lulling* lounging

But on his knees at meditation;
Not dallying with a brace of courtesans,
But meditating with two deep divines;
75 Not sleeping, to engross° his idle body,
But praying, to enrich his watchful soul.
Happy were England, would this virtuous prince
Take on his Grace the sovereignty thereof;
But sure I fear we shall not win him to it.

Mayor. Marry, God defend° his Grace should say us
80   nay!

Buckingham. I fear he will. Here Catesby comes
again.

Enter Catesby.

Now, Catesby, what says his Grace?

Catesby. He wonders to what end you have assemblèd
Such troops of citizens to come to him,
85 His Grace not being warned thereof before.
He fears, my lord, you mean no good to him.

Buckingham. Sorry I am my noble cousin should
Suspect me that I mean no good to him.
By heaven, we come to him in perfect love;
90 And so once more return and tell his Grace.
                              Exit [*Catesby*].
When holy and devout religious men
Are at their beads, 'tis much° to draw them thence,
So sweet is zealous contemplation.

Enter Richard aloft, between two Bishops.
          [*Catesby returns.*]

Mayor. See where his Grace stands 'tween two
clergymen!

Buckingham. Two props of virtue for a Christian
95   prince,
To stay him from the fall° of vanity;
And see, a book of prayer in his hand—

---

75 *engross* make fat   80 *defend* forbid   92 *much* hard   96 *fall*
falling into sin

True ornaments to know a holy man.
Famous Plantagenet, most gracious Prince,
Lend favorable ear to our requests,   100
And pardon us the interruption
Of thy devotion and right Christian zeal.

Richard. My lord, there needs no such apology.
I do beseech your Grace to pardon me,
Who, earnest in the service of my God,   105
Deferred the visitation of my friends.
But, leaving this, what is your Grace's pleasure?

Buckingham. Even that, I hope, which pleaseth God
     above
And all good men of this ungoverned isle.

Richard. I do suspect I have done some offense   110
That seems disgracious° in the city's eye,
And that you come to reprehend my ignorance.

Buckingham. You have, my lord. Would it might
     please your Grace,
On our entreaties, to amend your fault!

Richard. Else wherefore breathe I in a Christian
     land?   115

Buckingham. Know then it is your fault that you
     resign
The supreme seat, the throne majestical,
The scept'red office of your ancestors,
Your state° of fortune and your due of birth,
The lineal glory of your royal house,   120
To the corruption of a blemished stock;
Whiles, in the mildness of your sleepy thoughts,
Which here we waken to our country's good,
The noble isle doth want his proper limbs;
His face defaced with scars of infamy,   125
His royal stock graft° with ignoble plants,
And almost should'red in° the swallowing gulf
Of dark forgetfulness and deep oblivion.

111 *disgracious* displeasing   119 *state* high position   126 *graft*
grafted   127 *should'red in* jostled into

Which to recure,° we heartily solicit
130 Your gracious self to take on you the charge
And kingly government of this your land;
Not as protector, steward, substitute,
Or lowly factor° for another's gain,
But as successively,° from blood to blood,
135 Your right of birth, your empery,° your own.
For this, consorted with the citizens,
Your very worshipful and loving friends,
And by their vehement instigation,
In this just cause come I to move your Grace.

140 *Richard.* I cannot tell if to depart in silence
Or bitterly to speak in your reproof
Best fitteth my degree° or your condition.°
If not to answer, you might haply think
Tongue-tied ambition, not replying, yielded
145 To bear the golden yoke of sovereignty
Which fondly you would here impose on me.
If to reprove you for this suit of yours,
So seasoned° with your faithful love to me,
Then, on the other side, I checked° my friends.
150 Therefore, to speak, and to avoid the first,
And then, in speaking, not to incur the last,
Definitively° thus I answer you.
Your love deserves my thanks, but my desert
Unmeritable shuns your high request.
155 First, if all obstacles were cut away
And that my path were even° to the crown
As the ripe revenue and due of birth,
Yet so much is my poverty of spirit,°
So mighty and so many my defects,
160 That I would rather hide me from my greatness,
Being a bark to brook° no mighty sea,
Than in my greatness covet to be hid
And in the vapor of my glory smothered.

129 *recure* remedy 133 *factor* agent 134 *successively* by inheritance 135 *empery* supreme power 142 *degree* rank 142 *condition* status 148 *seasoned* given relish 149 *checked* should be rebuking 152 *Definitively* once and for all 156 *even* clear 158 *poverty of spirit* lack of self-confidence 161 *bark to brook* small ship able to endure

But, God be thanked, there is no need of me,
And much I need° to help you, were there need.   *165*
The royal tree hath left us royal fruit,
Which, mellowed by the stealing hours of time,
Will well become the seat of majesty
And make, no doubt, us happy by his reign.
On him I lay that you would lay on me,   *170*
The right and fortune of his happy stars,
Which God defend° that I should wring from him!

Buckingham. My lord, this argues conscience in your
    Grace,
But the respects thereof are nice° and trivial,
All circumstances well consideréd.   *175*
You say that Edward is your brother's son.
So say we too, but not by Edward's wife;
For first was he contract to Lady Lucy—
Your mother lives a witness to his vow—
And afterward by substitute betrothed   *180*
To Bona, sister to the King of France.
These both put off, a poor petitioner,
A care-crazed mother to a many sons,
A beauty-waning and distresséd widow,
Even in the afternoon of her best days,   *185*
Made prize and purchase° of his wanton eye,
Seduced the pitch° and height of his degree
To base declension° and loathed bigamy.
By her, in his unlawful bed, he got
This Edward, whom our manners call the Prince.   *190*
More bitterly could I expostulate,
Save that for reverence to some alive
I give a sparing limit to my tongue.
Then, good my lord, take to your royal self
This proffered benefit of dignity;°   *195*
If not to bless us and the land withal,
Yet to draw forth your noble ancestry

---

165 *need* lack   172 *defend* forbid   174 *respects thereof are nice*
considerations about it are too scrupulous   186 *purchase* booty
187 *pitch* high point (of a hawk's flight)   188 *base declension*
ignoble falling low   195 *benefit of dignity* gift of greatness

From the corruption of abusing times
Unto a lineal true-derivèd course.

200 *Mayor.* Do, good my lord; your citizens entreat you.

Buckingham. Refuse not, mighty lord, this proffered
love.

Catesby. O, make them joyful, grant their lawful suit!

Richard. Alas, why would you heap this care on me?
I am unfit for state and majesty.
205 I do beseech you take it not amiss,
I cannot nor I will not yield to you.

Buckingham. If you refuse it, as in love and zeal
Loath to depose the child, your brother's son—
As well we know your tenderness of heart
210 And gentle, kind, effeminate remorse,°
Which we have noted in you to your kindred
And egally° indeed to all estates—
Yet know, whe'r° you accept our suit or no,
Your brother's son shall never reign our king,
215 But we will plant some other in the throne
To the disgrace and downfall of your house;
And in this resolution here we leave you
Come, citizens. Zounds, I'll entreat no more!

Richard. O, do not swear, my lord of Buckingham.
Exeunt [Buckingham, Mayor, and Citizens].

Catesby. Call him again, sweet Prince, accept their
220 suit.
If you deny them, all the land will rue it.

Richard. Will you enforce me to a world of cares?
Call them again. I am not made of stone,
But penetrable to your kind entreaties,
225 Albeit against my conscience and my soul.

Enter Buckingham and the rest.

Cousin of Buckingham, and sage grave men,

210 *effeminate remorse* softhearted pity   212 *egally* equally   213
whe'r whether

Since you will buckle fortune on my back,
To bear her burden, whe'r I will or no,
I must have patience to endure the load;
But if black scandal or foul-faced reproach   230
Attend the sequel of your imposition,°
Your mere enforcement° shall acquittance° me
From all the impure blots and stains thereof;
For God doth know, and you may partly see,
How far I am from the desire of this.   235

Mayor. God bless your Grace! We see it and will say
    it.

Richard. In saying so you shall but say the truth.

Buckingham. Then I salute you with this royal title:
    Long live King Richard, England's worthy king!

All. Amen.   240

Buckingham. Tomorrow may it please you to be
    crowned?

Richard. Even when you please, for you will have
    it so.

Buckingham. Tomorrow then we will attend your
    Grace,
    And so most joyfully we take our leave.

Richard. [*To the Bishops*] Come, let us to our holy
    work again.   245
    Farewell, my cousin; farewell, gentle friends.
                                    Exeunt.

231 *imposition* laying on the burden   232 *Your mere enforcement*
the simple fact of your compulsion   232 *acquittance* release

ACT IV

Scene I. [*Before the Tower.*]

Enter the Queen, [Elizabeth,] the Duchess of
York, and Marquis [of] Dorset [at one door];
Anne, Duchess of Gloucester, [with Clarence's
daughter, at another door].

Duchess of York. Who meets us here? My niece°
    Plantagenet,
Led in the hand of her kind aunt of Gloucester!
Now, for my life, she's wand'ring to the Tower
On pure heart's love to greet the tender Prince.
Daughter, well met.

5 *Anne.*   God give your Graces both
    A happy and a joyful time of day!

Queen Elizabeth. As much to you, good sister!
    Whither away?

Anne. No farther than the Tower, and, as I guess,
Upon the like devotion° as yourselves,
10   To gratulate° the gentle princes there.

Queen Elizabeth. Kind sister, thanks. We'll enter all
    together.

IV.i.1 *niece* granddaughter   9 *devotion* purpose   10 *gratulate* greet
with joy

122

Enter the Lieutenant [Brakenbury].

And in good time here the Lieutenant comes.
Master Lieutenant, pray you, by your leave,
How doth the Prince, and my young son of York?

Lieutenant. Right well, dear madam. By your patience,   15
I may not suffer you to visit them;
The King hath strictly charged the contrary.

Queen Elizabeth. The King? Who's that?

Lieutenant.   I mean the Lord Protector.

Queen Elizabeth. The Lord protect him from that
     kingly title!
Hath he set bounds between their love and me?   20
I am their mother; who shall bar me from them?

Duchess of York. I am their father's mother; I will
     see them.

Anne. Their aunt I am in law, in love their mother.
Then bring me to their sights; I'll bear thy blame
And take thy office° from thee on my peril.   25

Lieutenant. No, madam, no; I may not leave° it so.
I am bound by oath, and therefore pardon me.
                              Exit Lieutenant.

Enter Stanley, [Earl of Derby].

Stanley. Let me but meet you, ladies, one hour hence,
And I'll salute your Grace of York as mother
And reverend looker-on of two fair queens.   30
[*To Anne*] Come, madam, you must straight to
     Westminster,
There to be crownèd Richard's royal queen.

Queen Elizabeth. Ah, cut my lace° asunder,
That my pent heart may have some scope to beat,
Or else I swoon with this dead-killing news!   35

Anne. Despiteful° tidings! O unpleasing news!

25 *take thy office* take over your duty   26 *leave* abandon   33 *lace*
bodice string   36 *Despiteful* cruel

Dorset. Be of good cheer; mother, how fares your
    Grace?

Queen Elizabeth. O Dorset, speak not to me, get thee
    gone!
    Death and destruction dogs thee at thy heels;
40   Thy mother's name is ominous to children.
    If thou wilt outstrip death, go cross the seas
    And live with Richmond, from° the reach of hell.
    Go hie thee, hie thee from this slaughterhouse,
    Lest thou increase the number of the dead
45   And make me die the thrall° of Margaret's curse,
    Nor mother, wife, nor England's counted queen.°

Stanley. Full of wise care is this your counsel, madam.
    Take all the swift advantage of the hours.
    You shall have letters from me to my son°
50   In your behalf, to meet you on the way.
    Be not ta'en tardy° by unwise delay.

Duchess of York. O ill-dispersing° wind of misery!
    O my accursèd womb, the bed of death!
    A cockatrice° hast thou hatched to the world,
55   Whose unavoided eye is murderous.

Stanley. Come, madam, come; I in all haste was sent.

Anne. And I with all unwillingness will go.
    O, would to God that the inclusive verge°
    Of golden metal that must round° my brow
60   Were red-hot steel to sear me to the brains!
    Anointed let me be with deadly venom
    And die ere men can say, "God save the Queen!"

Queen Elizabeth. Go, go, poor soul! I envy not thy
    glory.
    To feed my humor° wish thyself no harm.

65 *Anne.* No? Why, when he that is my husband now

42 *from* away from 45 *thrall* slave 46 *England's counted queen*
regarded as Queen of England 49 *son* i.e., his wife's son, Richmond 51 *ta'en tardy* caught napping 52 *ill-dispersing* scattering
evil 54 *cockatrice* fabulous monster, basilisk (see I.ii.150) 58
inclusive verge enclosing rim 59 *round* encircle 64 *feed my
humor* satisfy my mood

Came to me as I followed Henry's corse,
When scarce the blood was well washed from his
    hands
Which issuèd from my other angel husband
And that dear saint which then I weeping fol-
    lowed—
O, when, I say, I looked on Richard's face,   *70*
This was my wish: "Be thou," quoth I, "accursed
For making me, so young, so old a widow!°
And when thou wed'st, let sorrow haunt thy bed;
And be thy wife, if any be so mad,
More miserable by the life of thee   *75*
Than thou hast made me by my dear lord's death!"
Lo, ere I can repeat this curse again,
Within so small a time, my woman's heart
Grossly grew captive to his honey words
And proved the subject of mine own soul's curse, *80*
Which hitherto hath held mine eyes from rest;
For never yet one hour in his bed
Did I enjoy the golden dew of sleep,
But with his timorous dreams was still° awaked.
Besides, he hates me for my father Warwick,   *85*
And will, no doubt, shortly be rid of me.

Queen Elizabeth. Poor heart, adieu! I pity thy com-
    plaining.

Anne. No more than with my soul I mourn for yours.

Dorset. Farewell, thou woeful welcomer of glory!

Anne. Adieu, poor soul that tak'st thy leave of it!   *90*

Duchess of York. [*To Dorset*] Go thou to Richmond,
    and good fortune guide thee!
  [*To Anne*] Go thou to Richard, and good angels
    tend thee!
  [*To Queen Elizabeth*] Go thou to sanctuary, and
    good thoughts possess thee!
  I to my grave, where peace and rest lie with me!
  Eighty odd years of sorrow have I seen,   *95*

72 *so old a widow* a widow so aged by grief   84 *still* continually

And each hour's joy wracked° with a week of teen.°

Queen Elizabeth. Stay, yet look back with me unto the
    Tower.
    Pity, you ancient stones, those tender babes
    Whom envy hath immured within your walls,
100 Rough cradle for such little pretty ones!
    Rude ragged nurse, old sullen playfellow
    For tender princes, use my babies well!
    So foolish sorrow bids your stones farewell. *Exeunt.*

Scene II. [*The palace.*]

*Sound a sennet. Enter Richard, in pomp, Buck-
ingham, Catesby, Ratcliffe, Lovell, [a Page, and
others].*

King Richard. Stand all apart. Cousin of Buckingham!

Buckingham. My gracious sovereign?

King Richard. Give me thy hand.
                    Sound. [*He ascends the throne.*]
                        Thus high, by thy advice
    And thy assistance, is King Richard seated.
5   But shall we wear these glories for a day?
    Or shall they last, and we rejoice in them?

Buckingham. Still live they, and forever let them last!

King Richard. Ah, Buckingham, now do I play the
    touch°
    To try if thou be current gold indeed.
    Young Edward lives—think now what I would
10   speak.

Buckingham. Say on, my loving lord.

96 *wracked* ruined   96 *teen* grief   IV.ii.8 *touch* touchstone (used
to test gold)

King Richard. Why, Buckingham, I say I would be
　king.

Buckingham. Why, so you are, my thrice-renownèd
　lord.

King Richard. Ha! Am I king? 'Tis so; but Edward
　lives.

Buckingham. True, noble Prince.

King Richard.　　　　　　　　　O bitter consequence,°　15
　That Edward still should live true noble prince!
　Cousin, thou wast not wont to be so dull.
　Shall I be plain? I wish the bastards dead,
　And I would have it suddenly performed.
　What say'st thou now? Speak suddenly, be brief.　20

Buckingham. Your Grace may do your pleasure.

King Richard. Tut, tut, thou art all ice, thy kindness
　freezes.
　Say, have I thy consent that they shall die?

Buckingham. Give me some little breath, some pause,
　dear lord,
　Before I positively speak in this.　　　　　　　25
　I will resolve° you herein presently.
　　　　　　　　　　　　Exit Buckingham.

Catesby. [*Aside to another*] The King is angry. See,
　he gnaws his lip.

King Richard. I will converse° with iron-witted° fools
　And unrespective° boys. None are for me
　That look into me with considerate° eyes.　　　30
　High-reaching Buckingham grows circumspect.
　Boy!

Page. My lord?

King Richard. Know'st thou not any whom corrupting
　gold

15 *consequence* sequel　26 *resolve* answer　28 *converse* keep company　28 *iron-witted* dull-witted　29 *unrespective* heedless　30
considerate thoughtful

35   Will tempt unto a close exploit° of death?

Page. I know a discontented gentleman
　　Whose humble means match not his haughty spirit.
　　Gold were as good as twenty orators
　　And will, no doubt, tempt him to anything.

King Richard. What is his name?

40 *Page.*   His name, my lord, is Tyrrel.

King Richard. I partly know the man. Go call him
　　hither, boy.   *Exit [Page].*
　　The deep-revolving witty° Buckingham
　　No more shall be the neighbor to my counsels.
　　Hath he so long held out° with me, untired,
45 And stops he now for breath? Well, be it so.

Enter Stanley, [Earl of Derby].

How now, Lord Stanley? What's the news?

Stanley.   Know, my loving lord,
　　The Marquis Dorset, as I hear, is fled
　　To Richmond in the parts where he abides.
　　　　　　　　　　　　　　　　　[Stands aside.]

King Richard. Come hither, Catesby. Rumor it abroad
50 That Anne my wife is very grievous sick;
　　I will take order for her keeping close.
　　Inquire me out some mean poor gentleman,
　　Whom I will marry straight to Clarence' daughter.
　　The boy is foolish,° and I fear not him.
55 Look how thou dream'st! I say again, give out
　　That Anne my queen is sick and like to die.
　　About it; for it stands me much upon°
　　To stop all hopes whose growth may damage me.
　　　　　　　　　　　　　　　　　[Exit Catesby.]
　　I must be married to my brother's daughter,
60 Or else my kingdom stands on brittle glass.
　　Murder her brothers and then marry her!

---

35 *close exploit* secret deed   42 *deep-revolving witty* deeply-pon-
dering clever   44 *held out* kept up   54 *foolish* an idiot   57 *stands
me much upon* is very important to me

Uncertain way of gain! But I am in
So far in blood that sin will pluck on sin.
Tear-falling pity dwells not in this eye.

Enter Tyrrel.

Is thy name Tyrrel?   65

Tyrrel. James Tyrrel, and your most obedient subject.

King Richard. Art thou indeed?

Tyrrel.   Prove me, my gracious lord.

King Richard. Dar'st thou resolve to kill a friend of
    mine?

Tyrrel. Please° you;
    But I had rather kill two enemies.   70

King Richard. Why, there thou hast it! Two deep
    enemies,
    Foes to my rest and my sweet sleep's disturbers,
    Are they that I would have thee deal upon.
    Tyrrel, I mean those bastards in the Tower.

Tyrrel. Let me have open means to come to them,   75
    And soon I'll rid you from the fear of them.

King Richard. Thou sing'st sweet music. Hark, come
    hither, Tyrrel.
    Go, by this token. Rise, and lend thine ear. *Whispers.*
    There is no more but so. Say it is done,
    And I will love thee and prefer° thee for it.   80

Tyrrel. I will dispatch it straight.   *Exit.*

Enter Buckingham.

Buckingham. My lord, I have considered in my mind
    The late request that you did sound me in.

King Richard. Well, let that rest. Dorset is fled to
    Richmond.

Buckingham. I hear the news, my lord.   85

69 *Please* If it pleases   80 *prefer* advance

King Richard. Stanley, he is your wife's son. Well,
    look unto it.

Buckingham. My lord, I claim the gift, my due by
    promise,
    For which your honor and your faith is pawned:°
    Th' earldom of Hereford and the movables
90   Which you have promisèd I shall possess.

King Richard. Stanley, look to your wife; if she convey
    Letters to Richmond, you shall answer it.

Buckingham. What says your Highness to my just
    request?

King Richard. I do remember me, Henry the Sixth
95   Did prophesy that Richmond should be king
    When Richmond was a little peevish° boy.
    A king! Perhaps, perhaps.

Buckingham. My lord!

King Richard. How chance the prophet could not at
    that time
100   Have told me, I being by, that I should kill him?

Buckingham. My lord, your promise for the earldom!

King Richard. Richmond! When last I was at Exeter,
    The Mayor in courtesy showed me the castle,
    And called it Rugemont; at which name I started,
105   Because a bard of Ireland told me once
    I should not live long after I saw Richmond.

Buckingham. My lord!

King Richard. Ay, what's o'clock?

Buckingham. I am thus bold to put your Grace in
    mind
    Of what you promised me.

110 *King Richard.*   Well, but what's o'clock?

Buckingham. Upon the stroke of ten.

88 *pawned* pledged   96 *peevish* childish

King Richard.   Well, let it strike.

Buckingham. Why let it strike?

King Richard. Because that like a Jack° thou keep'st
    the stroke°
  Betwixt thy begging and my meditation.
  I am not in the giving vein today.   *115*

Buckingham. May it please you to resolve me in my
    suit.

King Richard. Thou troublest me; I am not in the vein.
            Exit [King Richard, and all but Buckingham].

Buckingham. And is it thus? Repays he my deep
    service
  With such contempt? Made I him king for this?
  O, let me think on Hastings, and be gone   *120*
  To Brecknock while my fearful head is on!   *Exit.*

[Scene III. *The palace.*]

Enter Tyrrel.

Tyrrel. The tyrannous and bloody act is done,
  The most arch° deed of piteous massacre
  That ever yet this land was guilty of.
  Dighton and Forrest, who I did suborn
  To do this piece° of ruthful° butchery,   *5*
  Albeit they were fleshed° villains, bloody dogs,
  Melted with tenderness and mild compassion,
  Wept like to children in their death's sad story.
  "O thus," quoth Dighton, "lay the gentle babes."
  "Thus, thus," quoth Forrest, "girdling one another   *10*

113 *Jack* (1) figure of a man on a clock, striking the hour (2)
knave 113 *thou keep'st the stroke* you keep on making a noise
IV.iii.2 *arch* extreme 5 *piece* masterpiece 5 *ruthful* piteous 6
fleshed experienced

Within their alabaster innocent arms.
Their lips were four red roses on a stalk
And in their summer beauty kissed each other.
A book of prayers on their pillow lay,
Which once," quoth Forrest, "almost changed my
15   mind;
But O, the devil"—there the villain stopped;
When Dighton thus told on: "We smotherèd
The most replenishèd° sweet work of Nature
That from the prime° creation e'er she framèd."
20 Hence both are gone with conscience and remorse
They° could not speak; and so I left them both,
To bear this tidings to the bloody King.

Enter [King] Richard.

And here he comes. All health, my sovereign lord!

King Richard. Kind Tyrrel, am I happy in thy news?

25 *Tyrrel.* If to have done the thing you gave in charge
Beget° your happiness, be happy then,
For it is done.

King Richard.   But didst thou see them dead?

Tyrrel. I did, my lord.

King Richard.   And buried, gentle Tyrrel?

Tyrrel. The chaplain of the Tower hath buried them;
30 But where (to say the truth) I do not know.

King Richard. Come to me, Tyrrel, soon at after-
supper,°
When thou shalt tell the process° of their death.
Meantime, but think how I may do thee good
And be inheritor of thy desire.
Farewell till then.

35 *Tyrrel.*   I humbly take my leave.   [*Exit.*]

King Richard. The son of Clarence have I pent up
close;

18 *replenishèd* complete   19 *prime* first   21 *They* i.e., which they
26 *Beget* cause   31 *aftersupper* late supper   32 *process* story

His daughter meanly have I matched in marriage;
The sons of Edward sleep in Abraham's bosom,°
And Anne my wife hath bid this world good night.
Now, for° I know the Britain° Richmond aims   40
At young Elizabeth, my brother's daughter,
And by that knot° looks proudly on the crown,
To her go I, a jolly thriving wooer.

Enter Ratcliffe.

Ratcliffe. My lord!

King Richard. Good or bad news, that thou com'st in
so bluntly?   45

Ratcliffe. Bad news, my lord. Morton is fled to Richmond,
And Buckingham, backed with the hardy Welshmen,
Is in the field, and still his power increaseth.

King Richard. Ely with Richmond troubles me more
near
Than Buckingham and his rash-levied° strength.   50
Come, I have learned that fearful commenting°
Is leaden servitor to dull delay;
Delay leads impotent and snail-paced beggary.°
Then fiery expedition° be my wing,
Jove's Mercury, and herald for a king!   55
Go muster men. My counsel is my shield;
We must be brief when traitors brave the field.

                                        Exeunt.

---

38 *Abraham's bosom* paradise   40 *for* because   40 *Britain* Breton
42 *knot* marriage tie   50 *rash-levied* hastily raised   51 *fearful commenting* timorous meditating   53 *beggary* bankruptcy   54 *expedition* speed

Scene [IV. *The palace.*]

Enter old Queen Margaret.

Queen Margaret. So now prosperity begins to mellow
　　And drop into the rotten mouth of death.
　　Here in these confines slily have I lurked
　　To watch the waning of mine enemies.
5　　A dire induction° am I witness to,
　　And will to France, hoping the consequence°
　　Will prove as bitter, black, and tragical.
　　Withdraw thee, wretched Margaret. Who comes
　　　here?　　　　　　　　　　　　　　　 [*Retires.*]

Enter Duchess [of York] and Queen [Elizabeth].

Queen Elizabeth. Ah, my poor princes, ah, my tender
　　　babes!
10　My unblown° flow'rs, new-appearing sweets!
　　If yet your gentle souls fly in the air
　　And be not fixed in doom perpetual,
　　Hover about me with your airy wings
　　And hear your mother's lamentation!

Queen Margaret. [*Aside*] Hover about her, say that
15　　right for right
　　Hath dimmed your infant morn to agèd night.

Duchess of York. So many miseries have crazed° my
　　　voice
　　That my woe-wearied tongue is still and mute.
　　Edward Plantagenet, why art thou dead?

Queen Margaret. [*Aside*] Plantagenet doth quit°
20　　Plantagenet,

IV.iv.5 *induction* opening scene　6 *consequence* following part　10
unblown unblossomed　17 *crazed* cracked　20 *quit* make up for

Edward for Edward pays a dying debt.

Queen Elizabeth. Wilt thou, O God, fly from such
    gentle lambs
And throw them in the entrails of the wolf?
When didst thou sleep when such a deed was done?

Queen Margaret. [*Aside*] When holy Harry died, and
    my sweet son.   25

Duchess of York. Dead life, blind sight, poor mortal
    living ghost,
Woe's scene, world's shame, grave's due by life
    usurped,
Brief abstract° and record of tedious days,
Rest thy unrest on England's lawful earth,
                                          [*Sits down.*]
Unlawfully made drunk with innocent blood!   30

Queen Elizabeth. Ah that thou wouldst as soon afford
    a grave
As thou canst yield a melancholy seat!
Then would I hide my bones, not rest them here.
Ah, who hath any cause to mourn but we?
                                   [*Sits down by her.*]

Queen Margaret. [*Comes forward*] If ancient sorrow
    be most reverend,   35
Give mine the benefit of seniory°
And let my griefs frown on the upper hand.°
If sorrow can admit society, [*Sits down with them.*]
Tell° o'er your woes again by viewing mine.
I had an Edward, till a Richard killed him;   40
I had a husband, till a Richard killed him.
Thou hadst an Edward, till a Richard killed him;
Thou hadst a Richard, till a Richard killed him.

Duchess of York. I had a Richard too, and thou didst
    kill him;
I had a Rutland too, thou holp'st° to kill him.   45

28 *abstract* summary   36 *seniory* seniority   37 *on the upper hand*
i.e., above all others   39 *Tell* count   45 *holp'st* helpedst

Queen Margaret. Thou hadst a Clarence too, and
    Richard killed him.
    From forth the kennel of thy womb hath crept
    A hellhound that doth hunt us all to death.
    That dog that had his teeth before his eyes
50   To worry lambs and lap their gentle blood,
    That foul defacer of God's handiwork,
    That excellent grand° tyrant of the earth
    That reigns in gallèd° eyes of weeping souls,
    Thy womb let loose to chase us to our graves.
55   O upright, just, and true-disposing° God,
    How do I thank thee that this carnal° cur
    Preys on the issue of his mother's body
    And makes her pewfellow° with others' moan!

Duchess of York. O Harry's wife, triumph not in my
    woes!
60   God witness with me I have wept for thine.

Queen Margaret. Bear with me; I am hungry for re-
    venge,
    And now I cloy me with beholding it.
    Thy Edward he is dead, that killed my Edward;
    Thy other Edward dead, to quit my Edward;
65   Young York he is but boot,° because both they
    Matched not the high perfection of my loss.
    Thy Clarence he is dead that stabbed my Edward,
    And the beholders of this frantic play,
    Th' adulterate° Hastings, Rivers, Vaughan, Grey,
70   Untimely smothered in their dusky graves.
    Richard yet lives, hell's black intelligencer,°
    Only reserved their factor° to buy souls
    And send them thither. But at hand, at hand,
    Ensues his piteous and unpitied end.
75   Earth gapes, hell burns, fiends roar, saints pray,
    To have him suddenly conveyed from hence.

---

52 *excellent grand* surpassingly chief   53 *gallèd* sore from rubbing
55 *true-disposing* justly ordaining   56 *carnal* carnivorous   58 *pew-fellow* companion   65 *but boot* only a makeweight   69 *adulterate*
adulterous   71 *intelligencer* secret agent   72 *Only reserved their
factor* kept alive merely as agent for the powers of hell

Cancel his bond of life, dear God, I pray,
That I may live and say, "The dog is dead."

Queen Elizabeth. O, thou didst prophesy the time
    would come
That I should wish for thee to help me curse   *80*
That bottled spider, that foul bunch-backed toad!

Queen Margaret. I called thee then vain flourish of
    my fortune;
I called thee then poor shadow, painted queen,
The presentation of but° what I was,
The flattering index° of a direful pageant,°   *85*
One heaved a-high° to be hurled down below,
A mother only mocked with two fair babes,
A dream of what thou wast, a garish° flag
To be the aim of every dangerous shot,
A sign of dignity, a breath, a bubble,   *90*
A queen in jest, only to fill the scene.
Where is thy husband now? Where be thy brothers?
Where be thy two sons? Wherein dost thou joy?
Who sues and kneels and says, "God save the
    Queen"?
Where be the bending peers that flatterèd thee?   *95*
Where be the thronging troops that followèd thee?
Decline° all this, and see what now thou art:
For happy wife, a most distressèd widow;
For joyful mother, one that wails the name;
For one being sued to, one that humbly sues;   *100*
For queen, a very caitiff° crowned with care;
For she that scorned at me, now scorned of me;
For she being feared of all, now fearing one;
For she commanding all, obeyed of none.
Thus hath the course of justice whirled about   *105*
And left thee but a very prey to time,
Having no more but thought of what thou wast
To torture thee the more, being what thou art.

---

84 *presentation of but* image only of   85 *flattering index* deceptive
prologue   85 *pageant* stage show   86 *a-high* on high   88 *garnish*
showy   97 *Decline* recite in order   101 *very caitiff* truly unhappy
wretch

Thou didst usurp my place, and dost thou not
110   Usurp the just proportion° of my sorrow?
Now thy proud neck bears half my burdened yoke,
From which even here I slip my wearied head
And leave the burden of it all on thee.
Farewell, York's wife, and queen of sad mischance!
115   These English woes shall make me smile in France.

Queen Elizabeth. O thou well skilled in curses, stay
awhile
And teach me how to curse mine enemies!

Queen Margaret. Forbear to sleep the nights, and fast
the days;
Compare dead happiness with living woe;
120   Think that thy babes were sweeter than they were
And he that slew them fouler than he is.
Bett'ring° thy loss makes the bad causer worse;
Revolving° this will teach thee how to curse.

Queen Elizabeth. My words are dull; O, quicken°
them with thine!

Queen Margaret. Thy woes will make them sharp and
125   pierce like mine.   *Exit [Queen] Margaret.*

Duchess of York. Why should calamity be full of
words?

Queen Elizabeth. Windy attorneys to their client's
woes,°
Airy succeeders of intestate joys,°
Poor breathing orators of miseries,
130   Let them have scope! Though what they will impart
Help nothing else, yet do they ease the heart.

Duchess of York. If so, then be not tongue-tied. Go
with me
And in the breath of bitter words let's smother
My damnèd son that thy two sweet sons smothered.

110 *just proportion* exact extent   122 *Bett'ring* magnifying   123
Revolving meditating on   124 *quicken* give life to   127 *attorneys
to their client's woes* spokesmen for the griefs of the one who employs them (i.e., words)   128 *succeeders of intestate joys* succes-
sors of joys which died without leaving a will

   The trumpet sounds. Be copious in exclaims.   135

Enter King Richard and his Train, [marching
with Drums and Trumpets].

King Richard. Who intercepts me in my expedition?°

Duchess of York. O, she that might have intercepted
   thee,
By strangling thee in her accursèd womb,
From all the slaughters, wretch, that thou hast done!

Queen Elizabeth. Hid'st thou that forehead with a
   golden crown   140
Where should be branded, if that right were right,
The slaughter of the prince that owed° that crown
And the dire death of my poor sons and brothers?
Tell me, thou villain-slave, where are my children?

Duchess of York. Thou toad, thou toad, where is thy
   brother Clarence?   145
And little Ned Plantagenet, his son?

Queen Elizabeth. Where is the gentle Rivers, Vaughan,
   Grey?

Duchess of York. Where is kind Hastings?

King Richard. A flourish, trumpets! Strike alarum,
   drums!
Let not the heavens hear these telltale women   150
Rail on the Lord's anointed. Strike, I say!
                Flourish. Alarums.
Either be patient and entreat me fair,°
Or with the clamorous report of war
Thus will I drown your exclamations.

Duchess of York. Art thou my son?   155

King Richard. Ay, I thank God, my father, and yourself.

Duchess of York. Then patiently hear my impatience.

---

136 *expedition* (1) campaign (2) haste   142 *owed* owned   152 *en-*
treat me fair treat me courteously

King Richard. Madam, I have a touch of your con-
dition°
That cannot brook the accent of reproof.

Duchess of York. O, let me speak!

160 *King Richard.*   Do then; but I'll not hear.

Duchess of York. I will be mild and gentle in my
words.

King Richard. And brief, good mother, for I am in
haste.

Duchess of York. Art thou so hasty? I have stayed°
for thee,
God knows, in torment and in agony.

165 *King Richard.* And came I not at last to comfort you?

Duchess of York. No, by the holy rood, thou know'st
it well,
Thou cam'st on earth to make the earth my hell.
A grievous burden was thy birth to me;
Tetchy° and wayward was thy infancy;
Thy schooldays frightful, desp'rate, wild, and furi-
170   ous;
Thy prime of manhood daring, bold, and venturous;
Thy age confirmed,° proud, subtle, sly, and bloody,
More mild, but yet more harmful, kind in hatred.
What comfortable hour canst thou name
175 That ever graced me with thy company?

King Richard. Faith, none but Humphrey Hour,° that
called your Grace
To breakfast once forth of my company.
If I be so disgracious° in your eye,
Let me march on and not offend you, madam.
Strike up the drum.

180 *Duchess of York.*   I prithee hear me speak.

---

158 *condition* disposition   163 *stayed* waited   169 *Tetchy* fretful
172 *age confirmed* maturity   176 *Humphrey Hour* (apparently the
name of a man, chosen for the play on *comfortable hour*)   178
disgracious displeasing

King Richard. You speak too bitterly.

Duchess of York.				Hear me a word;
For I shall never speak to thee again.

King Richard. So.

Duchess of York. Either thou wilt die by God's just
	ordinance
Ere from this war thou turn° a conqueror,			*185*
Or I with grief and extreme age shall perish
And never more behold thy face again.
Therefore take with thee my most grievous curse,
Which in the day of battle tire thee more
Than all the complete armor that thou wear'st!		*190*
My prayers on the adverse party fight!
And there the little souls of Edward's children
Whisper the spirits of thine enemies
And promise them success and victory!
Bloody thou art, bloody will be thy end;			*195*
Shame serves thy life and doth thy death attend.
						Exit.

Queen Elizabeth. Though far more cause, yet much
	less spirit to curse
Abides in me. I say amen to her.

King Richard. Stay, madam; I must talk a word with
	you.

Queen Elizabeth. I have no moe° sons of the royal
	blood							*200*
For thee to slaughter. For my daughters, Richard,
They shall be praying nuns, not weeping queens;
And therefore level° not to hit their lives.

King Richard. You have a daughter called Elizabeth,
Virtuous and fair, royal and gracious.			*205*

Queen Elizabeth. And must she die for this? O, let her
	live,
And I'll corrupt her manners,° stain her beauty,

185 *turn* return   200 *moe* more (in number)   203 *level* aim   207
manners habits

Slander myself as false to Edward's bed,
Throw over her the veil of infamy;
210   So she may live unscarred of bleeding slaughter,
I will confess she was not Edward's daughter.

King Richard. Wrong not her birth; she is a royal
princess.

Queen Elizabeth. To save her life, I'll say she is not so.

King Richard. Her life is safest only in her birth.

Queen Elizabeth. And only in that safety died her
215   brothers.

King Richard. Lo, at their birth good stars were opposite.

Queen Elizabeth. No, to their lives ill friends were
contrary.

King Richard. All unavoided° is the doom° of destiny.

Queen Elizabeth. True, when avoided grace° makes
destiny.
220   My babes were destined to a fairer death
If grace had blessed thee with a fairer life.

King Richard. You speak as if that I had slain my
cousins!

Queen Elizabeth. Cousins indeed, and by their uncle
cozened°
Of comfort, kingdom, kindred, freedom, life.
225   Whose hand soever lanced their tender hearts,
Thy head (all indirectly°) gave direction.
No doubt the murd'rous knife was dull and blunt
Till it was whetted on thy stone-hard heart
To revel in the entrails of my lambs.
230   But that still use° of grief makes wild grief tame,
My tongue should to thy ears not name my boys
Till that my nails were anchored in thine eyes;

---

218 *unavoided* inevitable   218 *doom* decree   219 *avoided grace*
i.e., the rejection of God's grace (by Richard)   223 *cozened* de-
frauded   226 *indirectly* underhandedly   230 *still use* continued
habit

And I, in such a desp'rate bay of death,
Like a poor bark of sails and tackling reft,
Rush all to pieces on thy rocky bosom.   235

King Richard. Madam, so thrive I in my enterprise
And dangerous success° of bloody wars
As I intend more good to you and yours
Than ever you and yours by me were harmed!

Queen Elizabeth. What good is covered with the face
of heaven,   240
To be discovered, that can do me good?

King Richard. Th' advancement of your children,
gentle lady.

Queen Elizabeth. Up to some scaffold, there to lose
their heads!

King Richard. Unto the dignity and height of fortune,
The high imperial type° of this earth's glory.   245

Queen Elizabeth. Flatter my sorrow with report of it.
Tell me, what state, what dignity, what honor
Canst thou demise° to any child of mine?

King Richard. Even all I have—ay, and myself and all
Will I withal° endow a child of thine,   250
So in the Lethe° of thy angry soul
Thou drown the sad remembrance of those wrongs
Which thou supposest I have done to thee.

Queen Elizabeth. Be brief, lest that the process° of
thy kindness
Last longer telling than thy kindness' date.°   255

King Richard. Then know that from my soul I love
thy daughter.

Queen Elizabeth. My daughter's mother thinks it with
her soul.

---

237 *success* result   245 *type* symbol   248 *demise* convey legally
250 *withal* with   251 *Lethe* river of oblivion   254 *process* story
255 *date* duration

King Richard. What do you think?

Queen Elizabeth. That thou dost love my daughter
from° thy soul.

260   So from thy soul's love didst thou love her brothers,
And from my heart's love I do thank thee for it.

King Richard. Be not so hasty to confound my mean-
ing.
I mean that with my soul I love thy daughter
And do intend to make her Queen of England.

Queen Elizabeth. Well then, who dost thou mean shall
265   be her king?

King Richard. Even he that makes her queen. Who
else should be?

Queen Elizabeth. What, thou?

King Richard.   Even so. How think you of it?

Queen Elizabeth. How canst thou woo her?

King Richard.   That would I learn of you,
As one being best acquainted with her humor.°

Queen Elizabeth. And wilt thou learn of me?

270 *King Richard.*   Madam, with all my heart.

Queen Elizabeth. Send to her by the man that slew her
brothers
A pair of bleeding hearts; thereon engrave
"Edward" and "York." Then haply will she weep;
Therefore present to her—as sometimes° Margaret
275   Did to thy father, steeped in Rutland's blood—
A handkerchief, which, say to her, did drain
The purple sap from her sweet brother's body,
And bid her wipe her weeping eyes withal.°
If this inducement move her not to love,
280   Send her a letter of thy noble deeds:
Tell her thou mad'st away her uncle Clarence,
Her uncle Rivers; ay, and for her sake

259 *from* apart from (i.e., not with)   269 *humor* disposition   274
sometimes once   278 *withal* with (it)

Mad'st quick conveyance° with her good aunt
Anne.

King Richard. You mock me, madam; this is not the
way
To win your daughter,

Queen Elizabeth.   There is no other way,   285
Unless thou couldst put on some other shape
And not be Richard that hath done all this.

King Richard. Say that I did all this for love of her.

Queen Elizabeth. Nay, then indeed she cannot choose
but hate thee,
Having bought love with such a bloody spoil.°   290

King Richard. Look what° is done cannot be now
amended.
Men shall deal unadvisedly° sometimes,
Which afterhours gives leisure to repent.
If I did take the kingdom from your sons,
To make amends I'll give it to your daughter.   295
If I have killed the issue of your womb,
To quicken your increase° I will beget
Mine issue of your blood upon your daughter.
A grandam's name is little less in love
Than is the doting title of a mother;   300
They are as children but one step below,
Even of your metal,° of your very blood,
Of all one pain, save for a night of groans
Endured of° her for whom you bid° like sorrow.
Your children were vexation to your youth,   305
But mine shall be a comfort to your age.
The loss you have is but a son being king,
And by that loss your daughter is made queen.
I cannot make you what amends I would;
Therefore accept such kindness as I can.   310
Dorset your son, that with a fearful soul

---

283 *conveyance* (1) carrying off (2) underhand dealing   290 *spoil*
destruction   291 *Look what* whatever   292 *shall deal unadvisedly*
are bound to act thoughtlessly   297 *quicken your increase* give
life to your offspring   302 *metal* substance   304 *of* by   304 *bid*
suffered

Leads discontented steps in foreign soil,
This fair alliance° quickly shall call home
To high promotions and great dignity.
315   The king that calls your beauteous daughter wife
Familiarly shall call thy Dorset brother.
Again shall you be mother to a king,
And all the ruins of distressful times
Repaired with double riches of content.
320   What! We have many goodly days to see.
The liquid drops of tears that you have shed
Shall come again, transformed to orient° pearl,
Advantaging their loan with interest
Of ten times double gain of happiness.
325   Go then, my mother, to thy daughter go;
Make bold her bashful years with your experience;
Prepare her ears to hear a wooer's tale.
Put in her tender heart th' aspiring flame
Of golden sovereignty; acquaint the Princess
330   With the sweet silent hours of marriage joys.
And when this arm of mine hath chastisèd
The petty rebel, dull-brained Buckingham,
Bound with triumphant garlands will I come
And lead thy daughter to a conqueror's bed;
335   To whom I will retail° my conquest won,
And she shall be sole victoress, Caesar's Caesar.

Queen Elizabeth. What were I best to say? Her father's
      brother
Would be her lord? Or shall I say her uncle?
Or he that slew her brothers and her uncles?
340   Under what title shall I woo for thee
That God, the law, my honor, and her love
Can make seem pleasing to her tender years?

King Richard. Infer° fair England's peace by this alli-
      ance.

Queen Elizabeth. Which she shall purchase with still-
      lasting war.

313 *alliance* marriage   322 *orient* shining   335 *retail* recount   343
Infer bring forward as an argument

King Richard. Tell her the King, that may command, entreats.   *345*

Queen Elizabeth. That at her hands which the King's King forbids.

King Richard. Say she shall be a high and mighty queen.

Queen Elizabeth. To wail the title, as her mother doth.

King Richard. Say I will love her everlastingly.

Queen Elizabeth. But how long shall that title "ever" last?   *350*

King Richard. Sweetly in force unto her fair life's end.

Queen Elizabeth. But how long fairly shall her sweet life last?

King Richard. As long as heaven and nature lengthens it.

Queen Elizabeth. As long as hell and Richard likes of it.

King Richard. Say I, her sovereign, am her subject low.   *355*

Queen Elizabeth. But she, your subject, loathes such sovereignty.

King Richard. Be eloquent in my behalf to her.

Queen Elizabeth. An honest tale speeds best being° plainly told.

King Richard. Then plainly to her tell my loving tale.

Queen Elizabeth. Plain and not honest is too harsh° a style.   *360*

King Richard. Your reasons are too shallow and too quick.

358 *speeds best being* succeeds best when it is   360 *harsh* discordant

Queen Elizabeth. O no, my reasons are too deep and
    dead;
    Too deep and dead, poor infants, in their graves.

King Richard. Harp not on that string, madam; that
    is past.

Queen Elizabeth. Harp on it still shall I till heart-
365   strings break.

King Richard. Now, by my George, my garter,° and
    my crown—

Queen Elizabeth. Profaned, dishonored, and the third
    usurped.

King Richard. I swear—

Queen Elizabeth.   By nothing, for this is no oath:
    Thy George, profaned, hath lost his lordly honor;
370   Thy garter, blemished, pawned his knightly virtue;
    Thy crown, usurped, disgraced his kingly glory.
    If something thou wouldst swear to be believed,
    Swear then by something that thou hast not
    wronged.

King Richard. Then by myself—

Queen Elizabeth.   Thyself is self-misused.

King Richard. Now by the world—

375 *Queen Elizabeth.*   'Tis full of thy foul wrongs.

King Richard. My father's death—

Queen Elizabeth.   Thy life hath it dishonored.

King Richard. Why then, by God—

Queen Elizabeth.   God's wrong is most of all.
    If thou didst fear to break an oath with him,
    The unity the King my husband made
380   Thou hadst not broken, nor my brothers died.
    If thou hadst feared to break an oath by him,

366 *George . . . garter* insignia of the Order of the Garter (a figure
of St. George and a velvet ribbon)

Th' imperial metal circling now thy head
Had graced the tender temples of my child,
And both the Princes had been breathing here,
Which now, two tender bedfellows for dust,   *385*
Thy broken faith hath made the prey for worms.
What canst thou swear by now?

King Richard.   The time to come.

Queen Elizabeth. That thou hast wrongèd in the time
    o'erpast;
For I myself have many tears to wash
Hereafter° time, for time past wronged by thee.   *390*
The children live whose fathers thou hast slaugh-
    tered,
Ungoverned° youth, to wail it in their age;
The parents live whose children thou hast butch-
    ered,
Old barren plants, to wail it with their age.
Swear not by time to come, for that thou hast   *395*
Misused ere used, by times ill-used o'erpast.

King Richard. As I intend to prosper and repent,
So thrive I in my dangerous affairs
Of hostile arms! Myself myself confound!°
Heaven and fortune bar me happy hours!   *400*
Day, yield me not thy light, nor, night, thy rest!
Be opposite all planets of good luck
To my proceeding if, with dear heart's love,
Immaculate devotion, holy thoughts,
I tender° not thy beauteous princely daughter!   *405*
In her consists my happiness and thine;
Without her, follows to myself and thee,
Herself, the land, and many a Christian soul,
Death, desolation, ruin, and decay.
It cannot be avoided but by this;   *410*
It will not be avoided but by this.
Therefore, dear mother—I must call you so—
Be the attorney of my love to her.
Plead what I will be, not what I have been;

390 *Hereafter* future   392 *Ungoverned* unguided   399 *confound*
ruin   405 *tender* look after tenderly

415   Not my deserts, but what I will deserve.
        Urge the necessity and state of times,°
        And be not peevish-fond° in great designs.

Queen Elizabeth. Shall I be tempted of the devil thus?

King Richard. Ay, if the devil tempt you to do good.

420 *Queen Elizabeth.* Shall I forget myself to be myself?°

King Richard. Ay, if yourself's remembrance wrong
        yourself.

Queen Elizabeth. Yet thou didst kill my children.

King Richard. But in your daughter's womb I'll bury
        them,
        Where in that nest of spicery° they will breed
425   Selves of themselves, to your recomforture.°

Queen Elizabeth. Shall I go win my daughter to thy
        will?

King Richard. And be a happy mother by the deed.

Queen Elizabeth. I go. Write to me very shortly,
        And you shall understand from me her mind.

King Richard. Bear her my truelove's kiss; and so
430   farewell.
                                Exit Queen [Elizabeth].
        Relenting fool, and shallow, changing woman!

                Enter Ratcliffe, [Catesby following].

        How now! What news?

Ratcliffe. Most mighty sovereign, on the western coast
        Rideth a puissant° navy; to our shores
435   Throng many doubtful hollow-hearted friends,
        Unarmed, and unresolved° to beat them back.
        'Tis thought that Richmond is their admiral;

416 *state of times* condition of affairs   417 *peevish-fond* obstinately
foolish   420 *myself to be myself* that I am I   424 *nest of spicery*
(alludes to the nest of the phoenix, a bird that periodically returned
to its fragrant nest, where it was consumed in flame and arose
renewed)   425 *recomforture* consolation   434 *puissant* powerful
436 *unresolved* irresolute

And there they hull,° expecting° but the aid
Of Buckingham to welcome them ashore.

King Richard. Some light-foot friend post° to the
   Duke of Norfolk: *440*
Ratcliffe, thyself—or Catesby; where is he?

Catesby. Here, my good lord.

King Richard.   -   Catesby, fly to the Duke.

Catesby. I will, my lord, with all convenient° haste.

King Richard. Ratcliffe, come hither. Post to Salisbury.
When thou com'st thither—[*To Catesby*] Dull un-
   mindful villain,   *445*
Why stay'st thou here and go'st not to the Duke?

Catesby. First, mighty liege, tell me your Highness'
   pleasure
What from your Grace I shall deliver to him.

King Richard. O, true, good Catesby. Bid him levy
   straight
The greatest strength and power that he can make   *450*
And meet me suddenly at Salisbury.

Catesby. I go.   *Exit.*

Ratcliffe. What, may it please you, shall I do at Salisbury?

King Richard. Why, what wouldst thou do there before I go?

Ratcliffe. Your Highness told me I should post before.   *455*

King Richard. My mind is changed.

          Enter Lord Stanley, [*Earl of Derby*].

                    Stanley, what news with you?

Stanley. None good, my liege, to please you with the
   hearing,

438 *hull* drift with the wind   438 *expecting* awaiting   440 *post*
hasten   443 *convenient* appropriate

Nor none so bad but well may be reported.

King Richard. Hoyday, a riddle! Neither good nor
    bad!
460 What need'st thou run so many miles about
    When thou mayest tell thy tale the nearest way?
    Once more, what news?

Stanley.   Richmond is on the seas.

King Richard. There let him sink, and be the seas on
    him!
    White-livered runagate,° what doth he there?

465 *Stanley.* I know not, mighty sovereign, but by guess.

King Richard. Well, as you guess?

Stanley. Stirred up by Dorset, Buckingham, and Mor-
    ton,
    He makes for England, here to claim the crown.

King Richard. Is the chair empty? Is the sword un-
    swayed?
470 Is the King dead, the empire unpossessed?
    What heir of York is there alive but we?
    And who is England's King but great York's heir?
    Then tell me, what makes he upon the seas?

Stanley. Unless for that, my liege, I cannot guess.

King Richard. Unless for that he comes to be your
475   liege,
    You cannot guess wherefore the Welshman comes.
    Thou wilt revolt and fly to him, I fear.

Stanley. No, my good lord; therefore mistrust me not.

King Richard. Where is thy power then to beat him
    back?
480 Where be thy tenants and thy followers?
    Are they not now upon the western shore,
    Safe-conducting the rebels from their ships?

464 *runagate* fugitive

Stanley. No, my good lord, my friends are in the
   north.

King Richard. Cold friends to me! What do they in
   the north
   When they should serve their sovereign in the west?   485

Stanley. They have not been commanded, mighty
   King.
   Pleaseth your Majesty to give me leave,
   I'll muster up my friends and meet your Grace
   Where and what time your Majesty shall please.

King Richard. Ay, thou wouldst be gone to join with
   Richmond.   490
   But I'll not trust thee.

Stanley.   Most mighty sovereign,
   You have no cause to hold my friendship doubtful.
   I never was nor never will be false.

King Richard. Go then and muster men; but leave be-
   hind
   Your son George Stanley. Look your heart be firm,   495
   Or else his head's assurance° is but frail.

Stanley. So deal with him as I prove true to you.
                                             Exit Stanley.

Enter a Messenger.

First Messenger. My gracious sovereign, now in Dev-
   onshire,
   As I by friends am well advertisèd,°
   Sir Edward Courtney and the haughty prelate,   500
   Bishop of Exeter, his elder brother,
   With many moe confederates, are in arms.

Enter another Messenger.

Second Messenger. In Kent, my liege, the Guilfords
   are in arms,

496 *assurance* security   499 *advertisèd* informed

And every hour more competitors°
505   Flock to the rebels, and their power grows strong.

Enter another Messenger.

Third Messenger. My lord, the army of great Buck-
    ingham—

King Richard. Out on ye, owls! Nothing but songs of
    death?   *He striketh him.*
    There, take thou that, till thou bring better news.

Third Messenger. The news I have to tell your Maj-
    esty
510   Is that by sudden floods and fall of waters
    Buckingham's army is dispersed and scattered,
    And he himself wand'red away alone,
    No man knows whither.

King Richard.   I cry thee mercy.
    There is my purse to cure that blow of thine.
515   Hath any well-advisèd friend proclaimed
    Reward to him that brings the traitor in?

Third Messenger. Such proclamation hath been made,
    my lord.

Enter another Messenger.

Fourth Messenger. Sir Thomas Lovell and Lord Mar-
    quis Dorset,
    'Tis said, my liege, in Yorkshire are in arms.
520   But this good comfort bring I to your Highness:
    The Britain° navy is dispersed by tempest.
    Richmond in Dorsetshire sent out a boat
    Unto the shore to ask those on the banks
    If they were his assistants, yea or no;
525   Who answered him they came from Buckingham
    Upon his party. He, mistrusting them,
    Hoised° sail and made his course again for Britain.°

---

504 *competitors* associates   521 *Britain* Breton   527 *Hoised* hoisted
527 *Britain* Brittany

King Richard. March on, march on, since we are up
   in arms,
  If not to fight with foreign enemies,
  Yet to beat down these rebels here at home.   *530*

Enter Catesby.

Catesby. My liege, the Duke of Buckingham is taken.
  That is the best news. That the Earl of Richmond
  Is with a mighty power landed at Milford
  Is colder news, but yet they must be told.

King Richard. Away towards Salisbury! While we rea-
   son here,   *533*
  A royal battle might be won and lost.
  Someone take order Buckingham be brought
  To Salisbury; the rest march on with me.
                       Flourish. Exeunt.

Scene [V. *Lord Stanley's house.*]

Enter [Lord Stanley, Earl of] Derby, and
Sir Christopher [Urswick, a chaplain].

Stanley. Sir Christopher, tell Richmond this from me:
  That in the sty of the most deadly boar
  My son George Stanley is franked up in hold;°
  If I revolt, off goes young George's head;
  The fear of that holds off my present aid.   *5*
  So get thee gone; commend me to thy lord.
  Withal say that the Queen hath heartily consented
  He should espouse Elizabeth her daughter.
  But tell me, where is princely Richmond now?

IV.v.3 *franked up in hold* penned up in custody (*frank*=sty)

Christopher. At Pembroke or at Harfordwest° in
10   Wales.

Stanley. What men of name resort to him?

Christopher. Sir Walter Herbert, a renownèd soldier,
Sir Gilbert Talbot, Sir William Stanley,
Oxford, redoubted Pembroke, Sir James Blunt,
15   And Rice ap Thomas, with a valiant crew,
And many other of great name and worth;
And towards London do they bend their power,
If by the way they be not fought withal.

Stanley. Well, hie thee to thy lord. I kiss his hand;
20   My letter will resolve° him of my mind.
                                        [*Gives letter.*]
Farewell.   *Exeunt.*

10 *Harfordwest* Haverfordwest   20 *resolve* inform

ACT V

Scene I. [*Salisbury. An open place.*]

*Enter Buckingham with [Sheriff and] Halberds,°
led to execution.*

Buckingham. Will not King Richard let me speak with
    him?

Sheriff. No, my good lord; therefore be patient.

Buckingham. Hastings, and Edward's children, Grey
    and Rivers,
  Holy King Henry and thy fair son Edward,
  Vaughan, and all that have miscarrièd   *5*
  By underhand corrupted foul injustice,
  If that your moody discontented souls
  Do through the clouds behold this present hour,
  Even for revenge mock my destruction!
  This is All Souls' day, fellow, is it not?   *10*

Sheriff. It is, my lord.

Buckingham. Why, then All Souls' day is my body's
    doomsday.
  This is the day which in King Edward's time
  I wished might fall on me when I was found
  False to his children and his wife's allies.   *15*

V.i.s.d. *Halberds* guards armed with long poleaxes

157

This is the day wherein I wished to fall
By the false faith of him whom most I trusted.
This, this All Souls' day to my fearful soul
Is the determined respite of my wrongs.°
20 That high All-seer which I dallied with
Hath turned my feignèd prayer on my head
And given in earnest what I begged in jest.
Thus doth he force the swords of wicked men
To turn their own points in their masters' bosoms.
25 Thus Margaret's curse falls heavy on my neck:
"When he," quoth she, "shall split thy heart with
      sorrow,
Remember Margaret was a prophetess."
Come lead me, officers, to the block of shame;
Wrong hath but wrong, and blame the due of
      blame.

                          Exeunt Buckingham with Officers.

Scene II. [*Camp near Tamworth.*]

*Enter Richmond, Oxford, Blunt, Herbert,
    and others, with Drum and Colors.*

Richmond. Fellows in arms and my most loving
      friends,
Bruised underneath the yoke of tyranny,
Thus far into the bowels° of the land
Have we marched on without impediment;
5   And here receive we from our father Stanley
Lines of fair comfort and encouragement.
The wretched, bloody, and usurping boar,
That spoiled your summer fields and fruitful vines,
Swills your warm blood like wash, and makes his
      trough

19 *determined respite of my wrongs* end of reprieve for my unjust
acts   V.ii.3 *bowels* center

In your emboweled° bosoms, this foul swine   10
Is now even in the center of this isle,
Near to the town of Leicester, as we learn.
From Tamworth thither is but one day's march.
In God's name cheerly on, courageous friends,
To reap the harvest of perpetual peace   15
By this one bloody trial of sharp war.

Oxford. Every man's conscience is a thousand men
To fight against this guilty homicide.

Herbert. I doubt not but his friends will turn to us.

Blunt. He hath no friends but what are friends for
    fear,   20
Which in his dearest need will fly from him.

Richmond. All for our vantage. Then in God's name
    march!
True hope is swift and flies with swallow's wings;
Kings it makes gods, and meaner creatures kings.
                                   Exeunt omnes.

[Scene III. *Bosworth Field.*]

*Enter King Richard in arms, with Norfolk,
    Ratcliffe, and the Earl of Surrey,
        [and Soldiers].*

King Richard. Here pitch our tent, even here in Bos-
    worth field.
My Lord of Surrey, why look you so sad?

Surrey. My heart is ten times lighter than my looks.

King Richard. My Lord of Norfolk!

Norfolk.   Here, most gracious liege.

10 *emboweled* ripped up

King Richard. Norfolk, we must have knocks; ha,
5   must we not?

Norfolk. We must both give and take, my loving lord.

King Richard. Up with my tent! Here will I lie to-
      night;
                [*Soldiers begin to set up the King's tent.*]
      But where tomorrow? Well, all's one for that.
      Who hath descried the number of the traitors?

10 *Norfolk.* Six or seven thousand is their utmost power.

King Richard. Why, our battalia° trebles that account;
      Besides, the King's name is a tower of strength,
      Which they upon the adverse faction want.°
      Up with the tent! Come, noble gentlemen,
15   Let us survey the vantage of the ground.
      Call for some men of sound direction.°
      Let's lack no discipline, make no delay,
      For, lords, tomorrow is a busy day.   *Exeunt.*

      *Enter Richmond, Sir William Brandon, Oxford,
            and Dorset, [Herbert, and Blunt].*

Richmond. The weary sun hath made a golden set
20   And by the bright tract° of his fiery car°
      Gives token of a goodly day tomorrow.
      Sir William Brandon, you shall bear my standard.
      Give me some ink and paper in my tent.
      I'll draw the form and model of our battle,
25   Limit° each leader to his several charge,
      And part in just proportion our small power.
      My Lord of Oxford, you, Sir William Brandon,
      And you, Sir Walter Herbert, stay with me.
      The Earl of Pembroke keeps° his regiment;
30   Good Captain Blunt, bear my good-night to him,
      And by the second hour in the morning
      Desire the Earl to see me in my tent.
      Yet one thing more, good Captain, do for me:

V.iii.11 *battalia* army   13 *want* lack   16 *direction* ability to give
orders   20 *tract* track   20 *car* chariot   25 *Limit* assign   29 *keeps*
stays with

Where is Lord Stanley quartered, do you know?

Blunt. Unless I have mista'en his colors much,   35
Which well I am assured I have not done,
His regiment lies half a mile at least
South from the mighty power of the King.

Richmond. If without peril it be possible,
Sweet Blunt, make some good means to speak with
  him   40
And give him from me this most needful note.

Blunt. Upon my life, my lord, I'll undertake it;
And so God give you quiet rest tonight!

Richmond. Good night, good Captain Blunt. [*Exit
  Blunt.*] Come, gentlemen,
Let us consult upon tomorrow's business.   45
Into my tent; the dew is raw and cold.
                    They withdraw into the tent.

        *Enter, [to his tent, King] Richard, Ratcliffe,
                Norfolk, and Catesby.*

King Richard. What is't o'clock?

Catesby.   It's suppertime, my lord;
It's nine o'clock.

King Richard.   I will not sup tonight.
Give me some ink and paper.
What, is my beaver° easier than it was?   50
And all my armor laid into my tent?

Catesby. It is, my liege; and all things are in readiness.

King Richard. Good Norfolk, hie thee to thy charge;
Use careful watch, choose trusty sentinels.

Norfolk. I go, my lord.   55

King Richard. Stir with the lark tomorrow, gentle
  Norfolk.

Norfolk. I warrant you, my lord.   *Exit.*

50 *beaver* face-guard of a helmet

King Richard. Catesby!

Catesby. My lord?

King Richard.   Send out a pursuivant-at-arms°
60   To Stanley's regiment; bid him bring his power
        Before sunrising, lest his son George fall
        Into the blind cave of eternal night.   [*Exit Catesby.*]
        Fill me a bowl of wine. Give me a watch.°
        Saddle white Surrey° for the field tomorrow.
65   Look that my staves° be sound and not too heavy.
        Ratcliffe!

Ratcliffe. My lord?

King Richard. Saw'st thou the melancholy Lord
    Northumberland?

Ratcliffe. Thomas the Earl of Surrey and himself,
70   Much about cockshut time,° from troop to troop
        Went through the army, cheering up the soldiers.

King Richard. So, I am satisfied. Give me a bowl of
    wine.
        I have not that alacrity of spirit
        Nor cheer of mind that I was wont to have.
                                        [*Wine brought.*]
75   Set it down. Is ink and paper ready?

Ratcliffe. It is, my lord.

King Richard. Bid my guard watch. Leave me. Rat-
    cliffe,
        About the mid of night come to my tent
        And help to arm me. Leave me, I say.
                        Exit Ratcliffe. [*King Richard sleeps.*]

Enter [*Stanley, Earl of*] *Derby, to Richmond in
    his tent,* [*Lords and Gentlemen attending*].

80   *Stanley.* Fortune and victory sit on thy helm!

---

59 *pursuivant-at-arms* minor herald   63 *watch* timepiece   64 *Surrey* (the name of a horse)   65 *staves* lances   70 *cockshut time* twilight

Richmond. All comfort that the dark night can afford
  Be to thy person, noble father-in-law!
  Tell me, how fares our loving mother?

Stanley. I by attorney bless thee from thy mother,
  Who prays continually for Richmond's good.   85
  So much for that. The silent hours steal on
  And flaky° darkness breaks within the east.
  In brief, for so the season° bids us be,
  Prepare thy battle early in the morning
  And put thy fortune to the arbitrament   90
  Of bloody strokes and mortal-staring° war.
  I, as I may—that which I would I cannot—
  With best advantage° will deceive the time°
  And aid thee in this doubtful shock of arms.
  But on thy side I may not be too forward,   95
  Lest, being seen, thy brother, tender George,
  Be executed in his father's sight.
  Farewell; the leisure° and the fearful time
  Cuts off the ceremonious vows of love
  And ample interchange of sweet discourse   100
  Which so long sund'red friends should dwell upon.
  God give us leisure for these rites of love!
  Once more adieu; be valiant, and speed well.

Richmond. Good lords, conduct him to his regiment.
  I'll strive with° troubled thoughts to take a nap, 105
  Lest leaden slumber peise° me down tomorrow
  When I should mount with wings of victory.
  Once more, good night, kind lords and gentlemen.
                        Exeunt. Manet Richmond.
  O thou whose captain I account myself,
  Look on my forces with a gracious eye!   110
  Put in their hands thy bruising irons of wrath,
  That they may crush down with a heavy fall
  The usurping helmets of our adversaries!
  Make us thy ministers of chastisement,

87 *flaky* streaked with light   88 *season* time   91 *mortal-staring* fatally glaring   93 *advantage* opportunity   93 *the time* the people of this time   98 *leisure* time available   105 *with* against   106 *peise* weigh

115　　That we may praise thee in the victory!
　　　To thee I do commend my watchful soul
　　　Ere I let fall the windows° of mine eyes.
　　　Sleeping and waking, O defend me still!   *Sleeps.*

Enter the Ghost of Prince Edward, son to Henry
the Sixth.

　　Ghost. (*To Richard*) Let me sit heavy on thy soul
　　　　tomorrow!
120　　Think how thou stab'st me in my prime of youth
　　　At Tewkesbury. Despair therefor° and die!
　　　(*To Richmond*) Be cheerful, Richmond; for the
　　　　wrongèd souls
　　　Of butchered princes fight in thy behalf.
　　　King Henry's issue,° Richmond, comforts thee.
　　　　　　　　　　　　　　　　　　　　　　[*Exit.*]

Enter the Ghost of Henry the Sixth.

　　Ghost. (*To Richard*) When I was mortal, my anointed
125　　　body
　　　By thee was punchèd full of deadly holes.
　　　Think on the Tower and me. Despair and die!
　　　Harry the Sixth bids thee despair and die!
　　　(*To Richmond*) Virtuous and holy, be thou con-
　　　　queror!
130　　Harry, that prophesied thou shouldst be king,
　　　Doth comfort thee in thy sleep. Live and flourish!
　　　　　　　　　　　　　　　　　　　　　　[*Exit.*]

Enter the Ghost of Clarence.

　　Ghost. [*To Richard*] Let me sit heavy in thy soul to-
　　　　morrow,
　　　I that was washed to death with fulsome wine,
　　　Poor Clarence, by thy guile betrayed to death.
135　　Tomorrow in the battle think on me,
　　　And fall° thy edgeless sword. Despair and die!

---

117 *windows* eyelids   121 *therefor* because of that   124 *issue* offspring   136 *fall* let fall

(*To Richmond*) Thou offspring of the house of
   Lancaster,
The wrongèd heirs of York do pray for thee.
Good angels guard thy battle! Live and flourish!
                                                [*Exit.*]

Enter the Ghosts of Rivers, Grey, and Vaughan.

Rivers. [*To Richard*] Let me sit heavy in thy soul tomorrow,   140
Rivers, that died at Pomfret! Despair and die!

Grey. Think upon Grey, and let thy soul despair!

Vaughan. Think upon Vaughan and with guilty fear
   Let fall thy lance: despair, and die!

All. (*To Richmond*) Awake, and think our wrongs in
   Richard's bosom   145
Will conquer him! Awake, and win the day!
                                              [*Exeunt.*]

Enter the Ghost of Hastings.

Ghost. [*To Richard*] Bloody and guilty, guiltily awake,
   And in a bloody battle end thy days!
Think on Lord Hastings. Despair and die!
   (*To Richmond*) Quiet untroubled soul, awake,
   awake!   150
Arm, fight, and conquer for fair England's sake!
                                                [*Exit.*]

Enter the Ghosts of the two young Princes.

Ghosts. (*To Richard*) Dream on thy cousins smoth-
   erèd in the Tower.
Let us be lead within thy bosom, Richard,
And weigh thee down to ruin, shame, and death.
Thy nephews' souls bid thee despair and die!   155
   (*To Richmond*) Sleep, Richmond, sleep in peace
   and wake in joy.
Good angels guard thee from the boar's annoy!°

157 *annoy* disturbance

Live, and beget a happy race of kings!
Edward's unhappy sons do bid thee flourish.

[Exeunt.]

Enter the Ghost of Lady Anne his wife.

Ghost. (*To Richard*) Richard, thy wife, that wretched
160   Anne thy wife,
That never slept a quiet hour with thee,
Now fills thy sleep with perturbations.
Tomorrow in the battle think on me,
And fall thy edgeless sword. Despair and die!
(*To Richmond*) Thou quiet soul, sleep thou a quiet
165   sleep.
Dream of success and happy victory!
Thy adversary's wife doth pray for thee.   *[Exit.]*

Enter the Ghost of Buckingham.

Ghost. (*To Richard*) The first was I that helped thee
to the crown;
The last was I that felt thy tyranny.
170   O, in the battle think on Buckingham,
And die in terror of thy guiltiness!
Dream on, dream on, of bloody deeds and death;
Fainting, despair; despairing, yield thy breath!
(*To Richmond*) I died for hope° ere I could lend
thee aid;
175   But cheer thy heart and be thou not dismayed.
God and good angels fight on Richmond's side,
And Richard falls in height of all his pride.   *[Exit.]*

Richard starteth up out of a dream.

King Richard. Give me another horse! Bind up my
wounds!
Have mercy, Jesu! Soft! I did but dream.
180   O coward conscience, how dost thou afflict me!
The lights burn blue. It is now dead midnight.

174 *for hope* because of hope (to help)

Cold fearful drops stand on my trembling flesh.
What do I fear? Myself? There's none else by.
Richard loves Richard: that is, I am I.
Is there a murderer here? No. Yes, I am.   *185*
Then fly. What, from myself? Great reason why!
Lest I revenge. What, myself upon myself?
Alack, I love myself. Wherefore? For any good
That I myself have done unto myself?
O no! Alas, I rather hate myself   *190*
For hateful deeds committed by myself.
I am a villain. Yet I lie, I am not.
Fool, of thyself speak well. Fool, do not flatter.
My conscience hath a thousand several° tongues,
And every tongue brings in a several tale,   *195*
And every tale condemns me for a villain.
Perjury, perjury in the highest degree,
Murder, stern murder in the direst degree,
All several sins, all used in each degree,
Throng to the bar, crying all, "Guilty! Guilty!"   *200*
I shall despair. There is no creature loves me;
And if I die, no soul will pity me.
Nay, wherefore should they, since that I myself
Find in myself no pity to myself?
Methought the souls of all that I had murdered   *205*
Came to my tent, and every one did threat
Tomorrow's vengeance on the head of Richard.

Enter Ratcliffe.

Ratcliffe. My lord!

King Richard. Zounds, who is there?

Ratcliffe. Ratcliffe, my lord; 'tis I. The early village
    cock   *210*
  Hath twice done salutation to the morn.
  Your friends are up and buckle on their armor.

King Richard. O Ratcliffe, I have dreamed a fearful
    dream!

194 *several* separate

What think'st thou, will our friends prove all true?

Ratcliffe. No doubt, my lord.

215 *King Richard.*   O Ratcliffe, I fear, I fear!

Ratcliffe. Nay, good my lord, be not afraid of shadows.

King Richard. By the apostle Paul, shadows tonight
Have struck more terror to the soul of Richard
Than can the substance of ten thousand soldiers
220 Armèd in proof° and led by shallow Richmond.
'Tis not yet near day. Come, go with me.
Under our tents I'll play the easedropper°
To see if any mean to shrink from me.
                    Exeunt Richard and Ratcliffe.

Enter the Lords to Richmond sitting in his tent.

Lords. Good morrow, Richmond.

Richmond. Cry mercy,° lords and watchful gentle-
225 men,
That you have ta'en a tardy sluggard here.

Lords. How have you slept, my lord?

Richmond. The sweetest sleep and fairest-boding
dreams
That ever ent'red in a drowsy head
230 Have I since your departure had, my lords.
Methought their souls whose bodies Richard mur-
dered
Came to my tent and cried° on victory.
I promise you my heart is very jocund
In the remembrance of so fair a dream.
235 How far into the morning is it, lords?

Lords. Upon the stroke of four.

Richmond. Why, then 'tis time to arm and give direction.

220 *proof* tested armor   222 *easedropper* eavesdropper   225 *Cry
mercy* (I) beg pardon   232 *cried* called aloud

His Oration to his Soldiers.

More than I have said, loving countrymen,
The leisure and enforcement of the time
Forbids to dwell upon; yet remember this: 240
God and our good cause fight upon our side;
The prayers of holy saints and wrongèd souls,
Like high-reared bulwarks, stand before our faces.
Richard except, those whom we fight against
Had rather have us win than him they follow.   245
For what is he they follow? Truly, gentlemen,
A bloody tyrant and a homicide;
One raised in blood and one in blood established;
One that made means° to come by what he hath,
And slaughterèd those that were the means to help
    him;   250
A base foul stone, made precious by the foil°
Of England's chair, where he is falsely set;
One that hath ever been God's enemy.
Then if you fight against God's enemy,
God will in justice ward° you as his soldiers;   255
If you do sweat to put a tyrant down,
You sleep in peace, the tyrant being slain;
If you do fight against your country's foes,
Your country's fat° shall pay your pains the hire;
If you do fight in safeguard of your wives,   260
Your wives shall welcome home the conquerors;
If you do free your children from the sword,
Your children's children quits° it in your age.
Then in the name of God and all these rights,
Advance your standards, draw your willing swords.   265
For me, the ransom° of my bold attempt
Shall be this cold corpse on the earth's cold face;
But if I thrive, the gain of my attempt
The least of you shall share his part thereof.   270
Sound drums and trumpets boldly and cheerfully;
God and Saint George! Richmond and victory!
                                        [*Exeunt.*]

---

249 *made means* contrived ways   251 *foil* setting for a gem   255
ward protect   259 *fat* abundance   263 *quits* repays   266 *the ran-
som* i.e., the price paid (if defeated)

Enter King Richard, Ratcliffe, and [Soldiers].

King Richard. What said Northumberland as touching
   Richmond?

Ratcliffe. That he was never trainèd up in arms.

King Richard. He said the truth; and what said Surrey then?

Ratcliffe. He smiled and said, "The better for our pur-
275   pose."

King Richard. He was in the right, and so indeed it is.
                              The clock striketh.
   Tell° the clock there. Give me a calendar.
   Who saw the sun today?

Ratcliffe.   Not I, my lord.

King Richard. Then he disdains to shine; for by the
   book
280   He should have braved° the east an hour ago.
   A black day will it be to somebody.
   Ratcliffe!

Ratcliffe. My lord?

King Richard.   The sun will not be seen today;
   The sky doth frown and lour upon our army.
285   I would these dewy tears were from the ground.
   Not shine today! Why, what is that to me
   More than to Richmond? For the selfsame heaven
   That frowns on me looks sadly upon him.

Enter Norfolk.

Norfolk. Arm, arm, my lord; the foe vaunts in the
   field.

King Richard. Come, bustle, bustle. Caparison my
290   horse.
   Call up Lord Stanley, bid him bring his power.
   I will lead forth my soldiers to the plain,
   And thus my battle shall be orderèd:

277 *Tell* count   280 *braved* made glorious

My foreward shall be drawn out all in length,
Consisting equally of horse and foot;   295
Our archers shall be placèd in the midst;
John Duke of Norfolk, Thomas Earl of Surrey,
Shall have the leading of this foot and horse.
They thus directed,° we will follow
In the main battle, whose puissance° on either side   300
Shall be well wingèd with our chiefest horse.
This, and Saint George to boot!° What think'st
  thou, Norfolk?

Norfolk. A good direction, warlike sovereign.
  This found I on my tent this morning.
                    He showeth him a paper.
  "Jockey° of Norfolk, be not so bold,   305
  For Dickon thy master is bought and sold."°

King Richard. A thing devisèd by the enemy.
  Go, gentlemen, every man unto his charge.
  Let not our babbling dreams affright our souls;
  Conscience is but a word that cowards use,   310
  Devised at first to keep the strong in awe;
  Our strong arms be our conscience, swords our
    law!
  March on, join bravely, let us to it pell-mell,
  If not to heaven, then hand in hand to hell.

                His Oration to his Army.

What shall I say more than I have inferred?   315
Remember whom you are to cope withal,
A sort° of vagabonds, rascals, and runaways,
A scum of Britains and base lackey peasants,
Whom their o'ercloyèd country vomits forth
To desperate ventures and assured destruction.   320
You sleeping safe, they bring to you unrest;
You having lands, and blest with beauteous wives,
They would distrain° the one, distain° the other.

---

299 *directed* arranged   300 *puissance* power   302 *to boot* to our
help   305 *Jockey* (nickname for John)   306 *bought and sold* betrayed for a bribe   317 *sort* set   323 *distrain* confiscate   323 *dis-
tain* dishonor

And who doth lead them but a paltry fellow,
325 Long kept in Britain° at our mother's cost,
A milksop, one that never in his life
Felt so much cold as over shoes in snow?
Let's whip these stragglers o'er the seas again,
Lash hence these overweening rags of France,
330 These famished beggars, weary of their lives,
Who, but for dreaming on this fond° exploit,
For want of means, poor rats, had hanged them-
    selves.
If we be conquerèd, let men conquer us,
And not these bastard Britains, whom our fathers
Have in their own land beaten, bobbed, and
335   thumped,
And in record left them the heirs of shame.
Shall these enjoy our lands? Lie with our wives?
Ravish our daughters? (*Drum afar off.*) Hark! I
    hear their drum.
Fight, gentlemen of England! Fight, bold yeomen!
340 Draw, archers, draw your arrows to the head!
Spur your proud horses hard and ride in blood!
Amaze the welkin° with your broken staves!

Enter a Messenger.

What says Lord Stanley? Will he bring his power?

Messenger. My lord, he doth deny to come.

345 *King Richard.* Off with his son George's head!

Norfolk. My lord, the enemy is past the marsh.
After the battle let George Stanley die.

King Richard. A thousand hearts are great within my
    bosom.
Advance our standards, set upon our foes!
350 Our ancient word of courage, fair Saint George,
Inspire us with the spleen° of fiery dragons!
Upon them! Victory sits on our helms.   *Exeunt.*

325 *Britain* Brittany   331 *fond* foolish   342 *welkin* sky   351 *spleen*
fierce spirit

[Scene IV. *Bosworth Field*.]

Alarum; excursions.° *Enter Catesby*
[*and Norfolk*].

Catesby. Rescue, my Lord of Norfolk, rescue, rescue!
   The King enacts more wonders than a man,
   Daring an opposite° to every danger.
   His horse is slain, and all on foot he fights,
   Seeking for Richmond in the throat of death.   5
   Rescue, fair lord, or else the day is lost!

Alarums. Enter [*King*] *Richard.*

King Richard. A horse! A horse! My kingdom for a
      horse!

Catesby. Withdraw, my lord; I'll help you to a horse.

King Richard. Slave, I have set my life upon a cast,°
   And I will stand the hazard° of the die.   10
   I think there be six Richmonds in the field;
   Five have I slain today instead of him.
   A horse! A horse! My kingdom for a horse!
                                          [*Exeunt.*]

V.iv.s.d. *excursions* sallies   3 *opposite* opponent   9 *cast* throw (of
dice)   10 *hazard* chance

[Scene V. *Bosworth Field*.]

*Alarum. Enter [King] Richard and Richmond;
they fight; Richard is slain.*

*Retreat° and flourish. Enter Richmond, [Stanley,
Earl of] Derby, bearing the crown, with divers
other Lords.*

Richmond. God and your arms be praised, victorious
friends!
The day is ours; the bloody dog is dead.

Stanley. Courageous Richmond, well hast thou acquit
thee.
Lo, here this long-usurpèd royalty
5   From the dead temples of this bloody wretch
Have I plucked off, to grace thy brows withal.
Wear it, enjoy it, and make much of it.

Richmond. Great God of heaven, say amen to all!
But tell me, is young George Stanley living?

10   *Stanley.* He is, my lord, and safe in Leicester town,
Whither, if it please you, we may now withdraw us.

Richmond. What men of name° are slain on either
side?

Stanley. John Duke of Norfolk, Walter Lord Ferrers,
Sir Robert Brakenbury, and Sir William Brandon.

15   *Richmond.* Inter their bodies as become their births.
Proclaim a pardon to the soldiers fled
That in submission will return to us;

V.v.s.d. *Retreat* trumpet signal to recall troops   12 *name* high rank

And then, as we have ta'en the sacrament,°
We will unite the White Rose and the Red.
Smile heaven upon this fair conjunction,°   20
That long have frowned upon their enmity!
What traitor hears me and says not amen?
England hath long been mad and scarred herself;
The brother blindly shed the brother's blood,
The father rashly slaughtered his own son,   25
The son, compelled, been butcher to the sire.
All this divided York and Lancaster,
Divided in their dire division,
O, now let Richmond and Elizabeth,
The true succeeders of each royal house,   30
By God's fair ordinance conjoin together!
And let their heirs, God, if thy will be so,
Enrich the time to come with smooth-faced peace,
With smiling plenty, and fair prosperous days!
Abate the edge° of traitors, gracious Lord,   35
That would reduce° these bloody days again
And make poor England weep in streams of blood!
Let them not live to taste this land's increase
That would with treason wound this fair land's
    peace!
Now civil wounds are stopped, peace lives again;   40
That she may long live here, God say amen!

                                              Exeunt.

                    FINIS

---

18 *ta'en the sacrament* taken a solemn oath (to marry Elizabeth
when he won the crown) 20 *conjunction* joining in marriage
35 *Abate the edge* blunt the sharp point 36 *reduce* bring back

Textual Note

Richard III, one of Shakespeare's most popular plays, appeared in eight quarto editions, more than any other Shakespeare play except *Henry IV, Part I*. The First Quarto (Q1) was entered for publication on October 20, 1597, as "The tragedie of kinge Richard the Third with the death of the Duke of Clarence." The actors of Shakespeare's company who reconstructed this text from memory left out over 200 lines and made many changes, but they preserved some lines omitted in the Folio, especially IV.ii.98–115. Printers added errors in each of the later quartos, dated 1598, 1602 (Q3), 1605, 1612, 1622 (Q6), 1629, and 1634.

The best text of the play appeared in 1623 in the First Folio (F). The printer, William Jaggard, had his compositors set up *Richard III* from a quarto marked with many corrections from an authentic manuscript. It used to be believed that this quarto was Q6, supplemented by an uncorrected quarto, Q3. In 1955, however, J. K. Walton, in *The Copy for the Folio Text of Richard III,* concluded that Q3, corrected, was the only quarto used for F. My collation of all variants in the first six quartos supports this conclusion. It is possible that both Q3 and Q6 were used, but that remains to be proved.

The present edition follows the readings of the First Folio except for the changes listed below. These changes have been made for definite reasons. First, the part of the Folio text containing III.i.1–168 seems to have been printed from Q3 without any correction from a manu-

script, and the Folio text from V.iii.49 to the end of the
play makes very few corrections. These few corrections
have been accepted, but the rest of the text in these passages is based on Q1, from which Q3 and F are here
derived. For example, the right reading "as" in III.i.123
appears in Q1, while "as, as," in F derives from the mis-
print "as as" in Q3. Second, the reading of Q1 is also
preferred, in any part of the play, to a different reading
which F merely reprints from Q3. Third, the present text
accepts 30 lines from Q1 which are not in F. Finally,
I have corrected errors and have made a few emendations.

The divisions into acts and scenes include all those
in the Folio, translated from Latin, and these further
scenes as marked in modern editions: III.v–vii, IV.iii, and
V.iii–v. Brackets set off these and other editorial additions.
Spelling, punctuation, and capitalization are modernized,
and speech prefixes are regularized. In the following list
of significant changes from the Folio, and from Q1 where
it is the basic text, the reading of the present text is given
in italics and the alternative reading of the Folio, or of
Q1 or Q3, in roman.

I.i.26 *spy* [Q1] see   42 s.d. *Clarence, guarded, and Brakenbury*
Clarence, and Brakenbury, guarded   45 *the* [Q1] th'   52 *for* [Q1]
but   65 *tempers him to this* [Q1] tempts him to this harsh   75 *to
her for his* [Q1] for her   103 *I* [Q1] I do   124 *the* [Q1] this [Q3]
133 *prey* [Q1] play   142 *What* [Q1] Where

I.ii.27 *life* death (cf. IV.i.75)   39 *stand* [Q1] Stand'st   60 *deed*
[Q1] Deeds   78 *a man* [Q1] man   80 *accuse* curse   154 *aspect*
[Q1] Aspects   195 *was man* [Q1] man was [Q3]   201 *Richard* [Q1,
not in F]   202 *Anne. To take . . . give* [Q1, not in F]   225 *Richard.
Sirs . . . corse* [Q1, not in F]   235 *at all* [Q1] withall [Q3]

I.iii.s.d. *Queen* [Q1] the Queene Mother   17 *come the lords* [Q1]
comes the Lord   108 s.d. *Enter old Queen Margaret* [after 109]
113 *Tell . . . said* [Q1, not in F]   114 *avouch* [Q1] auouch't   308
Queen Elizabeth [Q1 Qu.] Mar.   341, 349, 354 *First Murderer* Vil.
354 s.d. *Exeunt* [Q1 after 353, not in F]

I.iv.13 *Thence* [Q1] There   86 *First Murderer* 2 Mur.   89 *Second
Murderer* 1   122 *Faith* [Q1, not in F]   126 *Zounds* [Q1] Come

147 *Zounds* [Q1, not in F] 192–93 *to have . . . sins* [Q1] for any goodnesse 240 *And charged . . . other* [Q1, not in F] 266–70 *Which . . . distress* [not in Q; F inserts after 259]

II.i.5 *in* [Q1] to 7 *Rivers and Hastings* [Q1] Dorset and Riuers 39 *God* [Q1] heauen 40 *zeal* [Q1] loue 57 *unwittingly* [Q1] vn-willingly 59 *By* [Q1] To 109 *at* [Q1] and

II.ii.1 *Boy* [Q1] Edw. 3 *do you* [Q1] do 47 *have I* [Q1] haue 83 *weep* [Q1] weepes 84–85 *and so . . . Edward weep* [Q1, not in F] 142, 154 *Ludlow* [Q1] London 145 *Queen and Duchess of York. With all our hearts* [Q1, not in F]

II.iii.43 *Ensuing* [Q1] Pursuing (catchword "Ensuing")

II.iv.1 *hear* [Q1] heard [Q3] 21 *Archbishop* [Q1 Car.] Yor. 65 *death* [Q1] earth

III.i.s.d. *with others* [F] &c [Q1] 9 *Nor* [Q1] No 40 *God in heaven* [Q1] God [Q3] 43 *deep* [Q1] great [Q3] 56 *ne'er* [F] neuer [Q1] 57 *o'errule* [F] ouerrule [Q1] 60 s.d. *Exit* [not in Q1; after 59 in Q3 and F] 63 *seems* [Q1] thinkst [Q3] 78 *all-ending* [Q1] ending [Q3] 79 *ne'er* neuer [Q1 F] 87 *this* [Q1] his [Q3] 94 s.d. *and Cardinal* [F] Cardinall [Q1] 96 *loving* [Q1] noble [Q3] 97 *dread* [Q1] deare [Q3] 120 *heavy* [Q1] weightie [Q3] 123 *as* [Q1] as as [Q3] 141 *needs will* [Q1] will [Q3] 145 *grandam* [F] Granam [Q1] 149 *with* [Q1] and with 150 s.d. *A sennet* [F, not in Q1] *Hastings* Hast. Dors [Q1] Hastings, and Dorset [F] *and Catesby* [F, not in Q1] 154 *parlous* perillous [Q1 F] 160 *knowest* [Q1] know'st 161 *thinkest* [Q1] think'st 167 *thinkest* [Q1] think'st 167 *What will he?* [Q1] Will not hee?

III.ii.110 s.d. *He whispers in his ear* [Q1] Priest. Ile wait vpon your Lordship [cf. line 121]

III.iv.78 s.d. *Exeunt* [after 77] 81 *rase* [Q1] rowse

III.v.4 *wert* [Q1] were 104 *Penker* Peuker 105 s.d. *Exeunt* Exit 109 s.d. *Exit* [Q1] Exeunt

III.vii.218 *Zounds, I'll* [Q1] we will 219 *Richard. O . . . Buckingham* [Q1, not in F] 223 *stone* Stones 246 *cousin* [Q1] Cousins

IV.i. s.d. *Enter . . . another door* Enter the Queene, Anne Duchesse of Gloucester, the Duchesse of Yorke, and Marquesse Dorset 103 *sorrow* Sorrowes

IV.ii.71 *there* [Q1] then 89 *Hereford* [Q1] Hertford 97 *Perhaps, perhaps* [Q1] perhaps 98–115 *Buckingham. My lord . . . vein today* [Q1, not in F]

IV.iii.15 *once* [Q1] one 31 *at* [Q1] and

IV.iv.10 *unblown* [Q1] vnblowed 39 *Tell o'er . . . mine* Tell ouer

. . . mine [Q1, not in F]   45 *holp'st* hop'st   52 *That excellent . . .
earth* [after 53]   64 *Thy* [Q1] The   118 *nights . . . days* [Q1] night
. . . day* [Q3]   128 *intestate* [Q1] intestine   141 *Where* [Q1] Where't
200 *moe* [Q1] more [Q3]   268 *would I* [Q1] I would [Q3]   274
sometimes [Q1] sometime [Q3]   284 *this is* [Q1] this   323 *loan*
Loue   348 *wail* [Q1] vaile   364 *Harp . . . past* [after 365]   377 *God
. . . God's* [Q1] Heauen . . . Heanens (so misprinted)   392 *in* [Q1]
with   396 *o'erpast* [Q1] repast   417 *peevish-fond* peeuish found
423 *I'll* I   430 s.d. *Exit Queen* [after 429]   431 s.d. *Enter Ratcliffe*
[after "newes"]   444 *Ratcliffe* Catesby

IV.v.10 *Harfordwest* [Q1] Hertford-west [Q3]

V.i.11 *It is, my lord* [Q1] It is

V.ii.11 *center* [Q1] Centry

V.iii.28 *you* your   54 *sentinels* [F] centinell [Q1]   58 *Catesby* [Q1]
Ratcliffe   59 *Catesby* Rat. [Q1]   68 *Saw'st thou* [Q1] Saw'st   80 *sit*
[Q3] set [Q1]   83 *loving* [Q1] noble [Q3]   90 *the* [Q1] th'   101 *sun-
d'red* [F] sundried [Q1]   105 *thoughts* [Q1] noise   108 s.d. *Manet
Richmond* [F, not in Q1]   113 *The* [Q1] Th'   115 *the* [Q1] thy
[Q3]   118 s.d. *Enter . . . Sixth* [F] Enter the ghost of young Prince
Edward, sonne Harry the sixt, to Ri. [Q1]   126 *deadly holes* [Q1]
holes [Q3]   131 *thy sleep* [Q1] sleepe   132 *sit* [Q3] set [Q1]   139 s.d.
and Vaughan [F] Vaughan [Q1]   140 *Rivers* [Q3] King [Q1]   146
Will [Q3] Wel [Q1]   146 s.d.–151 *Enter . . . sake* [Q3; after line 159 in
Q1]   146 s.d. *Hastings* [Q1] L. Hastings [Q3]   152 *Ghosts* [F] Ghost
[Q1]   153 *lead* [Q1] laid [Q3]   155 *souls bid* [Q1] soule bids   159 s.d.
Lady Anne [Q1] Anne   162 *perturbations* [Q3] preturbations [Q1]
177 *falls* [Q1] fall   177 s.d. *starteth up out of a dream* [Q1] starts out of
his dreame   181 *now* [Q1] not [Q3]   184 *I am I* [Q3] I and I [Q1]
197 *Perjury, perjury* [Q1] Periurie [Q3]   197 *highest* [Q1] high'st
198 *direst* [Q1] dyr'st   200 *to the* [Q1] all to'th'   202 *will* [Q1]
shall [Q3]   203 *Nay* [F] And [Q1]   209 *Zounds, who is* [Q1] Who's
213–15 *King Richard. O Ratcliffe . . . my lord* [Q1, not in F]
223 *see* [Q1] heare [Q3]   223 s.d. *Exeunt Richard and Ratcliffe* [F]
Exeunt [Q1]   223 s.d. *Enter . . . in his tent* [F] Enter the Lordes to
Richmond [Q1]   224 *Lords* [Lo. Q1] Richm.   233 *heart* [F] soule
[Q1]   251 *foil* [Q1] soile [Q3]   256 *sweat* [Q1] sweare [Q3]
271 s.d. *Ratcliffe, and* [Rat. &c Q1] Ratcliffe, and Catesby   276 s.d.
The clock striketh [Q1] Clocke strikes   283 *not* [Q3] nor [Q1]
294 *drawn out all* [Q1] drawne [Q3]   298 *this* [Q1] the [Q3]
302 *boot* [Q3] bootes [Q1]   304 s.d. *He . . . paper* [Q1, not in F]
308 *unto* [Q1] to   310 *Conscience is but* [Q1] For Conscience is
313 *to it* [Q1] too't   314 s.d. *His . . . Army* [Q1, not in F]   320 *ventures* aduentures [Q1]   321 *to you* [Q1] you to [Q3]   323 *distrain*
restraine [Q1]   336 *in* [Q1] on [Q3]   339 *Fight, gentlemen* [Q1]

Right Gentlemen [Q3]   339 *bold* [Q1] boldly [Q3]   342 s.d. *Enter a Messenger* [F, not in Q1]   352 *helms* [Q1] helpes [Q3]   352 s.d. *Exeunt* [Q1, not in F]

V.iv.6 s.d. *Alarums.* [F, not in Q1]

V.v.s.d. *Retreat . . . Lords* [F] then retrait being sounded. Enter Richmond, Darby, bearing the crowne, with other Lords, &c [Q1]   4 *this . . . royalty* [Q1] these . . . Royalties   7 *Wear it, enjoy it* [Q1] Weare it [Q3]   11 *if it please you, we may now* [Q1] (if you please) we may   13 *Stanley* [Der. F, not in Q1]   32 *their* [Q1] thy [Q3]   41 s.d. *Exeunt* [F, not in Q1]

The Sources of *Richard the Third*

Shakespeare found the fullest account of Richard in Raphael Holinshed's *Chronicles* (second edition, 1587). Holinshed reprinted most of Sir Thomas More's *History of King Richard the Third* (written about 1513–14, printed in 1557) and wove in further information from Polydore Vergil's *Anglica Historia* (1534), Edward Hall's *The Union of the Two Noble and Illustre Families of Lancaster and York* (1548), and Richard Grafton's *Chronicles* of 1543 and 1569. Shakespeare added a few points from his own reading of Hall or Grafton, and a few from "The Tragedy of Clarence" in *The Mirror for Magistrates* (1559). The rest he drew from Holinshed or invented for himself.

The historical Richard was not so black as he was painted; it is still an unsolved question whether he committed any of the murders charged against him by his enemies. But Shakespeare was dramatizing the Richard of the Tudor historians, and they had no doubt that Richard was a murderer and a tyrant. More wrote that he "spared no man's death whose life withstood his purpose"; Hall declared that if he had not usurped the throne, he would have been "much praised and beloved, as he is now abhorred and vilipended." By the time Shakespeare wrote, Richard had already been staged as a Senecan villain in *Richardus Tertius,* a Latin play acted at Cambridge, and in *The True Tragedy of Richard the Third,* which Shakespeare quotes in *Hamlet*. More's vivid history, however, furnished the chief stimulus to Shakespeare's imagination.

The character sketch of Richard by More is here quoted in his own words, which Holinshed borrowed with little change. Holinshed followed More's *History* in the main up to the point where it ended, with the flight of Buckingham, and he used Hall and other authorities to continue the story.

SIR THOMAS MORE

from The History of King Richard the Third

Richard Duke of York . . . was with many nobles of the realm at Wakefield slain, leaving three sons, Edward, George, and Richard. . . . Edward, revenging his father's death, deprived King Henry and attained the crown. George Duke of Clarence was a goodly noble prince . . . heinous treason was there laid to his charge, and finally, were he faulty, were he faultless, attainted was he by Parliament and judged to the death, and thereupon hastily drowned in a butt of malmsey; whose death King Edward (albeit he commanded it), when he wist it was done, piteously bewailed and sorrowfully repented.

Richard, the third son, of whom we now entreat, was in wit and courage equal with either of them, in body and prowess far under them both; little of stature, ill-featured of limbs, crookbacked, his left shoulder much higher than his right, hard-favored of visage, and such as is in states called warly [i.e., in great men called warlike], in other men otherwise; he was malicious, wrathful, envious, and, from afore his birth, ever froward. It is for truth reported that the Duchess his mother had so much ado in her travail that she could not be delivered of him uncut, and that he came into the world with the feet forward, as men be borne outward, and (as the fame runneth) also not untoothed; whether men of hatred report above the truth, or else that nature changed her course in his beginning, which in the course of his life many things unnaturally committed. None evil captain was he in the war, as to which his disposition was more meetly

than for peace. Sundry victories had he, and sometimes
overthrows, but never in default, as for his own person,
either of hardiness or politic order; free was he called of
dispense, and somewhat above his power liberal, with
large gifts he got him unsteadfast friendship, for which he
was fain to pill and spoil in other places and got him
steadfast hatred. He was close and secret, a deep dis-
simuler, lowly of countenance, arrogant of heart, out-
wardly companiable [i.e., friendly] where he inwardly
hated, not letting to kiss whom he thought to kill; dis-
piteous and cruel, not for evil will alway, but ofter for
ambition, and either for the surety or increase of his
estate. Friend and foe was much what indifferent, where
his advantage grew; he spared no man's death whose life
withstood his purpose. He slew with his own hands King
Henry the Sixth, being prisoner in the Tower, as men
constantly say, and that without commandment or knowledge of the King, which would undoubtedly, if he had
intended that thing, have appointed that butcherly office to
some other than his own born brother. Some wise men
also ween that his drift, covertly conveyed, lacked not in
helping forth his brother of Clarence to his death; which
he resisted openly, howbeit somewhat (as men deemed)
more faintly than he that were heartily minded to his
wealth. And they that thus deem think that he long time
in King Edward's life forethought to be king in case that
the King his brother (whose life he looked that evil diet
should shorten) should happen to decease (as in deed
he did) while his children were young. And they deem
that for this intent he was glad of his brother's death
the Duke of Clarence, whose life must needs have hin-
dered him so intending, whether the same Duke of
Clarence had kept him true to his nephew the young
King, or enterprised to be king himself. But of all this
point is there no certainty, and whoso divineth upon conjectures may as well shoot too far as too short.

RAPHAEL HOLINSHED

from *Chronicles of England, Scotland, and Ireland*

[At Mortimer's Cross in 1461] the sun (as some write)
appeared to the Earl of March [Edward] like three suns,
and suddenly joined altogether in one. Upon which sight
he took such courage that he, fiercely setting on his enemies, put them to flight; and for this cause men imagined
that he gave the sun in his full brightness for his badge
or cognizance. . . .

[In 1464] it was thought meet by him and those of his
council that a marriage were provided for him in some
convenient place; and therefore was the Earl of Warwick
sent over into France to demand the Lady Bona, daughter
to Lewis Duke of Savoy and sister to the Lady Carlot,
then Queen of France; which Bona was at that time in
the French court.

The Earl of Warwick, coming to the French King, then
lying at Tours, was of him honorably received and right
courteously entertained. His message was so well liked
. . . that the matrimony on that side was clearly assented
to. . . . But here consider the old proverb to be true
which saith that marriage goeth by destiny. For, during
the time that the Earl of Warwick was thus in France
and (according to his instructions) brought the effect of
his commission to pass, the King, being on hunting in
the forest of Wychwood besides Stony Stratford, came
for his recreation to the manor of Grafton, where the
Duchess of Bedford then sojourned, wife to Sir Richard
Woodville Lord Rivers, on whom was then attendant a
daughter of hers called the Lady Elizabeth Grey, widow

of Sir John Grey, knight, slain at the last battle of St. Albans. . . .

This widow, having a suit to the King for such lands as her husband had given her in jointure, so kindled the King's affection towards her that he not only favored her suit, but more her person; for she was a woman of a more formal countenance than of excellent beauty, and yet both of such beauty and favor that with her sober demeanor, sweet looks, and comely smiling (neither too wanton, nor too bashful), besides her pleasant tongue and trim wit, she so allured and made subject unto her the heart of that great prince that, after she had denied him to be his paramour, with so good manner and words so well set as better could not be devised, he finally resolved with himself to marry her. . . .

But yet the Duchess of York his mother letted this match as much as in her lay; and when all would not serve, she caused a precontract to be alleged, made by him with Lady Elizabeth Lucy. But all doubts resolved, all things made clear, and all cavilations avoided, privily in a morning he married the said Lady Elizabeth Grey at Grafton beforesaid, where he first began to fancy her. And in the next year after she was with great solemnity crowned queen at Westminster. Her father also was created Earl Rivers and made high constable of England, her brother Lord Anthony was married to the sole heir of Thomas Lord Scales; Sir Thomas Grey, son to Sir John Grey the Queen's first husband, was created Marquis Dorset. . . .

The Earl of Warwick, being a far-casting prince, perceived somewhat in the Duke of Clarence whereby he judged that he bare no great good will towards the King his brother; and thereupon, feeling his mind by such talk as he of purpose ministered, understood how he was bent, and so won him to his purpose; and for better assurance of his faithful friendship he offered him his eldest daughter in marriage. . . . The Duke of Clarence being come to Calais with the Earl of Warwick, after he had sworn on the sacrament to keep his promise and pact made with the said Earl whole and inviolate, he married the Lady

Isabel, eldest daughter to the Earl, in Our Lady's Church there. . . .

Edward Prince of Wales wedded Anne, second daughter to the Earl of Warwick. . . .

The Earl of Pembroke . . . brought the child [Henry Tudor] with him to London to King Henry the Sixth; whom when the King had a good while beheld, he said to such princes as were with him: "Lo, surely this is he to whom both we and our adversaries, leaving the possession of all things, shall hereafter give room and place." So this holy man showed before the chance that should happen, that this Earl Henry, so ordained by God, should in time to come (as he did indeed) have and enjoy the kingdom and whole rule of this realm of England. . . .

[Henry VI's son Edward was taken prisoner at the battle of Tewkesbury,] whom incontinently George Duke of Clarence, Richard Duke of Gloucester, Thomas Grey Marquis Dorset, and William Lord Hastings, that stood by, suddenly murdered; for the which cruel act, the more part of the doers in their latter days drank of the like cup, by the righteous justice and due punishment of God. . . .

Moreover, here is to be remembered that poor King Henry the Sixth, a little before deprived (as ye have heard) of his realm and imperial crown, was now in the Tower spoiled of his life, by Richard Duke of Gloucester (as the constant fame ran), who (to the intent that his brother King Edward might reign in more surety) murdered the said King Henry with a dagger. . . .

The dead corpse on the Ascension Even was conveyed with bills and glaives pompously (if you will call that a funeral pomp) from the Tower to the church of St. Paul, and there laid on a bier or coffin barefaced; the same in presence of the beholders did bleed; where it rested the space of one whole day. From thence he was carried to the Blackfriars, and bled there likewise; and on the next day after, it was conveyed in a boat, without priest or clerk, torch or taper, singing or saying, unto the monastery of Chertsey, distant from London fifteen miles, and there was it first buried. . . .

Some have reported that the cause of [the death of

Clarence] . . . rose of a foolish prophecy, which was, that after King Edward one should reign whose first letter of his name should be a *G*. Wherewith the King and Queen were sore troubled and began to conceive a grievous grudge against this duke, and could not be in quiet till they had brought him to his end. And as the devil is wont to encumber the minds of men which delight in such devilish fantasies, they said afterward that that prophecy lost not his effect when, after King Edward, Gloucester usurped his kingdom. . . .

But sure it is that, although King Edward were consenting to his death, yet he much did both lament his infortunate chance and repent his sudden execution; insomuch that when any person sued to him for the pardon of malefactors condemned to death, he would accustomably say and openly speak: "Oh infortunate brother, for whose life not one would make suit." . . .

King Edward in his life, albeit that this dissension between his friends somewhat irked him, yet in his good health he somewhat the less regarded it, because he thought whatsoever business should fall between them, himself should alway be able to rule both the parties.

But in his last sickness, when he perceived his natural strength so sore enfeebled that he despaired all recovery, then he, considering the youth of his children, albeit he nothing less mistrusted than that that happened, yet well foreseeing that many harms might grow by their debate, while the youth of his children should lack discretion of themselves and good counsel of their friends, of which either party should counsel for their own commodity, and rather by pleasant advice to win themselves favor than by profitable advertisement to do the children good, he called some of them before him that were at variance, and in especial the Lord Marquis Dorset, the Queen's son by her first husband.

So did he also William the Lord Hastings, a noble man, then Lord Chamberlain, against whom the Queen specially grudged, for the great favor the King bare him; and also for that she thought him secretly familiar with the King in wanton company. Her kindred also bare him sore, as well for that the King had made him captain of Calais, which office the Lord Rivers, brother to the Queen, claimed of the King's former promise, as for divers other great gifts which he received, that they looked for. When these lords, with divers other of both the parties, were come in presence, the King, lifting up himself, and underset with pillows, as it is reported, on this wise said unto them.

"My lords, my dear kinsmen and allies, in what plight I lie you see, and I feel. . . . Wherefore in these last words that ever I look to speak with you, I exhort you and require you all, for the love that you have ever borne to me, for the love that I have ever borne unto you, for the love that Our Lord beareth to us all, from this time forward (all griefs forgotten) each of you love other. Which I verily trust you will, if ye anything earthly regard, either God or your king, affinity or kindred, this realm, your own country, or your own surety." And therewithal the King, no longer enduring to sit up, laid him down on his right side, his face towards them; and none was there present that could refrain from weeping.

But the lords recomforting him with as good words as they could, and answering for the time as they thought to stand with his pleasure, there in his presence, as by their words appeared, each forgave other and joined their hands together, when (as it after appeared by their deeds) their hearts were far asunder. As soon as the King was departed, the noble Prince his son drew toward London, which at the time of his decease kept his household at Ludlow in Wales. . . .

The Duke of Gloucester soon set on fire them that were of themselves easy to kindle, and in specially twain, Edward Duke of Buckingham and William Lord Hastings then Chamberlain, both men of honor and of great power, the one by long succession from his ancestry, the other by his office and the King's favor. These two, not bearing each to other so much love, as hatred both unto the Queen's part, in this point accorded together with the Duke of Gloucester that they would utterly remove from the King's company all his mother's friends, under the name of their enemies.

Upon this concluded the Duke of Gloucester, understanding that the lords which at that time were about the King intended to bring him up to his coronation accompanied with such power of their friends, that it should be hard for him to bring his purpose to pass without the gathering and great assembly of people and in manner of open war, whereof the end (he wist) was doubtful, and in which, the King being on their side, his part should have the face and name of a rebellion; he secretly therefore by divers means caused the Queen to be persuaded and brought in the mind that it neither were need, and also should be jeopardous, the King to come up strong. . . .

The Queen, being in this wise persuaded, such word sent unto her son, and unto her brother, being about the King; and over that the Duke of Gloucester himself and other lords, the chief of his band, wrote unto the King so reverently and to the Queen's friends there so lovingly that they, nothing earthly mistrusting, brought the King up in great haste, not in good speed, with a sober company. Now was the King in his way to London gone from Northampton, when these Dukes of Gloucester and Buckingham came thither, where remained behind the Lord Rivers, the King's uncle, intending on the morrow to follow the King and to be with him at Stony Stratford. . . .

But even by and by in his presence they picked a quarrel to the Lord Richard Grey, the King's other brother by his mother, saying that he, with the Lord Marquis his brother and the Lord Rivers his uncle, had compassed to rule the King and the realm. . . .

Unto which words the King answered: "What my brother Marquis hath done I cannot say, but in good faith I dare well answer for mine uncle Rivers and my brother here, that they be innocent of any such matter." "Yea, my liege" (quoth the Duke of Buckingham), "they have kept their dealing in these matters far from the knowledge of your good Grace." And forthwith they arrested the Lord Richard and Sir Thomas Vaughan, knight, in the King's presence. . . . The Duke of Gloucester . . .

sent the Lord Rivers and the Lord Richard with Sir Thomas Vaughan into the north country into divers places to prison, and afterward all to Pomfret, where they were in conclusion beheaded.

In this wise the Duke of Gloucester took upon himself the order and governance of the young King, whom with much honor and humble reverence he conveyed upward towards the city. But anon the tidings of this matter came hastily to the Queen a little before the midnight following, and that in the sorest wise, that the King her son was taken, her brother, her son, and her other friends arrested, and sent no man wist whither, to be done with God wot what. With which tidings the Queen in great flight and heaviness . . . got herself in all the haste possible with her younger son and her daughters out of the palace of Westminster, in which she then lay, into the Sanctuary, lodging herself and her company there in the Abbot's place. . . .

When the King approached near to the city, Edmund Shaw, goldsmith, then Mayor, with William White and John Matthew, Sheriffs, and all the other aldermen in scarlet, with five hundred horse of the citizens, in violet, received him reverently at Hornsey, and riding from thence accompanied him into the city, which he entered the fourth day of May, the first and last year of his reign. But the Duke of Gloucester bare him in open sight so reverently to the Prince, with all semblance of lowliness, that from the great obloquy in which he was so late before, he was suddenly fallen in so great trust that at the council next assembled he was made the only man chosen and thought most meet to be Protector of the King and his realm, so that (were it destiny or were it folly) the lamb was betaken to the wolf to keep. . . .

[Richard said to the council:] "Wherefore me thinketh it were not worst to send unto the Queen, for the redress of this matter, some honorable trusty man, such as both tendereth the King's weal and the honor of his council, and is also in favor and credence with her. For all which considerations, none seemeth more meetly than our reverend father here present, my Lord Cardinal. . . . And

if she be percase so obstinate, and so precisely set upon
her own will, that neither his wise and faithful advertisement cannot move her, nor any man's reason content her,
then shall we, by mine advice, by the King's authority
fetch him out of that prison and bring him to his noble
presence, in whose continual company he shall be so
well cherished and so honorably entreated that all the
world shall to our honor and her reproach perceive that
it was only malice, frowardness, or folly that caused her
to keep him there." . . .

[The Archbishop said:] "God forbid that any man
should for anything earthly enterprise to break the im-
munity and liberty of the sacred sanctuary, that hath
been the safeguard of so many a good man's life. And
I trust (quoth he) with God's grace, we shall not need
it. But for any manner need I would not we should do
it." . . .

[Buckingham argued that the Prince] "neither is, nor
can be, a sanctuary man . . . he must ask it himself that
must have it. . . . And verily, I have often heard of sanctuary men, but I never heard erst of sanctuary children." . . .

When the Lord Cardinal, and these other lords with
him, had received this young duke, they brought him
into the Star Chamber, where the Protector took him in
his arms and kissed him, with these words: "Now welcome, my lord, even with all my very heart." And he
said in that of likelihood as he thought. Thereupon forthwith they brought him unto the King his brother into the
Bishop's palace at Paul's, and from thence through the
city honorably into the Tower, out of the which after
that day they never came abroad. When the Protector
had both the children in his hands, he opened himself
more boldly, both to certain other men, and also chiefly
to the Duke of Buckingham. . . .

Then it was agreed that the Protector should have the
Duke's aid to make him king, and that the Protector's
only lawful son should marry the Duke's daughter, and
that the Protector should grant him the quiet possession
of the earldom of Hereford, which he claimed as his in-

heritance, and could never obtain it in King Edward's time.

Besides these requests of the Duke, the Protector of his own mind promised him a great quantity of the King's treasure and of his household stuff. And when they were thus at a point between themselves, they went about to prepare for the coronation of the young King, as they would have it seem. And that they might turn both the eyes and minds of men from perceiving of their drifts otherwhere, the lords being sent for from all parts of the realm came thick to that solemnity. But the Protector and the Duke, after that they had sent the Lord Cardinal, the Archbishop of York then Lord Chancellor, the Bishop of Ely, the Lord Stanley, and the Lord Hastings then Lord Chamberlain, with many other noble men, to commune and devise about the coronation in one place, as fast were they in another place, contriving the contrary, and to make the Protector king.

To which council albeit there were adhibited very few, and they were secret, yet began there, here and there abouts, some manner of muttering among the people, as though all should not long be well, though they neither wist what they feared, nor wherefore; were it that, before such great things, men's hearts of a secret instinct of nature misgive them, as the sea without wind swelleth of himself sometime before a tempest. . . .

The Lord Stanley, that was after Earl of Derby, wisely mistrusted it, and said unto the Lord Hastings that he much misliked these two several councils. "For while we" (quoth he) "talk of one matter in the tone place, little wot we whereof they talk in the tother place."

"My lord" (quoth the Lord Hastings), "on my life never doubt you; for while one man is there, which is never thence, never can there be thing once moved that should sound amiss toward me, but it should be in mine ears ere it were well out of their mouths." This meant he by Catesby, which was of his near secret counsel. . . . In whom if the Lord Hastings had not put so special trust, the Lord Stanley and he had departed with divers other lords, and broken all the dance, for many ill signs

that he saw, which he now construes all to the best. So
surely thought he that there could be none harm toward
him in that council intended where Catesby was. And of
truth the Protector and the Duke of Buckingham made
very good semblance unto the Lord Hastings and kept
him much in company. And undoubtedly the Protector
loved him well and loath was to have lost him, saving for
fear lest his life should have quailed their purpose.

For which cause he moved Catesby to prove with some
words cast out afar off whether he could think it possible to win the Lord Hastings unto their part. But Catesby
. . . reported unto them that he found him so fast, and
heard him speak so terrible words, that he durst no further break. . . .

Whereupon soon after . . . many lords assembled in
the Tower and there sat in council, devising the honorable solemnity of the King's coronation. . . . These lords
so sitting together communing of this matter, the Protector came in amongst them, first about nine of the clock,
saluting them courteously and excusing himself that he
had been from them so long, saying merrily that he had
been a sleeper that day.

After a little talking with them, he said unto the Bishop
of Ely: "My lord, you have very good strawberries at
your garden in Holborn; I require you let us have a mess
of them." "Gladly, my lord" (quoth he), "would God I
had some better thing as ready to your pleasure as that!"
And therewithal in all the haste he sent his servant for a
mess of strawberries. The Protector set the lords fast in
communing and thereupon, praying them to spare him
for a little while, departed thence. And soon after one
hour, between ten and eleven he returned into the chamber amongst them all, changed with a wonderful sour
angry countenance, knitting the brows, frowning and fret-
ting, and gnawing on his lips, and so sat him down in his
place.

All the lords were much dismayed and sore marveled
at this manner of sudden change, and what thing should
him ail. Then, when he had sitten still a while, thus he
began: "What were they worthy to have that compass

and imagine the destruction of me, being so near of blood unto the King, and Protector of his royal person and his realm?". . . Then the Lord Chamberlain (as he that for the love between them thought he might be boldest with him) answered and said that they were worthy to be punished as heinous traitors, whatsoever they were. And all the other affirmed the same. "That is" (quoth he) "yonder sorceress my brother's wife, and other with her" (meaning the Queen). . . .

Then said the Protector: "Ye shall all see in what wise that sorceress and that other witch of her counsel, Shore's wife, with their affinity, have by their sorcery and witchcraft wasted my body." And therewith he plucked up his doublet sleeve to his elbow upon his left arm, where he showed a wearish withered arm, and small; as it was never other.

Hereupon every man's mind sore misgave them, well perceiving that this matter was but a quarrel. . . . Natheless, the Lord Chamberlain (which from the death of King Edward kept Shore's wife . . .) answered and said: "Certainly, my lord, if they have so heinously done, they be worthy heinous punishment."

"What!" (quoth the Protector), "thou servest me, I ween, with ifs and with ands; I tell thee they have so done, and that I will make good on thy body, traitor." . . . And anon the Protector said to the Lord Hastings: "I arrest thee, traitor." "What! me, my lord?" (quoth he). "Yea, thee, traitor," quoth the Protector. . . . whom the Protector bade speed and shrive him apace, "for by St. Paul" (quoth he), "I will not to dinner till I see thy head off." It booted him not to ask why, but heavily took a priest at adventure and made a short shrift. . . .

A marvelous case is it to hear either the warnings of that he should have voided, or the tokens of that he could not void. For the self night next before his death the Lord Stanley sent a trusty messenger unto him at midnight in all the haste, requiring him to rise and ride away with him, for he was disposed utterly no longer to bide, he had so fearful a dream; in which him thought that a boar with his tusks so rased them both by the heads that the blood ran about both their shoulders. And forsomuch as the Protector gave the boar for his cognizance, this dream made so fearful an impression in his heart that he was thoroughly determined no longer to tarry, but had his horse ready, if the Lord Hastings would go with him, to ride yet so far the same night that they should be out of danger ere day.

"Ha, good Lord!" (quoth the Lord Hastings to this messenger), "leaneth my lord thy master so much to such trifles and hath such faith in dreams . . . ? Tell him it is plain witchcraft to believe in such dreams, which if they were tokens of things to come, why thinketh he not that we might be as likely to make them true by our going, if we were caught and brought back, as friends fail fliers? for then had the boar a cause likely to rase us with his tusks. . . . And therefore go to thy master (man) and commend me to him, and pray him be merry and have no fear; for I ensure him I am as sure of the man that he wotteth of as I am of mine own hand." . . .

Certain is it also that in riding towards the Tower, the same morning in which he was beheaded, his horse twice or thrice stumbled with him, almost to the falling. . . . The same morning, ere he was up, came a knight unto him, as it were of courtesy, to accompany him to the council; but of truth sent by the Protector to haste him thitherwards. . . .

This knight (I say), when it happened the Lord Chamberlain by the way to stay his horse and commune a while with a priest whom he met in the Tower street, brake his tale and said merrily to him: "What, my lord, I pray you come on; whereto talk you so long with that priest? You have no need of a priest yet"; and therewith he laughed upon him, as though he would say, "Ye shall have soon." . . .

Upon the very Tower wharf, so near the place where his head was off soon after, there met he with one Hastings, a pursuivant of his own name. . . . And therefore he said: "Ha, Hastings, art thou remembered when I met thee here once with an heavy heart?" "Yea, my lord" (quoth he), "that remember I well, and thanked be

God they got no good nor you no harm thereby." "Thou wouldst say so" (quoth he), "if thou knewest as much as I know, which few know else as yet, and moe shall shortly." That meant he by the lords of the Queen's kindred that were taken before and should that day be beheaded at Pomfret; which he well wist, but nothing ware that the ax hung over his own head. "In faith, man" (quoth he), "I was never so sorry, nor never stood in so great dread in my life, as I did when thou and I met here. And lo how the world is turned: now stand mine enemies in the danger . . . and I never in my life so merry, nor never in so great surety." . . .

Now flew the fame of this lord's death swiftly through the city, and so forth further about like a wind in every man's ear. But the Protector, immediately after dinner, intending to set some color upon the matter, sent in all the haste for many substantial men out of the city into the Tower.

Now at their coming, himself with the Duke of Buckingham stood harnessed in old ill-faring briganders, such as no man should ween that they would vouchsafe to have put upon their backs except that some sudden necessity had constrained them. And then the Protector showed them that the Lord Chamberlain, and other of his conspiracy, had contrived to have suddenly destroyed him and the Duke, there the same day in the council. And what they intended further was as yet not well known. Of which their treason he never had knowledge before ten of the clock the same forenoon, which sudden fear drove them to put on for their defense such harness as came next to hand. And so had God holpen them that the mischief turned upon them that would have done it. And this he required them to report.

Every man answered him fair, as though no man mistrusted the matter, which of truth no man believed. Yet for the further appeasing of the people's minds he sent immediately after dinner in all the haste one herald of arms with a proclamation to be made through the city in the King's name, containing that the Lord Hastings, with divers other of his traitorous purpose, had before conspired the same day to have slain the Lord Protector and the Duke of Buckingham, sitting in the council. . . .

Now was this proclamation made within two hours after that he was beheaded, and it was so curiously indited, and so fair written in parchment, in so well a set hand, and therewith of itself so long a process, that every child might well perceive that it was prepared before. . . .

Now was it so devised by the Protector and his council that the self day in which the Lord Chamberlain was beheaded in the Tower of London, and about the selfsame hour, was there (not without his assent) beheaded at Pomfret the fore-remembered lords and knights that were taken from the King at Northampton and Stony Stratford. Which thing was done in the presence and by the order of Sir Richard Ratcliffe, knight, whose service the Protector specially used in that counsel and in the execution of such lawless enterprises, as a man that had been long secret with him, having experience of the world and a shrewd wit, short and rude in speech, rough and boisterous of behavior, bold in mischief, as far from pity as from all fear of God.

This knight, bringing them out of the prison to the scaffold and showing to the people about that they were traitors, . . . caused them hastily, without judgment, process, or manner of order, to be beheaded, and without other earthly guilt but only that they were good men, too true to the King, and too nigh to the Queen. . . .

Now then . . . it was by the Protector and his council concluded that this Dr. Shaw should in a sermon at Paul's Cross signify to the people that neither King Edward himself, nor the Duke of Clarence, were lawfully begotten, nor were not the very children of the Duke of York. . . . Then showed he that his very right heir of his body lawfully begotten was only the Lord Protector. For he declared then that King Edward was never lawfully married unto the Queen, but was before God husband unto Dame Elizabeth Lucy, and so his children bastards. . . . But the Lord Protector, he said, the very noble Prince, the special pattern of knightly prowess, as well in all princely behavior as in the lineaments and favor of his visage represented the very face of the noble Duke his father. "This is," quoth he, "the father's own figure, this is his own countenance, the very print of his visage, the sure undoubted image, the plain express likeness of that noble Duke." . . .

Then, on the Tuesday following this sermon, there came to the Guildhall in London the Duke of Buckingham, [who urged the citizens] "to make humble petition to the most puissant Prince, the Lord Protector, that it may like his Grace (at our humble request) to take upon him the guiding and governance of this realm. . . ."

When the Duke had said, and looked that the people, whom he hoped that the Mayor had framed before, should, after this proposition made, have cried, "King Richard, King Richard!" all was hushed and mute, and not one word answered thereunto. Wherewith the Duke was marvelously abashed, and, taking the Mayor nearer to him, with other that were about him privy to that matter, said unto them softly, "What meaneth this, that the people be so still?" "Sir" (quoth the Mayor), "percase they perceive you not well" . . . and said that the people had not been accustomed there to be spoken unto, but by the Recorder, which is the mouth of the city, and haply to him they will answer. . . . But the Recorder so tempered his tale that he showed everything as the Duke's words, and no part his own. . . . At the last in the nether end of the hall an ambushment of the Duke's servants . . . began suddenly at men's backs to cry out, as loud as their throats would give, "King Richard, King Richard!" and threw up their caps in token of joy. . . . Now when the Duke and the Mayor saw this manner, they wisely turned it to their purpose and said it was a goodly cry and a joyful, to hear every man with one voice, no man saying nay. . . .

Then, on the morrow after, the Mayor with all the aldermen and chief commoners of the city, in their best manner appareled, assembling themselves together, resorted unto Baynard's Castle, where the Protector lay. To which place repaired also (according to their appointment) the Duke of Buckingham, and divers noble men with him, beside many knights and other gentlemen. And thereupon the Duke sent word unto the Lord Protector of the being there of a great and honorable company to move a great matter unto his Grace. Whereupon the Protector made difficulty to come out unto them, but if he first knew some part of their errand, as though he doubted and partly mistrusted the coming of such a number unto him so suddenly, without any warning or knowledge whether they came for good or harm.

Then the Duke . . . sent unto him by the messenger such loving message again . . . that at the last he came forth of his chamber, and yet not down unto them, but stood above in a gallery over them [Grafton and Hall add: with a bishop on every hand of him], where they might see him and speak to him, as though he would not yet come too near them till he wist what they meant. And thereupon the Duke of Buckingham first made humble petition unto him on the behalf of them all that his Grace would pardon them. . . .

When the Duke had this leave and pardon to speak, then waxed he bold to show him their intent . . . and finally to beseech his Grace that it would like him, of his accustomed goodness and zeal unto the realm, now with his eye of pity to behold the long-continued distress and decay of the same. . . . All which he might well do by taking upon him the crown and governance of this realm, according to his right and title lawfully descended unto him. . . .

When the Protector had heard the proposition, he looked very strangely thereat, and answered: that, all were it that he partly knew the things by them alleged to be true, yet such entire love he bare unto King Edward and his children . . . that he could not find it in his heart in this point to incline to their desire. For in all other nations, where the truth were not well known, it should peradventure be thought that it were his own ambitious mind and device to depose the Prince and take himself the crown. . . .

Upon this answer given, the Duke . . . showed aloud unto the Protector . . . that the realm was appointed King

Edward's line should not any longer reign upon them. . . .
These words much moved the Protector. . . .

But when he saw there was none other way, but that
either he must take it, or else he and his both go from it,
he said unto the lords and commons: "Sith we perceive
well that all the realm is so set . . . we be content and
agree favorably to incline to your petition and request,
and (according to the same) here we take upon us the
royal estate . . ."

With this there was a great shout, crying, "King
Richard, King Richard!" . . .

King Richard, after his coronation, . . . sent one John
Greene (whom he specially trusted) unto Sir Robert
Brakenbury, Constable of the Tower, with a letter, and
credence also, that the same Sir Robert should in any
wise put the two children to death. . . . Who plainly answered that he would never put them to death, to die
therefor. With which answer John Greene, returning, recounted the same to King Richard at Warwick yet in his
way. Wherewith he took such displeasure and thought
that the same night he said unto a secret page of his:
"Ah! whom shall a man trust? Those that I have brought
up myself, those that I had weened would most surely
serve me, even those fail me and at my commandment
will do nothing for me." "Sir" (quoth his page), "there
lieth one on your pallet without that I dare well say, to
do your Grace pleasure the thing were right hard that
he would refuse." Meaning this by Sir James Tirrell. . . .

King Richard arose. . . . And calling up Sir James,
brake to him secretly his mind in this mischievous matter.
In which he found him nothing strange. Wherefore on
the morrow he sent him to Brakenbury with a letter, by
which he was commanded to deliver Sir James all the
keys of the Tower for one night, to the end he might
there accomplish the King's pleasure in such things as he
had given him commandment. After which letter delivered, and the keys received, Sir James appointed the
night next ensuing to destroy them, devising before and
preparing the means. . . .

For Sir James Tirrell devised that they should be mur-

dered in their beds. To the execution whereof he appointed Miles Forrest, one of the four that kept them,
a fellow fleshed in murder beforetime. To him he joined
one John Dighton, his own horsekeeper, a big, broad,
square, and strong knave.

Then all the other being removed from them, this
Miles Forrest and John Dighton about midnight (the
seely children lying in their beds) came into the chamber
and, suddenly lapping them up among the clothes, so
to-bewrapped them and entangled them, keeping down
by force the featherbed and pillows hard unto their
mouths, that within a while, smothered and stifled, their
breath failing, they gave up to God their innocent souls
into the joys of heaven, leaving to the tormentors their
bodies dead in the bed. Which after that the wretches
perceived, first by the struggling with the pains of death,
and after, long lying still, to be thoroughly dead, they laid
their bodies naked out upon the bed and fetched Sir
James to see them; which, upon the sight of them,
caused those murderers to bury them at the stair foot,
meetly deep in the ground, under a great heap of stones.

Then rode Sir James in great haste to King Richard
and showed him all the manner of the murder; who gave
him great thanks . . . they say that a priest of Sir Robert
Brakenbury's took up the bodies again and secretly in
terred them. . . .

Some have I heard say that the Duke [of Buckingham],
a little before his coronation, among other things required
of the Protector the Duke of Hereford's lands, to the
which he pretended himself just inheritor. And forsomuch as the title which he claimed by inheritance was
somewhat interlaced with the title to the crown by the
line of King Henry before deprived, the Protector conceived such indignation that he rejected the Duke's request with many spiteful and minatory words. Which so
wounded his heart with hatred and mistrust that he never
after could endure to look aright on King Richard, but
ever feared his own life. . . .

The Duke . . . prepared open war against him . . .
Sir Edward Courtney and Peter his brother, Bishop of

Exeter, raised another army in Devonshire and Cornwall. In Kent Richard Gilford and other gentlemen collected a great company of soldiers and openly began war. . . .

The Duke of Buckingham, accompanied with a great power of wild Welshmen, . . . [was separated from them by a flood,] was of necessity compelled to fly . . . and he fell infortunately into the hands of the foaming boar, that tore him in pieces with his tusks. . . .

But when he had confessed the whole fact and conspiracy, upon All Souls' Day, without arraignment or judgment, he was at Salisbury, in the open market place, on a new scaffold beheaded and put to death. . . .

Henry Earl of Richmond prepared an army of five thousand manly Bretons and forty well-furnished ships . . . the Earl approached to the south part of the realm of England, even at the mouth of the haven of Poole in the county of Dorset, where he might plainly perceive all the sea banks and shores garnished and furnished with men of war and soldiers, appointed and deputed there to defend his arrival and landing. . . .

The Earl of Richmond, suspecting their flattering request to be but a fraud (as it was indeed) . . . [returned to Brittany]. . . .

King Richard [at Exeter] . . . went about the city and viewed the seat of the same, and at length he came to the castle; and when he understood that it was called Rugemont, suddenly he fell into a dump and (as one astonied) said: "Well, I see my days be not long." He spake this of a prophecy told him, that when he came once to Richmond he should not long live after; which fell out in the end to be true, not in respect of this castle, but in respect of Henry Earl of Richmond. . . .

[Richard] revolved in his wavering mind how great a fountain of mischief toward him should spring if the Earl of Richmond should be advanced to the marriage of his niece . . . he himself would rather take to wife his cousin and niece the Lady Elizabeth. . . . Wherefore he sent to the Queen (being in sanctuary) divers and often messengers, which first should excuse and purge him of all things before against her attempted or procured, and after should so largely promise promotions innumerable, and benefits, not only to her, but also to her son Lord Thomas, Marquis Dorset, that they should bring her (if it were possible) into some wanhope, or (as men say) into a fool's paradise.

The messengers, being men both of wit and gravity, so persuaded the Queen with great and pregnant reasons, and what with fair and large promises, that she began somewhat to relent, and to give to them no deaf ear; insomuch that she faithfully promised to submit and yield herself fully and frankly to the King's will and pleasure. . . .

After this he procured a common rumor (but he would not have the author known) to be published and spread abroad among the common people, that the Queen [Anne] was dead; to the intent that she, taking some conceit of this strange fame, should fall into some sudden sickness or grievous malady; and to prove, if afterwards she should fortune by that or any other ways to lose her life, whether the people would impute her death to the thought or sickness, or thereof would lay the blame to him. . . .

But howsoever that it fortuned, either by inward thought and pensiveness of heart, or by infection of poison (which is affirmed to be most likely), within few days after, the Queen departed out of this transitory life. . . .

Amongst the noble men whom he most mistrusted, these were the principal: . . . the Lord Stanley, because he was joined in matrimony with the Lady Margaret, mother to the Earl of Richmond. . . . For when the said Lord Stanley would have departed into his country to visit his family and to recreate and refresh his spirits (as he openly said, but the truth was, to the intent to be in a perfect readiness to receive the Earl of Richmond at his first arrival in England), the King in no wise would suffer him to depart before he had left as an hostage in the court George Stanley, Lord Strange, his first-begotten son and heir. . . .

[When Richmond invaded England,] the whole army

came before the town of Tamworth; and . . . he privily
departed again from his host to the town of Atherstone,
where the Lord Stanley and Sir William his brother with
their bands were abiding. There the Earl came first to
his father-in-law, in a little close, where he saluted him
and Sir William his brother; and after divers and friendly
embracings, each rejoiced of the state of other and suddenly were surprised with great joy, comfort, and hope
of fortunate success in all their affairs and doings. Afterward they consulted together how to give battle to King
Richard, if he would abide, whom they knew not to be
far off with an huge host. . . .

King Richard, which was appointed now to finish his
last labor by the very divine justice and providence of
God (which called him to condign punishment for his
mischievous deserts), marched to a place meet for two
battles to encounter, by a village called Bosworth, not far
from Leicester; and there he pitched his field on a hill
called Anne Beame, refreshed his soldiers, and took
his rest.

The fame went that he had the same night a dreadful
and terrible dream; for it seemed to him, being asleep,
that he did see divers images like terrible devils, which
pulled and haled him, not suffering him to take any quiet
or rest. The which strange vision not so suddenly struck
his heart with a sudden fear, but it stuffed his head and
troubled his mind with many busy and dreadful imaginations. For incontinent after, his heart being almost
damped, he prognosticated before the doubtful chance
of the battle to come; not using the alacrity and mirth of
mind and countenance as he was accustomed to do before he came toward the battle. And lest that it might
be suspected that he was abashed for fear of his enemies,
and for that cause looked so piteously, he recited and
declared to his familiar friends in the morning his wonderful vision and fearful dream. . . .

[Richmond's army] exceeded not five thousand men,
beside the power of the Stanleys, whereof three thousand
were in the field under the standard of Sir William Stanley. The King's number was double so much and more.

When both these armies were thus ordered, and all men ready to set forward, King Richard called his chieftains together and to them said as followeth.

The oration of King Richard the Third to the chieftains of his army. . . .

"Ye see . . . how a company of traitors, thieves, outlaws, and runagates of our own nation be aiders and partakers of his feat and enterprise, ready at hand to overcome and oppress us. You see also what a number of beggarly Bretons and fainthearted Frenchmen be with him arrived to destroy us, our wives and children. . . .

"And to begin with the Earl of Richmond, captain of this rebellion, he is a Welsh milksop, a man of small courage and of less experience in martial acts and feats of war, brought up by my mother's means and mine, like a captive in a close cage, in the court of Francis, Duke of Brittany. . . . Now, St. George to borrow, let us set forward. . . ."

The oration of King Henry the Seventh to his army:

"If ever God gave victory to men fighting in a just quarrel . . . I doubt not but God will rather aid us (yea, and fight for us) than see us vanquished and overthrown by such as neither fear him nor his laws, nor yet regard justice or honesty. . . . For what can be a more honest, goodly, or godly quarrel than to fight against a captain, being an homicide and murderer of his own blood or progeny, an extreme destroyer of his nobility? . . .

"Therefore labor for your gain and sweat for your right. . . . And this one thing I assure you, that in so just and good a cause, and so notable a quarrel, you shall find me this day rather a dead carrion upon the cold ground than a free prisoner on a carpet in a lady's chamber. . . . And therefore in the name of God and St. George, let every man courageously advance forth his standard." . . .

When King Richard saw the Earl's company was passed the marsh, he did command with all haste to set upon them. . . . Now being inflamed with ire and vexed with outrageous malice, he put his spurs to his horse and rode out of the side of the range of his battle, leaving the vanguard fighting, and like a hungry lion ran with spear in rest toward him. The Earl of Richmond . . . gladly proffered to encounter with him body to body and man to man. . . . King Richard's men were driven back and fled, and he himself, manfully fighting in the middle of his enemies, was slain, and (as he worthily had deserved) came to a bloody death, as he had led a bloody life. . . .

In this battle . . . of the nobility were slain John, Duke of Norfolk, which was warned by divers to refrain from the field, insomuch that the night before he should set forward toward the King, one wrote this rhyme upon his gate:

> Jack of Norfolk, be not too bold,
> For Dickon thy master is bought and sold. . . .

King Richard (as the fame went) might have escaped and gotten safeguard by fleeing. For . . . when the loss of the battle was imminent and apparent, they brought to him a swift and a light horse, to convey him away. He, which was not ignorant of the grudge and ill will that the common people bare toward him, casting away all hope of fortunate success and happy chance to come, answered (as men say) that on that day he would make an end of all battles, or else there finish his life. . . .

When the Earl had thus obtained victory, and slain his mortal enemy, he kneeled down and rendered to almighty God his hearty thanks . . . he not only praised and lauded his valiant soldiers, but also gave unto them his hearty thanks. . . . Then the people rejoiced, and clapped their hands, crying up to heaven, "King Henry, King Henry!"

When the Lord Stanley saw the good will and gladness of the people, he took the crown of King Richard, which was found amongst the spoil in the field, and set it on the Earl's head. . . .

Anon after, he assembled together the sage councilors of the realm, in which council, like a prince of just faith and true of promise, to avoid all civil discord, he appointed a day to join in marriage with the Lady Elizabeth, heir of the house of York, with his noble person, heir to the line of Lancaster. . . . By reason of which marriage, peace was thought to descend out of heaven into England. . . .

Commentaries

CHARLES LAMB

Letter to Robert Lloyd

I am possessed with an admiration of the genuine Richard, his genius, and his mounting spirit, which no consideration of his cruelties can depress. Shakspeare has not made Richard so black a Monster as is supposed. Wherever he is monstrous, it was to conform to vulgar opinion. But he is generally a Man. Read his most exquisite address to the Widowed Queen to court her daughter for him—the topics of maternal feeling, of a deep knowledge of the heart, are such as no monster could have supplied. Richard must have *felt* before he could feign so well; tho' ambition choked the good seed. I think it the most finished piece of Eloquence in the world; of *persuasive* oratory far above Demosthenes, Burke, or any man, far exceeding the courtship of Lady Anne. Her relenting is barely natural, after all; the more perhaps S[hakespeare]'s merit to make *impossible* appear *probable*, but the *Queen's consent* (taking in all the circumstances and topics, *private and public* . . .) is probable. . . . This observation applies to many other parts. All the inconsistency is, that Shakspeare's better genius was forced to struggle against the prejudices which made a monster of Richard. He set out to paint a *monster*, but his human sympathies produced a *man*. [1801]

From *Charles Lamb and the Lloyds*, ed. E. V. Lucas. London: Smith, Elder, & Company, 1898.

CHARLES LAMB

from Cooke's "Richard the Third"

We are ready to acknowledge that this actor presents
us with a very original and very forcible portrait (if
not of the *man Richard,* whom Shakspeare drew, yet)
of the *monster Richard,* as he exists in the *popular idea,*
in *his own exaggerated* and *witty self-abuse,* in the over-
strained representations of the parties who were *sufferers*
by his *ambition;* and, above all, in the impertinent and
wretched *scenes,* so absurdly foisted in by some who have
thought themselves capable of adding to what *Shakspeare*
wrote.

But of Mr. Cooke's *Richard:*

1st, *His predominant and masterly simulation.*

He has a tongue can wheedle with the DEVIL.

It has been the policy of that ancient and gray simulator, in
all ages, to hide his *horns* and *claws.* The *Richard* of Mr.
Cooke perpetually obtrudes *his.* We see the effect of his
deceit uniformly *successful,* but we do not comprehend
how it *succeeds.* We can put ourselves, by a very common fiction, into the place of the individuals upon whom
it acts, and say, that, in the like case, we should not have
been alike credulous. The hypocrisy is too glaring and
visible. It resembles more the shallow cunning of a mind
which is its own dupe than the profound and practiced
art of so powerful an intellect as *Richard's.* It is too ob-
streperous and loud, breaking out into *triumphs* and
plaudits at its own success, like an unexercised *novitiate*

From *The Works of Charles Lamb,* ed. William MacDonald. London:
J. M. Dent, 1903, Vol. III.

to *tricks.* It has none of the silent confidence and steady self-command of the *experienced politician;* it possesses none of that *fine address* which was necessary to have betrayed the heart of *Lady Anne,* or even to have imposed upon the duller wits of the Lord *Mayor* and *Citizens.*

2ndly, *His habitual jocularity,* the effect of buoyant spirits and an elastic mind, rejoicing in its own powers and in the success of its machinations. This quality of unstrained mirth accompanies *Richard* and is a prime feature in his character. It never leaves him; in plots, in stratagems, and in the midst of his bloody devices, it is perpetually driving him upon wit and jests and personal satire, fanciful allusions, and quaint felicities of phrase. It is one of the chief artifices by which the consummate master of dramatic effect has contrived to soften the horrors of the scene, and to make us contemplate a bloody and vicious character with delight. Nowhere, in any of his plays, is to be found so much of sprightly colloquial dialogue, and soliloquies of genuine humor, as in *Richard.* This character of unlabored mirth Mr. Cooke seems entirely to pass over, and substitutes in its stead the coarse, taunting humor and clumsy merriment of a low-minded assassin.

3dly, *His personal deformity.*—When the *Richard* of Mr. Cooke makes allusions to his own *form,* they seem accompanied with *unmixed distaste* and *pain,* like some obtrusive and *haunting* idea— But surely the *Richard* of Shakspeare mingles in these allusions a perpetual reference to his own powers and capacities, by which he is enabled to surmount these petty objections; and the joy of a defect *conquered,* or *turned* into an advantage, is one cause of these very allusions, and of the satisfaction with which his mind recurs to them. These allusions themselves are made in an ironical and good-humored spirit of exaggeration—the most bitter of them are to be found in his self-congratulating soliloquy spoken in the very moment and crisis of joyful exultation on the success of his unheard-of courtship.

[1802]

CHARLES LAMB

from *On the Tragedies of Shakespeare, Considered with Reference to Their Fitness for Stage Representation*

Not one of the spectators who have witnessed Mr. C[ooke]'s exertions in that part, but has come away with a proper conviction that Richard is a very wicked man and kills little children in their beds, with something like the pleasure which the giants and ogres in children's books are represented to have taken in that practice; moreover, that he is very close and shrewd and devilish cunning, for you could see that by his eye.

But is in fact this the impression we have in reading the Richard of Shakspeare? Do we feel anything like disgust, as we do at that butcherlike representation of him that passes for him on the stage? A horror at his crimes blends with the effect that we feel, but how is it qualified, how is it carried off, by the rich intellect which he displays, his resources, his wit, his buoyant spirits, his vast knowledge and insight into characters, the poetry of his part—not an atom of all which is made perceivable in Mr. C[ooke]'s way of acting it. Nothing but his crimes, his actions, is visible; they are prominent and staring. The murderer stands out, but where is the lofty genius, the man of vast capacity—the profound, the witty, accomplished Richard?   [1811]

From *The Works of Charles Lamb,* ed. William MacDonald. London: J. M. Dent, 1903, Vol. III.

LILY B. CAMPBELL

The Tragical Doings of King Richard III

The play of *Richard III,* antedating in its composition the historical dramas that we have been studying, is of special interest for two reasons: first, it shows where tragedy and history meet; and second, it reveals an author writing without a clear distinction between these genres in mind. The play can with justification be classed as either tragedy or history, and Shakespeare's first editors did not resolve the dilemma. It was first published in quarto in 1597 with the title:

> The Tragedy of King Richard the Third. Containing, his treacherous plots against his brother Clarence: the pittie-full murther of his innocent nephews: his tyrannicall usurpation; with the whole course of his detested life, and most deserved death.

The five subsequent quartos which preceded the folio gathering of the plays bore the same title. The editors of the First Folio put it with the "Histories," though in this unique instance they departed from custom by retaining the term *"tragedy"* when printing the head-title:

> The Tragedy of Richard the Third: with the landing of Earle Richmond, and the battell at Bosworth Field.

From *Shakespeare's "Histories": Mirrors of Elizabethan Policy* by Lily B. Campbell. San Marino, California: The Huntington Library, 1947. Copyright 1947 by the Huntington Library. Reprinted by permission of the Huntington Library. The footnotes have been abridged.

In order to understand this play, then, it is necessary to distinguish the elements of tragedy from those of the history play with which they are combined, and to do so we must again recall the fundamental distinctions between the two genres. An earlier chapter pointed out that the plays listed by Shakespeare's editors as histories are derived from the same chronicles that furnished material for *Lear* and *Macbeth*. Furthermore, Shakespearean tragedy, like most Elizabethan tragedy, deals with those of high estate and is therein not differentiated from history, for it remained true that, as Raleigh said, "the markes, set on private men, are with their bodies cast into the earth; and their fortunes, written only in the memories of those that lived with them." In his histories and his tragedies alike Shakespeare patterned a moral universe in which the wages of sin is death; in both genres he acted as a register of God's judgments. Yet Macbeth kills his king and usurps a throne, and his tale is classified as a tragedy by Shakespeare's editors: Bolingbroke usurps a throne, his king is killed, and the story is classed as a history. We think of Macbeth as a murderer; of Henry IV as a rebel who usurped a throne. Neither the source material, the characters, nor the divine vengeance which the plays record can, therefore, be held to account for the difference between tragedy and history. For that difference, as I have earlier indicated, we must look to the old division of morals into private and public, a division most clearly explained among the poets by Spenser in his letter to Raleigh, for Spenser proposed to portray in the first twelve books of *The Faerie Queene* the twelve private moral virtues in Arthur before he became king and "to frame the other part of polliticke vertues in his person, after that hee came to be king." He also proposed to present Queen Elizabeth both as the Faerie Queene and as Belphoebe, "considering she beareth two persons, the one of a most royall Queene or Empresse, the other of a most vertuous and beautifull Lady." This was the distinction laid down by philosophers and observed by poets, a distinction between private and political virtue, which marked the difference between the realms of ethics and of politics. Tragedy deals with an ethical world; history with a political world. In tragedy God avenges private sins; in history the King of kings avenges public sins, those of king and subject alike.

In classifying Shakespeare's *Richard III,* then, we need to consider the over-all impression. The killing of the little princes in the Tower, rather than the illegal seizing of the throne, haunts the playgoer. Clarence's dream of divine vengeance, rather than the right of the House of York to rule, fills the mind and stirs the emotions. We accept Richard's labeling of himself as a villain, and when Richmond describes him as "a bloody tyrant and a homicide," we think more of the shed blood than of tyranny. These are impressions left by a tragedy rather than a history play. We need to ask why and wherefore.

One answer to these questions is to be found in Richard's own words when, waking from his last night of dreams, in which the ghosts of his murdered victims have passed before him, he cries out:

> Perjury, perjury, in the high'st degree:
> Murder, stern murder, in the dir'st degree;
> All several sins, all us'd in each degree,
> Throng to the bar, crying all, Guilty! Guilty!

Now perjury and murder are sins which brand Richard or any man a villain, a sinner against the moral order; but they are not sins which identify him as a traitor, a regicide, an usurper, a tyrant. Perjury and murder are, moreover, not only the sins which Richard commits with each of his victims in turn; they are also the sins which doom the other sinners in the play to divine vengeance. So much do these two sins dominate the play that the moral pattern becomes repetitious and at times almost loses its cumulative horror.

Also there is in *Richard III* the same portrayal and analysis of passion which characterize Shakespearean tragedy elsewhere. Ambition compels Richard, as it does Macbeth, to murder that he may gain a throne. Fear compels him, as it does Macbeth, to murder to keep the

throne. Even the murderer becomes surfeited with his
own crimes. The *Mirror for Magistrates* had represented
Richard as saying:

> But what thing may suffise unto the bloudy man,
> The more he bathes in bloud, the bloudier he is alway:

and Shakespeare later wrote the same idea into words
for Macbeth:

> I am in bloud
> Stepp'd in so far, that, should I wade no more,
> Returning were as tedious as go o'er.

He writes like words here for Richard III:

> But I am in
> So far in blood that sin will pluck on sin.

But each step in blood brings new perturbation to Richard's soul. Like Macbeth, he has murdered sleep, and
his queen complains:

> For never yet one hour in his bed
> Did I enjoy the golden dew of sleep,
> But with his timorous dreams was still awak'd.

Yet fear urges him on to new crimes. He arranges with
Tyrrel to kill the little princes in the Tower:

> two deep enemies,
> Foes to my rest and my sweet sleep's disturbers . . .

And Tyrrel, like another Exton, promises, "I'll rid you
from the fear of them." His last night is a night of dream-
riding ghosts, and roused by Ratcliff to the day of battle,
he protests, "O Ratcliff, I fear, I fear!" Answering Ratcliff's plea not to be afraid of shadows, he confesses:

> By the apostle Paul, shadows tonight
> Have struck more terror to the soul of Richard

Than can the substance of ten thousand soldiers
Armed in proof, and led by shallow Richmond!

In contrast, the Richmond whom he must encounter has
had

The sweetest sleep and fairest-boding dreams
That ever entered in a drowsy head,

and his heart "is very jocund" in the remembrance. The
picture of the destructive power of passion in *Richard III*
is a cruder one than Shakespeare was later to achieve in
Macbeth, but in the other characters as well as in Richard
himself its corrosive effect is exhibited and analyzed.

Emphasizing moral rather than political sins and re-
vealing passion as both motivating sin and punishing it
by the perturbation of the soul, *Richard III* also shares
with the other Shakespearean tragedies a deep concern
with the problem of revenge. The contemporary discussion of revenge, as I have shown elsewhere, was built
upon the Biblical authority for a jealous God who had
said "Vengeance is mine." Three kinds of vengeance were
posited on the basis of this Biblical authority: God's vengeance for sin; public vengeance executed by the ruler
or his representative acting as the agent of God in admin-
istering justice and punishing sin; and private vengeance
which usurps the authority of God and is, therefore, for-
bidden.[1]

In *Richard III* the murder of Clarence and the execution of Hastings are made the occasions for long discussions of private revenge in relation to divine vengeance
and public vengeance. Clarence, it will be remembered,
was condemned by his brother, King Edward IV, but
"the order was revers'd," and Clarence is actually killed
by the hirelings of Richard, who sees in him an impediment in his path to the throne. The murderers at first pretend to come on an order from the King, and I quote
from the impassioned debate between them and their vic-

[1] See my "Theories of Revenge in Renaissance England," *Modern
Philology,* XXVIII (1931), 281–96.

tim Shakespeare's most detailed statement of the whole
Elizabethan philosophy of vengeance. Clarence makes
clear from the first the difference between private vengeance and public vengeance, delegated by God to his
vice-gerent to be executed under law for the public weal:

> *Clarence.* Are you drawn forth, among a world of men,
>   To slay the innocent? What is my offense?
>   Where is the evidence that doth accuse me?
>   What lawful quest have given their verdict up
>   Unto the frowning judge? or who pronounc'd
>   The bitter sentence of poor Clarence' death?
>   Before I be convict by course of law,
>   To threaten me with death is most unlawful.
>   I charge you, as you hope to have redemption
>   By Christ's dear blood shed for our grievous sins,
>   That you depart and lay no hands on me!
>   The deed you undertake is damnable.
>
> *First Murderer.* What we will do we do upon command.
>
> *Second Murderer.* And he that hath commanded is our king.
>
> *Clarence.* Erroneous vassals! the great King of kings
>   Hath in the table of His law commanded
>   That thou shalt do no murder. Will you then
>   Spurn at His edict, and fulfill a man's?
>   Take heed; for He holds vengeance in His hand,
>   To hurl upon their heads that break His law.
>
>   . . . .
>
> *First Murderer.* How canst thou urge God's dreadful law
>   to us,
>   When thou hast broke it in such dear degree?
>
> *Clarence.* . . . .
>   If God will be avenged for the deed,
>   O, know you yet, He doth it publicly.
>   Take not the quarrel from His powerful arm;
>   He needs no indirect or lawless course
>   To cut off those that have offended Him.

Even the King has no right to exact private revenge, but
as the murderers reveal the fact that not Edward, but

Richard, is the author of their deed, Clarence calls upon
them to relent and save their souls, asking

> And are you yet to your own souls so blind
> That you will war with God by murdering me?

The murderers do not relent, but no sooner is the deed
committed than the Second Murderer cries, as does many
another murderer in Shakespeare's tragedies:

> How fain, like Pilate, would I wash my hands
> Of this most grievous murder—

The case of Hastings is also presented at length to show
the heinousness of private revenge, here disguised as public revenge. Hastings, betrayed by Catesby, is reported
unwilling to see young Edward V deprived of his throne.
Without due process of law and on the obviously
trumped-up charge that he has succeeded Edward IV as
the protector of Jane Shore, who is accused along with
Queen Elizabeth of having through witchcraft brought
harm to his deformed body, Richard orders the death of
Hastings. Anticipating the suspicion which his action may
cause, he justifies the huggermugger execution to the Lord
Mayor of London:

> What, think you we are Turks or infidels?
> Or that we would, against the form of law,
> Proceed thus rashly in the villain's death,
> But that the extreme peril of the case,
> The peace of England, and our persons' safety,
> Enforc'd us to this execution?

The mayor is amenable to such reasoning, but Buckingham feels it wise to share the blame with lesser folk who
do their master's bidding too enthusiastically:

> Yet had we not determin'd he should die,
> Until your lordship came to see his end;
> Which now the loving haste of these our friends,
> Something against our meanings, have prevented: ...

The audience is already aware of the reason why Hastings
has been hurried to his death, but a scrivener is introduced
to enforce the lesson by explaining that the writing out
of the precedent and the indictment had anticipated the
accusation and seizure of Hastings by many hours, and
he queries:

> Who is so gross,
> That cannot see this palpable device?
> Yet who so bold, but says he sees it not?

The introduction of the long dialogue between Clarence
and his murderers and the intrusion of the scrivener with
his undramatic but pointed speech make evident Shakespeare's special interest in revenge in this play.

The matter of the divine vengeance which is inexorably
meted out for sin is, moreover, associated with the un-
stinted use of the supernatural in divers ways throughout
the play. The wounds of King Henry VI bleed in the
presence of his murderer. Prophecies contribute to the
imprisonment of the Duke of Clarence, and his terrible
dream warns him of his doom. Stanley dreams of Hastings' downfall. Hastings' horse stumbles three times. The
littler of the princes senses the presence of the ghost of
his uncle Clarence in the Tower. Richard accuses Jane
Shore and the queen of witchcraft. The ghosts of those
whom he has murdered disturb Richard's dreams and
give comfort to his foe the night before Bosworth Field.
Most important of all, the plot of the play is woven as a
web of curses and their fulfillment, and the sense of a
divine vengeance exacting a measured retribution for each
sin is ever-present.

However, God may and often does make use of an
evil instrument in the execution of His divine vengeance,
and Richard, like Tamburlaine, functions as the scourge
of God.[2] His first murder in the play is that of his brother

---

2 See R. W. Battenhouse, *Marlowe's Tamburlaine* (Nashville, 1941),
where the Elizabethan conception of God's use of a wicked man as a
scourge is discussed at length.

Clarence. The third part of *Henry VI* showed Clarence
going over to the side of King Henry in support of Warwick against Edward IV and marrying Warwick's younger
daughter. It showed him later forsworn as he rejoined his
brother's forces. Now we hear Richard, pretending pity
for him and commenting unctuously:

> Poor Clarence did forsake his father, Warwick;
> Ay, and forswore himself, which Jesu pardon!

Margaret tries to close his speech with a curse before
Richard can finish it, and she apparently makes herself
heard in heaven—or hell—with her "Which God revenge,"
for Clarence dreams of a descent "Unto the kingdom of
perpetual night":

> The first that there did greet my stranger-soul
> Was my great father-in-law, renowned Warwick,
> Who spoke aloud, "What scourge for perjury
> Can this dark monarchy afford false Clarence?"

Then appeared the slaughtered Prince of Wales, son of
Henry VI, "A shadow like an angel, with bright hair,"
who "squeak'd out aloud":

> "Clarence is come, false, fleeting, perjur'd Clarence,
> That stabb'd me in the field by Tewksbury:
> Seize on him Furies, take him into torment!"

Shattered by his dream, Clarence sorrows to his keeper:

> I have done those things,
> That now give evidence against my soul,
> For Edward's sake; and see how he requites me!
> O God! If my deep prayers cannot appease Thee,
> But thou wilt be aveng'd on my misdeeds,
> Yet execute Thy wrath in me alone; . . .

Clarence is murdered before an Elizabethan audience that
knew his last prayer had not been answered, for the destruction of his wife and children by Henry VII and

Henry VIII, who feared their possible claims to the throne, was an oft-told tale.

King Edward IV, learning of the death of Clarence, which he had commanded and then unavailingly counter-manded, cries out in horror:

> O God, I fear thy justice will take hold
> On me, and you, and mine, and yours for this!

Like King John and King Henry IV he bitterly chides those who have failed to advise him and check him, but he acknowledges his own sin, and Richard assents, "God will revenge it." King Edward dies, and those who heard his words are soon themselves experiencing the justice of God administered through Richard's malice.

Anne calls down the wrath of God upon the wife of Richard III and thereby curses her future self. Buckingham calls upon God to take vengeance if he be not true to England's queen and so curses himself. Edward on his deathbed warns the rival factions gathered about him to swear peace:

> Take heed you dally not before your king;
> Lest He that is the supreme King of kings
> Confound your hidden falsehood, and award
> Either of you to be the other's end.

Both factions perjure themselves, heedless of the warning, and upon them both the supreme King of kings takes vengeance through Richard's evil acts.

The poor, distracted Margaret, queen to Henry VI, is taunted by Richard as one who suffers the fate to which she was doomed by his father's curses:

> The curse my noble father laid on thee,
> When thou didst crown his warlike brows with paper,
> And with thy scorns drew'st rivers from his eyes,
> And then, to dry them, gav'st the Duke a clout
> Steep'd in the faultless blood of pretty Rutland—
> His curses, then from bitterness of soul
> Denounc'd against thee, are all fall'n upon thee;

And God, not we, hath plag'd thy bloody deed.

But Margaret in her turn pronounces her dreadful anathe-
mas upon those who have wronged her. She cries out for
King Edward's death because her king was murdered to
make this Yorkist king. She begs God to let Queen Elizabeth die "neither mother, wife, nor England's queen"
that justice may prevail and her own loss of child, husband, and kingdom be paid for. For all those who stood
by when her son was murdered:

> God I pray Him,
> That none of you may live his natural age,
> But by some unlook'd accident cut off!

And her prayers are answered, even her prayer for the
young Edward V:

> Edward thy son, that now is Prince of Wales,
> For Edward my son, that was Prince of Wales,
> Die in his youth by like untimely violence!

Her raucous demands for justice shock us, and the execution of that justice horrifies us, but they contribute to the
pattern of the play.

In his turn God's evil executioner of his justice must
feel the vengeance of the King of kings, and when he
does, we see the working out of yet more of Margaret's
awful curses:

> If heaven hath any grievous plague in store,
> Exceeding those that I can wish upon thee,
> O, let them keep it till thy sins be ripe,
> And then hurl down their indignation
> On thee, the troubler of the poor world's peace!
> The worm of conscience still begnaw thy soul!
> Thy friends suspect for traitors while thou livest,
> And take deep traitors for thy dearest friends!
> No sleep close up that deadly eye of thine,
> Unless it be while some tormenting dream
> Affrights thee with a hell of ugly devils!

Richard's device of closing the curse with her name before
she can close it with his is unavailing, for Margaret's
curses foretell the manner of his punishment. His doom
does not come upon him till his sins are ripe. Conscience
gnaws his soul, and he never sleeps without horrible
dreams. He distrusts his best friends and discards true
advisers. He makes friends with traitors. His last night is
a night of horror, and he meets his death ignominiously
on foot, his horse having been killed under him in the
course of the battle.

It is the God of the Old Testament that must be supposed to rule in such a moral order as Shakespeare here
depicts, but it is a moral order. The justice is that of an
eye for an eye, a Prince of Wales for a Prince of Wales.
Prayers that are offered as curses by those with hatred
in their hearts are answered by a divine justice without
pity. The stage should indeed be hung with black for the
presentation of this play. But it was a play that rounded
out the cycle of history in which the crown was snatched
from the House of Lancaster by unruly Yorkist hands,
only to be lost by the third heir to the importunate Richmond. Holinshed explained:

> And as it thus well appeared, that the house of Yorke
> shewed itselfe more bloudie in seeking to obteine the
> kingdome, than that of Lancaster in usurping it: so it
> came to passe, that the Lords vengeance appeared more
> heavie towards the same than towards the other, not
> ceassing till the whole issue male of the said Richard duke
> of Yorke was extinguished. For such is Gods justice,
> to leave no unrepentant wickednesse unpunished, as es-
> peciallie in this caitife Richard the third, not deserving
> so much as the name of a man, muche lesse of a king,
> most manifestlie appeareth.[3]

Thus Shakespeare pictured the dominating sins in the
play as perjury and murder, sins against the moral order.
He portrayed and analyzed the passion of ambition that
caused Richard to sin and the passion of fear that at the
same time punished him for his sins and forced him to

3 *Chronicles*, III, 761.

wade still further in blood. He inserted nonhistorical scenes developing the Elizabethan philosophy of revenge. He used the supernatural to enhance the horror of the play and to contribute to the impression of a divine vengeance meting out punishment for sin. He showed God's revenge exacted through the agency of the evil Richard, who was nevertheless held to account for his evil-doing. He made use of pathos in the death of the royal children. These are the common methods of Shakespearean tragedy, and they justify those who hold *Richard III* to be a tragedy.

But on the other hand, Shakespeare's editors can also be justified for putting *Richard III* among the histories. Except for the epilogue spoken by Richmond there are, of course, no great speeches on political abstractions such as the later history plays contained, or such as are to be found in *The True Tragedie of Richard the Third*. Unlike *King John* and *Richard II* and *Henry IV*, the play presents the usurpation of a throne and the punishment of the usurper without expounding the political sins involved. Yet Richard is, as Richmond says, a bloody tyrant and an usurper, and his crimes constitute offenses against the common weal for which the great King of kings takes vengeance. Thus though Clarence and Hastings are the victims of Richard's private vengeance, their deaths are made to emphasize the particular sinfulness of private vengeance executed, under the cloak of public vengeance, by one who serves as God's vice-gerent. And the pattern of sin and punishment is a political as well as a moral pattern, for murder and perjury are motivated by political purposes. The God who demands vengeance is, furthermore, the same God who presides as King of kings. In this play, as I have said, we see where tragedy and history meet.

A. P. ROSSITER

Angel with Horns: The Unity of "Richard III"

"Let's write 'good angel' on the devil's horn"
—*Measure for Measure*, II.iv.16

In the Second Part of *Henry IV* (III.i) the King and
Warwick are talking away the midnight, or the King's
insomnia; and the King remembers how Richard spoke
like a prophet of the future treachery of the Percies.
Warwick replies that those who look for rotations in history can indeed appear to be prophets:

> There is a history in all men's lives,
> Figuring the nature of the times deceas'd;
> The which observ'd, a man may prophesy,
> With a near aim, of the main chance of things
> As yet not come to life, who in their seeds
> And weak beginnings lie intreasured.
> Such things become the hatch and brood of time.

Richard, he explains, had observed "the necessary form"
of the events he had seen happen; and from that he could
"create a perfect guess" of some that were to ensue as
"the hatch and brood of time."

From *Angel with Horns and Other Shakespeare Lectures* by A. P.
Rossiter. London: Longmans, Green & Co., Limited, 1961; New York:
Theatre Arts Books, 1961. © 1961 by Longmans, Green & Co., Limited.
Reprinted by permission of Longmans, Green & Co., Limited, and The-
atre Arts Books.

Men have always looked for such a predictability in history: it gives the illusion of a comfortably ordered world. They have also often read—and written—historical records to show that the course of events has been guided by a simple process of divine justice, dispensing rewards and punishments here on earth and seeing to it that the wicked do *not* thrive like the green bay tree (as the Psalmist thought), and that virtue is not "triumphant only in theatrical performances" (as the humane Mikado put it: being a Gilbertian Japanese, not an Elizabethan Christian). The story matter of the Henry VI plays and of *Richard III* accepted both of these comforting and comfortable principles.

When I say "story matter" I mean what the Chronicles gave the author (or authors) of these four plays, and I wish to remain uncommitted as to whether their *plots* (and especially that of *Richard III*) work entirely within those reassuring limitations.

I am averse to source study, as material for lectures. Yet sad experience of human nature (and perhaps of historians) leads me to remind you how the Richard III myth ("story") came to reach Shakespeare. In the play, you remember, the Bishop of Ely, Morton, plots with Buckingham and runs away to join Richmond (Henry Tudor). He duly became one of Henry's ministers; and Thomas More grew up in his household—and later wrote the life of Richard III. It would only be human if Morton recounted all the worst that was ever said of the master he had betrayed: it is not surprising that Edward Halle should accept More's account, in writing his vast book on the "noble and illustre families of Lancastre and York"; and still more human that Raphael Holinshed (whom no one could call a historian) should copy extensively from Halle—and so leave room for all those since Horace Walpole who have had doubts about the historical character of this terrible monarch and the events of his times.

To think that we are seeing anything like sober history in this play is derisible naïvety. What we are offered is a formally patterned sequence presenting two things: on the one hand, a rigid Tudor *schema* of retributive justice

(a sort of analogy to Newton's Third Law in the field of
moral dynamics: "Action and reaction are equal and
opposite"); and, on the other, a huge triumphant stage
personality, an early old masterpiece of the art of rhetorical stage writing, a monstrous being incredible in any
sober, historical scheme of things—Richard himself.

I will talk about the first, first. The basic pattern of
retributive justice (or God's vengeance) is well enough
illustrated in Holinshed, in the passage telling how Prince
Edward (Henry VI's son and Margaret's) was murdered
at the Battle of Tewkesbury. The Prince was handed over
to Edward IV on the proclamation of a promise that he
would not be harmed; he was brought before the King,
asked why he "durst so presumptuously enter into his
realm" and replied courageously "To recover my father's
kingdom and heritage" (and more to that purpose)—but
let Holinshed say the rest:

> At which words king Edward said nothing, but with his
> hand thrust him from him, or (as some saie) stroke him
> with his gantlet; whom incontinentlie, George duke of
> Clarence, Richard duke of Glocester, Thomas Greie mar-
> quesse Dorcet, and William lord Hastings, that stood by,
> suddenlie murthered; for the which cruell act, the more
> part of the dooers in their latter daies dranke of the like
> cup, by the righteous iustice and due punishment of God.

There you have the notional pattern, in little, of the
whole framework of *Richard III*: Clarence—"false, fleeting, perjur'd Clarence" (who took the sacrament to remain true to Henry VI of Lancaster and deserted him);
Gray—one of the group of Queen Elizabeth Woodeville's
relations, who fall to Richard and Buckingham next after
Clarence; Hastings, who says he will see "this crown of
mine hewn from its shoulders/Before I see the crown so
foul misplaced" (on Richard's head)—and *does* (if a
man can be said to see his own decapitation). Holinshed
really understates the matter in writing "the more part of
the dooers . . . dranke of the like cup"; for of those he
names, everyone did. On the one hand, that is what
Richard III is about: what it is composed of. A heavy-

handed justice commends the ingredients of a poisoned [cup].

This notional pattern of historic events rigidly determined by a mechanical necessity is partly paralleled by, partly modified by, the formal patterns of the episodes (or scenes) and the language. By "formal patterns" I mean the unmistakably iterated goings-on in scenes so exactly parallel that if the first *is* passable on a modern stage as quasi-realistic costume-play stuff, the second (repeating it always *more* unrealistically) cannot be. The two wooing scenes (Richard with Anne and Elizabeth) are the simplest case; but in the lamentation scenes—where a collection of bereft females comes together and goes through a dismal catalogue of *Who was Who* and *Who has lost Whom* (like a gathering of historical Mrs. Gummidges, each "thinking of the old 'un" with shattering simultaneity)—there, even editors have found the proceedings absurd; and readers difficult. When Queen Margaret, for example, says:

> I had an Edward, till a Richard kill'd him;
> I had a husband, till a Richard kill'd him:
> Thou hadst an Edward, till a Richard kill'd him;
> Thou hadst a Richard, till a Richard kill'd him.
>
> (IV.iv.40–43)

a reader may *just* keep up (and realize that the last two are the Princes in the Tower, so that Queen Elizabeth is being addressed); but when the Duchess of York takes up with

> I had a Richard too, and thou didst kill him;
> I had a Rutland too, thou holp'st to kill him,

it is likely that you are lost, unless your recollection of a *Henry VI* and the ends of Richard, Duke of York and his young son (Edmund) is unusually clear.

It is not only the iteration of scene that is stylized: the stiffly formal manipulation of echoing phrase and sequence of words within the scenes is even more unrealistic. A

closely related parallelism exists in the repeated occur-
rence of a sort of "single-line traffic" in sentences: the
classicist's *stichomythia*. One speaker takes from the other
exactly the same ration of syllables, and rejoins as if under
contract to repeat the form of the given sentence as
exactly as possible, using the maximum number of the
same words or their logical opposites, or (failing that)
words closely associated with them. I describe the game
pedantically, because it *is* an exact and scientific game with
language, and one of the graces and beauties of the play
Shakespeare wrote. If we cannot accept the "patterned
speech" of *Richard III,* its quality must remain unknown
to us. "Early work" is an evasive, criticism-dodging term.
Early it may be; but the play is a triumphant contrivance
in a manner which cannot properly be compared with
that of any other tragedy—nor of any history, except
3 Henry VI (where the manner takes shape, and particu-
larly in III.ii) and *King John* (which is not half so well
built or integrated as this).

I have emphasized the stylization of verbal patterning
(with its neatly overexact adjustments of stroke to stroke,
as in royal tennis), because the sequence of most of the
important events offers very much the same pattern. I
might remark, in passing, that these verbal devices were
offering to the Elizabethans an accomplished English
equivalent to the neat dexterities they admired in Seneca
(a point made by T. S. Eliot years ago; though he did
not examine how the dramatic ironies of the action run
in parallel with these counterstroke reversals of verbal
meaning, and form a kind of harmony). But we miss
something more than Shakespeare's rhetorical game of
tennis if merely irritated by, e.g.:

Anne: I would I knew thy heart.

Richard: 'Tis figured in my tongue.

Anne: I fear me, both are false.

Richard: Then never man was true.

Those reversals of intention (*heart-tongue; false-true*)

are on precisely the pattern of the repeated reversals of
human expectation, the reversals of events, the anticipated
reversals (foreseen only by the audience), which make
"dramatic irony." The patterned speech of the dialogue
—the wit that demonstrates that a sentence is but a cheveril glove, quickly turned the other way—is fundamentally
one with the ironic patterns of the plot. "Dramatic irony"
here is verbal *peripeteia*.

You will see that simply exemplified if you read Buckingham's speech at the beginning of Act II, where he calls
a curse on himself if ever he goes back on his reconciliation with the Queen (and is quite specific about it); then
turn straight to his last lines in V.i, when he is on the
way to execution: "That high All-seer, which I dallied
with." He has got exactly what he asked for. He did not
mean the words he used, but they have been reversed
into actuality, in exactly the same way as verbal terms
are reversed in the tennis-court game of rhetoric.

The same irony plays all over *Richard III*. It lurks like
a shadow behind the naïvely self-confident Hastings; it
hovers a moment over Buckingham when Margaret warns
him against "yonder dog" (Richard), and, on Richard's
asking what she said, he replies, "Nothing that I respect,
my gracious lord" (I.iii.295)—and this at a time when
Buckingham is under no threat whatsoever.

Its cumulative effect is to present the personages as
existing in a state of total and terrible uncertainty. This
is enhanced if we know the details of what comes into
the play from *3 Henry VI,* but is there even if we know
only a few bare essentials of what has gone before. We
need to know who Margaret is; how Lancaster has been
utterly defeated, and King Henry and his son murdered;
how Clarence betrayed his King and returned to the
Yorkists; and how Richard, his younger brother, has
already marked him as his immediate obstruction on his
intended way to the crown. We need to know too that the
Duchess of York is mother to that unrewarding trio,
Edward IV, Clarence, Gloucester; that Edward IV has
married an aspiring commoner, Elizabeth Grey (*née*
Woodeville); and that she has jacked up her relations

into nobility. Beyond those half-dozen facts we do not
need back-reference to *3 Henry VI* for any but the finer
points—so far as the essential ironies of the plot go.

Far more important than these details is the simple
overriding principle derived from the Tudor historians:
that England rests under a chronic curse—the curse of
faction, civil dissension, and fundamental anarchy, result-
ing from the deposition and murder of the Lord's Anointed
(Richard II) and the usurpation of the House of Lancaster. The savageries of the Wars of the Roses follow logi-
cally (almost theologically) from that; and Elizabeth's
"All-seeing heaven, what a world is this!" says but half.
It is a world of absolute and hereditary moral ill, in which
everyone (till the appearance of Richmond-Tudor in
Act V) is tainted with the treacheries, the blood and the
barbarities of civil strife, and internally blasted with the
curse of a moral anarchy which leaves but three human
genera: the strong in evil, the feebly wicked, and the help-
lessly guilt-tainted (such as the Princes, Anne—all those
despairing, lamenting women, whose choric wailings are
a penitential psalm of guilt and sorrow: England's guilt,
the individual's sorrow). The "poor painted Queen's"
"What a world" needs supplementing with the words of
the pessimistically clear-sighted Third Citizen:

> All may be well; but, if God sort it so,
> 'Tis more than we deserve or I expect.
>
> (II.iii.36–37)

I have in effect described the meaning of the framework
of the play: presented it as "moral history," to be interpreted in abstract terms. But the play itself is also a sym-
phonic structure which I can only describe in terms of
music: a rhetorical symphony of five movements, with
first and second subjects and some Wagnerian leitmotifs.
The play-making framework is Senecan revenge, the char-
acterization largely Marlovian; but the orchestration is not
only original, but unique. It can be sketched like this.

The first movement employs five "subjects": Richard
himself, his own overture; the wooing theme (to be re-

peated in the fourth movement); Richard among his
enemies (repeating the duplicity with which he has fooled
Clarence); Margaret's curse; and the long dying fall of
Clarence. It occupies the whole of Act I.

The second movement includes Act II and scenes i–iv
of Act III. It begins with the King's feeble peacemaking
—in which Buckingham invites his curse—and its other
subjects are: a lamentation after the King's death (repeated in the fourth movement); the fall of the curse on
Rivers, Grey, and Vaughan (when the curse is remembered), and on Hastings (the curse briefly recalled again).
The future subject of Richard's moves against the Princes
is introduced between-whiles.

The third movement cuts across the act divisions and
runs from III.v to IV.iii. Its main subject is the Glouces-
ter-Buckingham plot for the crown, with the magnificently
sardonic fooling of the London *bourgeoisie* with a crisis-
scare, a brace of bishops, and the headline story that
here is a highly respectable unlibidinous monarch for
decent England. On its success, Anne is called to be
Queen, and thus to meet the curse she herself called
on Richard's wife before he wooed her in that humor
and won her (the first movement is here caught up).
Buckingham now makes himself one of Richard's future
victims by showing reluctance for the plot against the
Princes, and Richard throws him off with a snub. The
Princes are dealt with (the account of Forrest and Deigh-
ton echoing that of the murderers of Clarence, one of
whom had a temporary conscience); and Richard concludes with a brisk summary and prospectus:

> The sons of Edward sleep in Abraham's bosom,
> And Anne my wife hath bid this world good night;

and so, since Richmond plans to marry "young Elizabeth,
my brother's daughter," "To her go I, a jolly thriving
wooer" (Richard's last jocularity). The movement ends
with the first murmurs of Richmond. Previously there has
been slipped in the trivial-sounding prophecy about "Ruge-
mount," besides Henry VI's prophecy (IV.ii.94 ff.). The

flight of the Bishop of Ely (Morton) really troubles Richard.

The fourth movement brings down the curse on Buckingham (V.i is obviously misplaced, so the movement runs from IV.iv to V.i inclusive). Mainly it repeats themes heard before: with a long lamentation scene (the Blake-like weeping Queens); a repetition of Margaret's curse with the curse of Richard's mother added; the second wooing scene; the subject of Nemesis repeated by Buckingham. In it the sound of Richmond's advance has become clearer; and Richard's self-command and certainty begin to waver.

The fifth movement is all at Bosworth: the fall of the curse on Richard himself. There is the dream-prologue of the procession of contrapuntal Ghosts (including all those so qualified from the four previous movements) and, like all ghosts, they are reminiscent and repetitive. The play ends with the epilogue to the Wars of the Roses—spoken by Queen Elizabeth's grandfather—calling a blessing on the English future, and inverting the opening lines of Richard's prologue:

> Now is the winter of our discontent
> Made glorious summer . . .

The deliberateness of this highly controlled workmanship needs but little comment. I shall take up a single musical phrase: one that intertwines its plangent undertones throughout the whole symphony, a true leitmotif.

At first sight, Clarence's dream (I.iv.9 ff.) appears to contribute little to the play, nothing to the plot; and it may seem a rhetorical indulgence, even if we accept Mr. Eliot's judgment that it shows "a real approximation in English to the magnificence of Senecan Latin at its best. . . . The best of Seneca has here been absorbed into English."[1] But first recollect the setting. Clarence has been sent to the Tower, by the machinations of the Queen's party (so he thinks), and he is confident that his brother

---

[1] *Selected Essays*, 1932, p. 90; reprinted from Introduction to *Seneca His Tenne Tragedies*, 1927.

Richard will stand good friend to him. He believes Richard's worried "We are not safe, Clarence; we are not safe"; cannot possibly see the ironical joke Richard is cracking with himself; has no idea that he has been first on Richard's list since that moment in *3 Henry VI* (V.vi) when his brother muttered, "Clarence, beware; thou keep'st me from the light."[2] (A line that follows a passage predetermining the gulling of both Clarence and Anne to follow:

> I have no brother, I am like no brother;
> And this word "love," which graybeards call divine,
> Be resident in men like one another,
> And not in me! I am myself alone.)

Clarence had not been there to hear that: knows nothing of the typically sharp reversal of Richard's solemnly hypocritical fooling now with:

> Go tread the path that thou shalt ne'er return.
> Simple, plain Clarence, I do love thee so
> That I will shortly send thy soul to heaven,
> If heaven will take the present at our hands. (I.i.117–20)

Clarence has his nightmare in the Tower: a vision prophetic of doom, and thick with curdled guilt. He dreams that Richard blunderingly knocks him overboard from a vessel; he drowns; goes to hell; and his guilt-sick mind spews up its own evil:

> *Keeper:* Awak'd you not in this sore agony?
>
> *Clarence:* No, no, my dream was lengthen'd after life.
> O, then began the tempest to my soul!
> I pass'd, methought, the melancholy flood
> With that sour ferryman which poets write of,
> Unto the kingdom of perpetual night.

[2] This contradicts R. G. Moulton, *Shakespeare as a Dramatic Artist*, 1885 (p. 92), who says Richard is *not* "ambitious" (as Macbeth is): "never found dwelling upon the prize in view." This presumes a complete disconnection between *3 Henry VI* and *Richard III*. No such assumption is acceptable nowadays—nor was it sensible even then.

> The first that there did greet my stranger soul
> Was my great father-in-law, renowned Warwick,
> Who spake aloud "What scourge for perjury
> Can this dark monarchy afford false Clarence?"
> And so he vanish'd. Then came wand'ring by
> A shadow like an angel, with bright hair
> Dabbled in blood, and he shriek'd out aloud
> "Clarence is come—false, fleeting, perjur'd Clarence,
> That stabb'd me in the field by Tewkesbury.
> Seize on him, Furies, take him unto torment!"
>
> (I.iv.42–57)

It is as fine a passage in that style as English can offer: calculated to leave its solemn music in even half-attentive ears. In the second movement of the play (II.ii.43 ff.), Queen Elizabeth announces the King's death:

> If you will live, lament; if die, be brief,
> That our swift-winged souls may catch the King's,
> Or like obedient subjects follow him
> To his new kingdom of ne'er-changing night.

It is scarcely a proper-wifely expectation of the fate of her husband's spirit: but the echo of "Unto the kingdom of perpetual night" is the effect intended, not Elizabeth's notions. The actors who put together the Q. text of 1597 showed that they appreciated, if clumsily, the author's intention. They made it "To his new kingdom of perpetuall rest": catching the echo rightly, while missing the point.

The same "dark monarchy" awaits all these people: they are the living damned. That is the translation of this echo-technique of leitmotifs; and why I call the play's anatomy "musical." Nor is that all: the phrase returns again. But before I come to that, remark how Hastings philosophizes on his fall at the end of the second movement:

> O momentary grace of mortal men,
> Which we more hunt for than the grace of God!
> Who builds his hope in air of your good[3] looks

[3] Qq. faire.

Lives like a drunken sailor on a mast,
Ready with every nod to tumble down
Into the fatal bowels of the deep.   (III.iv.95–100)

We have heard that surging rhythm before. And with it
the feeling of being aloft, in air, unbalanced: the rhythm
of Clarence dreaming:

As we pac'd along
Upon the giddy footing of the hatches,
Methought that Gloucester stumbled, and in falling
Struck me, that thought to stay him, overboard
Into the tumbling billows of the main.   (I.iv.16–20)

Pattern repeats pattern with remarkable exactitude. "Into
the fatal bowels of the deep" is where the giddy Hastings
also goes. "O Lord, methought what pain it was to drown"
might be extended to all these desperate swimmers in the
tide of pomp and history. The elaboration of the dream
is no mere exercise in fine phrase on Latin models: it
offers a symbol of choking suspense above black depths
(the ocean, and perpetual night) which epitomizes the
"momentary grace" of all these "mortal men" and women.
And the sea as figure of "the destructive element" appears
again in Elizabeth's lines in the second wooing scene:

But that still use of grief makes wild grief tame,
My tongue should to thy ears not name my boys
Till that my nails were anchor'd in thine eyes;
And I, in such a desp'rate bay of death,
Like a poor bark, of sails and tackling reft,
Rush all to pieces on thy rocky bosom.   (IV.iv.230–35)

"Bay" of death suggests also an animal at bay; just
plausibly relevant, since Richard (the boar) would be at
bay when she *could* scratch his eyes out. But the repetition of the rather too emphatic anchors and the eyes from
Clarence's dream is much more striking.

You will find a further echo of the "night motif" in the
last movement. Richard suspects Stanley (confusingly
also called Derby), and reasonably so: for he was hus-

band to the Countess of Richmond, Henry Tudor's mother, the famous Lady Margaret Beaufort; and therefore keeps his son, George Stanley, as hostage. Before Bosworth, he sends a brisk message to warn the father of the black depths beneath the son; and again Shakespeare sounds his doom music from the Clarence sequence:

> bid him bring his power
> Before sunrising, lest his son George fall
> Into the blind cave of eternal night.   (V.iii.60–62)

Need I remark that Clarence was "George" too, and lightly called that by Richard when he was afraid that King Edward might die before he signed his brother's death warrant?

> He cannot live, I hope, and must not die
> Till George be packed with post horse up to heaven.
>   (I.i.145–46)

I could further exemplify the play's tight-woven artistry by taking up that very remarkable prose-speech on "conscience" by Clarence's Second Murderer (I.iv.136 ff.), and following the word into Richard's troubled mind in Act V before Margaret's curse attains its last fulfillment. But to reduce attention to Richard himself in his own play, beyond what I am already committed to by my insistence on taking the play as a *whole* (as a dramatic pattern, not an exposition of "character"), would be to do it—and Shakespeare—an injustice.

Richard Plantagenet is alone with Macbeth as the Shakespearean version of the thoroughly bad man in the role of monarch and hero; he is unique in combining with that role that of the diabolic humorist. It is this quality which makes it an inadequate account to say that the play is "moral history," or that the protagonists are the personality of Richard and the curse of Margaret (or what it stood for in orthodox Tudor thinking about retributive justice in history)—for all that these opposed "forces" *are* central throughout. The first movement establishes both, and emphatically. First, Richard, stumping down the stage on his unequal legs, forcing his hitched-up left shoulder and his withered arm on us, till we realize that *this* is what the "winter of our discontent" in *3 Henry VI* has produced, *this* the proper "hatch and brood of time"; and then, Richard established, his cruel and sardonic effectiveness demonstrated on Clarence and Anne, there arises against his brazen Carl Orff-like music the one voice he quails before (if but slightly): the subdominant notes of Margaret and her prophecy of doom, to which the ghosts will walk in the visionary night before Bosworth. It is a conflict between a spirit and a ghost: between Richard, the spirit of ruthless will, of daemonic pride, energy and self-sufficiency, of devilish gusto and *Schadenfreude* (he *enjoys* wickedness even when it is of no practical advantage to his ambitions or to securing himself by murder: it may be only wickedness in *words,* but the spirit revealed is no less evilly exultant for that); and the ghost, as I call her—for what else is Margaret, Reignier's daughter picked up on a battlefield by Suffolk and married to that most etiolated of Shakespeare's husbands, Henry VI, but the living ghost of Lancaster, the walking dead, memorializing the long, cruel, treacherous, bloody conflict of the years of civil strife and pitiless butchery?

You can, of course, see more there if you will. Make her the last stage or age of woman-in-politics: she who has been beautiful, fiercely passionate, queenly, dominating, master of armies, *generalissima*; now old, defeated, empty of everything but fierce bitterness, the illimitable bitterness and rancor of political zeal. What did Yeats write of *his* equivalent symbol? It is in "A Prayer for my Daughter." For her he prays:

> An intellectual hatred is the worst,
> So let her think opinions are accursed.
> Have I not seen the loveliest woman born
> Out of the mouth of Plenty's horn,
> Because of her opinionated mind
> Barter that horn and every good

> By quiet natures understood
> For an old bellows full of angry wind?

Margaret is that, if you like; but, not to go beyond Shakespeare, I cannot but think that when the old Duchess of
York sits down upon the ground for the second lamentation scene (to tell "sad stories of the death of kings"),
the *author's* mind ran more upon Margaret as he wrote:

> Dead life, blind sight, poor mortal living ghost, . . .
> Brief abstract and record of tedious days,
> Rest thy unrest on England's lawful earth,
> Unlawfully made drunk with innocent blood.
>   (IV.iv.26, 28–30)

Here Shakespeare devises a new variation on the Senecan
visitant from another world howling for revenge, by making the specter nominal flesh and blood; the tune of the
Dance of Death to which all dance to damnation is played
by Margaret; and one aspect of the play is our watching
the rats go into the Weser, compelled by that fatal tune.

But Richard himself is not simply the last and most important (and worst) of the victims—if those justly destroyed can be called "victims." That is just where the
label "moral history" is inadequate. For Richard has
grown a new dimension since his abrupt and remarkable
development in *3 Henry VI*: he has become a wit, a
mocking comedian, a "vice of kings"—but with a clear
inheritance from the old Vice of the Moralities: part symbol of evil, part comic devil, and chiefly, on the stage,
the generator of roars of laughter at wickednesses
(whether of deed or word) which the audience would
immediately condemn in real life. On the one hand, his
literary relations with the Senecan "Tyrant" (author of
"In regna mea Mors impetratur," etc.) are clear enough;
as they are with the Elizabethan myth of "the murderous
Machiavel" ("feared am I more than loved/Let me be
feared," etc.): enough has been written on them. But
only the medieval heritage—from the comic devils with
their *Schadenfreude,* and the Vice as comic inverter of

order and decency—can fully explain the new Richard of this apparent sequel to the *Henry VI* series.

I have said that the Christian pattern imposed on history gives the simple plot of a cast accursed, where all are evil beings, all deserve punishment. Look, then, with a believing Tudor eye, and ought you not to *approve* Richard's doings? *Per se,* they are the judgment of God on the wicked; and he

> *Ein Teil von jener Kraft*
> *Die stets das Böse will, und stets das Gute schafft.*[4]

But that is not all. Richard's sense of humor, his function as clown, his comic irreverences and sarcastic or sardonic appropriations of things to (at any rate) *his* occasions: all those act as underminers of our assumed naïve and proper Tudor principles; and we are on his side much rather because he makes us (as the Second Murderer put it) "take the devil in [our] mind," than for any "historical-philosophical-Christian-retributional" sort of motive. In this respect a good third of the play is a kind of grisly *comedy*; in which we meet the fools to be taken in on Richard's terms, see them with his mind, and rejoice with him in their stultification (in which execution is the ultimate and unanswerable practical joke, the absolutely final laugh this side of the Day of Judgment). Here, Richard is a middle-term between Barabas, the Jew of Malta (*c.* 1590) and Volpone (1606). He inhabits a world where everyone deserves everything he can do to them; and in his murderous practical joking he is *inclusively* the comic exposer of the mental shortcomings (the intellectual and moral deformities) of this world of beings depraved and besotted. If we forget to pity them awhile (and he does his best to help us), then his impish spirit urges us towards a positive reversal of "Christian charity" until the play's fourth movement (which is when the Elizabethan spectator began to back out, I take it)—or even beyond that point.

[4] "A part of that Power which always wills evil and yet always brings about good." (Goethe's *Faust*)

An aspect of Richard's appeal, which has, I fancy,
passed relatively unexamined,[5] is one that we can be confident that William Shakespeare felt and reflected on. I
mean the appeal of the actor: the talented being who can
assume every mood and passion at will, at all events to
the extent of making others believe in it. Beyond question, all our great actors have regarded the part as a fine
opportunity. The extent to which the histrionic art (as
Shakespeare thought and felt about it) contributed to the
making of this great stage figure is to me more interesting.

The specific interest here is the *power* that would be
in the hands of an actor consummate enough to make
(quite literally) "all the world a stage" and to work on
humanity by the perfect simulation of every feeling: the
appropriate delivery of every word and phrase that will
serve his immediate purpose; together with the complete
dissimulation of everything that might betray him
(whether it be his intentions, or such obstructive feelings
as compunction, pity or uncertainty of mind). This appears at once when Gloucester first takes shape as the
man self-made to be King, in the long soliloquy in *3
Henry VI* (III.ii). The closing lines are specifically on
histrionic genius:

> Why, I can smile, and murder whiles I smile,
> And cry "Content!" to that which grieves my heart,
> And wet my cheeks with artificial tears,
> And frame my face to all occasions.

And then, after a little bragging prospectus on his intended deadliness, he ends:

> I can add colors to the chameleon,
> Change shapes with Protheus for advantages,
> And set the murderous Machiavel to school.
> Can I do this, and cannot get a crown?
> Tut, were it farther off, I'll pluck it down.

---

5 [J. Middleton Murry, *Shakespeare*, 1936, pp. 125–26, quotes the
theatrical metaphors and remarks briefly on the conception of Richard
as an actor.]

M. R. Ridley notes here that "Machiavelli . . . seems to have been to the Elizabethans a type of one who advocated murder as a method of cold-blooded policy."[6] It is true that that marks off one point of difference between the "Senecan" tyrant-villainy (which is primarily for revenge) and the "Machiavellian" (which is for power, or self-aggrandizement: "We that are great, our own self-good still moves us"): though I do not think that the distinction can be maintained, if you read Seneca. But surely Ridley's note misses the point, in its context? What the "Machiavel" allusion represents is, I believe, Shakespeare's recognition that the program set before the Prince in *Il Principe* is one that demands exactly those histrionic qualities I have just described: a lifelong, unremitting vigilance in relentless simulation and impenetrable deception. There, precisely, lies the super-humanity of the Superman. The will-to-power is shorn of its effective power without it. He is an *artist* in evil.

Now Richard in his own play shows this power—these powers—to perfection. Except to the audience, he is invisible; but the audience he keeps reminded not only of his real intentions, but equally of his actor's artistries. The bluff plain Englishman, shocked at ambitious go-getters and grievingly misunderstood, is perfectly "done" before the Queen's relations:

> Because I cannot flatter and look fair,
> Smile in men's faces, smooth, deceive, and cog,
> Duck with French nods and apish courtesy,
> I must be held a rancorous enemy.
> Cannot a plain man live and think no harm
> But thus his simple truth must be abus'd
> With silken, sly, insinuating Jacks? (I.iii.47–53)

A little later, it is: "I am too childish-foolish for this world," (*ibid.*, 141); and even: "I thank my God for my humility" (II.i.74).

Then, left to himself and the audience, after egging on all their quarrels:

6 *New Temple* ed., p. 140.

But then I sigh and, with a piece of Scripture,
Tell them that God bids us do good for evil.
And thus I clothe my naked villainy
With odd old ends stol'n forth of holy writ,
And seem a saint when most I play the devil.
                                    (I.iii.333–37)

The stage direction, *"Enter two Murderers,"* caps this
nicely. It is not simply that Richard is a hypocrite and
(like other stage villains) tells us so. The actor's tech-
nique of "asides" is the essence of his chuckling private
jokes—made to "myself alone." (You might say that
Shakespeare is giving not merely "the acting of drama,"
but also "the drama of consummate *acting*").

The same reminders, nudging the audience's attention,
appear in his swift-switched actual asides: e.g., his thoroughly unholy reception of his mother's blessing, spoken
as he gets up off his dutiful knees:

Amen! And make me die a good old man!
That is the butt end of a mother's blessing;
I marvel that her Grace did leave it out.
                                    (II.ii.109–11)

Or, again, we have Richard's insinuating equivocations in
talking to the prattling little Princes; in one of which he
acknowledges his theatrical-historical legacy from the Moralities: "Thus, like the formal vice, Iniquity,/I moralize
two meanings in one word." (III.i.82–83). Over and
above this there is that striking passage (III.v.1–11)
where he and Buckingham are working up a crisis (appearing ill-dressed in old rusty armor, as if they had
armed in desperate haste), when Richard specifically in-
quires whether Buckingham can "do the stage tragedian":

  Richard. Come, cousin, canst thou quake and change thy
      color,
    Murder thy breath in middle of a word,
    And then again begin, and stop again,
    As if thou wert distraught and mad with terror?

> *Buckingham.* Tut, I can counterfeit the deep tragedian;
>> Speak and look back, and pry on every side,
>> Tremble and start at wagging of a straw,
>> Intending deep suspicion. Ghastly looks
>> Are at my service, like enforced smiles;
>> And both are ready in their offices
>> At any time to grace my stratagems.

It is all sardonically jocular; but nothing shows more clearly the artist's delight in his craft: call it illusion or deception, it makes no odds. It is this dexterity that his other rapid reversals of tone keep us aware of; whether he is half-amazedly rejoicing in his conquest of Anne, or poking unfilial fun at his mother (a performance more shocking to Elizabethans than to our more child-foolish days).

Yet again, there is that admirable moment when the Londoners are being fooled into believing that he must be persuaded to be king; when Buckingham pretends to lose patience, with "Zounds, I'll entreat no more." And Richard, bracketed aloft with two Bishops, is distressed: "O, do not swear, my lord of Buckingham." (III.vii. 219). (It is like the moment in *Eric or Little by Little* (ch. 8) when Eric refers to the usher as a "surly devil"; and the virtuous Russell exclaims: "O Eric, that is the first time that I have heard you swear.") It is this unholy jocularity, the readiness of sarcastic, sardonic, profane, and sometimes blasphemous wit, the demonic gusto of it all, which not only wins the audience over to accepting the Devil as hero, but also points us towards the central paradox of the play. And, through that, to a full critical awareness of its unity: with a few remarks on which I shall conclude.

To begin with Richard. On the face of it, he is the demon-Prince, the cacodemon born of hell, the misshapen toad, etc. (all things ugly and ill). But through his prowess as actor and his embodiment of the comic Vice and impish-to-fiendish humor, he offers the false as more attractive than the true (the actor's function), and the ugly and evil as admirable and amusing (the clown's game of value reversals). You can say, "We don't take him seriously." I reply, "That is exactly what gets most of his acquaintances into Hell: just what the devil-clown relies on." But he is not only this demon incarnate, he is in effect God's agent in a predetermined plan of divine retribution: the "scourge of God." Now by Tudor-Christian historical principles, this plan is *right*. Thus, in a real sense, Richard is a king who "can do no wrong"; for in the pattern of the justice of divine retribution on the wicked, he functions as an avenging angel. Hence my paradoxical title, "Angel with Horns."

The paradox is sharpened by what I have mainly passed by: the repulsiveness, humanely speaking, of the "justice." God's will it may be, but it sickens us: it is as pitiless as the Devil's (who is called in to execute it). The contrast with Marlowe's painless, dehumanized slaughterings in *Tamburlaine* is patent.

This over-all system of *paradox* is the play's unity. It is revealed as a constant displaying of inversions, or reversals of meaning: whether we consider the verbal patterns (the *peripeteias* or reversals of act and intention or expectation); the antithesis of false and true in the histrionic character; or the constant inversions of irony. Those verbal capsizings I began by talking about, with their deliberate reversals to the opposite meaning in equivocal terms, are the exact correlatives of both the nature of man (or man in power: Richard) and of the nature of events (history); and of language too, in which all is conveyed.

But, start where you will, you come back to history; or to the pattern made out of the conflict of two "historical myths." The orthodox Tudor myth made history God-controlled, divinely prescribed and dispensed, to move things towards a God-ordained perfection: Tudor England. Such was the *frame* that Shakespeare took. But the total effect of Shakespeare's "plot" has quite a different effect from Halle: a very different meaning. Dr. Duthie may write, "But there is no doubt that Shakespeare saw history in the same light as Halle saw it."[7] I

7 G. I. Duthie, *Shakespeare*, 1951, p. 118.

say there *is* doubt. Dover Wilson has nothing to offer but what he summarizes from Moulton, but his last sentence points my doubting way: "it appears, to me at least, unlikely that Shakespeare's 'main end' in *Richard III* was to show the working out of God's will in English history.' "[8] (The quotation he is discussing is from Tillyard's *Shakespeare's History Plays* [1944], p. 208.) He can go no further because his own limitations on *Henry IV* inhibit his ever observing that the comic Richard has no more place in Halle's scheme than Falstaff has.

The other myth is that of Richard the Devil-King: the Crookback *monstrum deforme, ingens* whom Shakespeare *found* as a ready-made Senecan tyrant and converted into a quite different inverter of moral order: a ruthless, demonic comedian with a most un-Senecan sense of humor and the seductive appeal of an irresistible gusto, besides his volcanic Renaissance energies. They are themselves demoralizing: *Tapfer sein ist gut*[9] is the antithesis of a Christian sentiment.

The outcome of this conflict of myths was Shakespeare's display of constant inversions of meaning; in all of which, two systems of meaning impinge and go over to their opposites, like the two "ways" of the cheveril glove. This applies equally to words and word-patterns; to the actor-nature; to dramatic ironies; and to events, as the hatch and brood of time, contrasted with opposite expectations.

As a result of the paradoxical ironic structure built from these inversions of meaning—built above all by Richard's demonic appeal—the naïve, optimistic, "Christian" principle of history, consoling and comfortable, modulates into its opposite. The "Christian" system of retribution is undermined, counterbalanced, by historic irony. (Do I need to insist that the coupling of "Christian" and "retribution" itself is a paradox? That the God of vengeance is *not* a Christian God; that his opposite is a God of mercy who has no representation in this play. If I do, I had better add that the so-called "Christian"

8 *Richard III* (*New Cambridge* ed., 1954), p. xlv.
9 "To be bold is good."

frame is indistinguishable from a pagan one of Nemesis
in which the "High all-seer" is a Fate with a cruel sense
of humor.)

But do not suppose I am saying that the play is a "de-
bunking of Tudor myth," or that Shakespeare is disprov-
ing it. He is not "proving" anything: not even that "Blind
belief is sure to err/And scan his works in vain" (though
I think that is *shown,* nevertheless). Contemporary
"order"-thought spoke as if naïve faith saw true: God
was above God's Englishmen and ruled with justice—
which meant summary vengeance. This historic myth offered absolutes, certainties. Shakespeare in the Histories
always leaves us with relatives, ambiguities, irony, a process thoroughly dialectical. Had he entirely accepted the
Tudor myth, the frame and pattern of order, his way
would have led, I suppose, towards writing *moral history*
(which is what Dr. Tillyard and Dr. Dover Wilson and
Professor Duthie have made *out* of him). Instead, his
way led him towards writing *comic history*. The former
would never have taken him to tragedy: the latter (para-
doxically) did. Look the right way through the cruel-
comic side of Richard and you glimpse Iago. Look back
at him through his energy presented as evil, and you see
Macbeth. And if you look at the irony of men's struggles
in the nets of historic circumstance, the ironies of their
pride and self-assurance, you will see Coriolanus; and you
are past the great tragic phase and back in history again.

Suggested References

The number of possible references is vast and grows alarmingly. (The *Shakespeare Quarterly* devotes one issue each year to a list of the previous year's work, and *Shakespeare Survey* —an annual publication—includes a substantial review of recent scholarship, as well as an occasional essay surveying a few decades of scholarship on a chosen topic.) Though no works are indispensable, those listed below have been found especially helpful.

1. Shakespeare's Times

Byrne, M. St. Clare. *Elizabethan Life in Town and Country.* Rev. ed. New York: Barnes & Noble, 1961. Chapters on manners, beliefs, education, etc., with illustrations.

Joseph, B. L. *Shakespeare's Eden: The Commonwealth of England, 1558–1629.* New York: Barnes & Noble, 1971. An account of the social, political, economic, and cultural life of England.

Schoenbaum, S. *Shakespeare: The Globe and the World.* New York: Oxford University Press, 1979. A readable, handsomely illustrated book on the world of the Elizabethans.

Shakespeare's England. 2 vols. London: Oxford University Press, 1916. A large collection of scholarly essays on a wide variety of topics (e.g. astrology, costume, gardening, horsemanship), with special attention to Shakespeare's references to these topics.

Stone, Lawrence. *The Crisis of the Aristocracy, 1558–1641,* abridged edition. London: Oxford University Press, 1967.

2. Shakespeare

Barnet, Sylvan. *A Short Guide to Shakespeare.* New York: Harcourt Brace Jovanovich, 1974. An introduction to all of the works and to the dramatic traditions behind them.

Bentley, Gerald E. *Shakespeare: A Biographical Handbook*. New Haven, Conn.: Yale University Press, 1961. The facts about Shakespeare, with virtually no conjecture intermingled.

Bush, Geoffrey. *Shakespeare and the Natural Condition*. Cambridge, Mass.: Harvard University Press, 1956. A short, sensitive account of Shakespeare's view of "Nature," touching most of the works.

Chambers, E. K. *William Shakespeare: A Study of Facts and Problems*. 2 vols. London: Oxford University Press, 1930. An invaluable, detailed reference work; not for the casual reader.

Chute, Marchette. *Shakespeare of London*. New York: Dutton, 1949. A readable biography fused with portraits of Stratford and London life.

Clemen, Wolfgang H. *The Development of Shakespeare's Imagery*. Cambridge, Mass.: Harvard University Press, 1951. (Originally published in German, 1936.) A temperate account of a subject often abused.

Granville-Barker, Harley. *Prefaces to Shakespeare*. 2 vols. Princeton, N.J.: Princeton University Press, 1946–47. Essays on ten plays by a scholarly man of the theater.

Harbage, Alfred. *As They Liked It*. New York: Macmillan, 1947. A long, sensitive essay on Shakespeare, morality, and the audience's expectations.

Kernan, Alvin B., ed. *Modern Shakespearean Criticism: Essays on Style, Dramaturgy, and the Major Plays*. New York: Harcourt Brace Jovanovich, 1970. A collection of major formalist criticism.

————. "The Plays and the Playwrights." In *The Revels History of Drama in English*, general editors Clifford Leech and T. W. Craik. Vol. III. London: Methuen, 1975. A book-length essay surveying Elizabethan drama with substantial discussions of Shakespeare's plays.

Schoenbaum, S. *Shakespeare's Lives*. Oxford: Clarendon Press, 1970. A review of the evidence, and an examination of many biographies, including those by Baconians and other heretics.

————. *William Shakespeare: A Compact Documentary Life*. New York: Oxford University Press, 1977. A readable presentation of all that the documents tell us about Shakespeare.

Traversi, D. A. *An Approach to Shakespeare*. 3rd rev. ed. 2 vols. New York: Doubleday, 1968–69. An analysis of the plays beginning with words, images, and themes, rather than with characters.

Van Doren, Mark. *Shakespeare*. New York: Holt, 1939. Brief, perceptive readings of all of the plays.

3. Shakespeare's Theater

Beckerman, Bernard. *Shakespeare at the Globe, 1599–1609*. New York: Macmillan, 1962. On the playhouse and on Elizabethan dramaturgy, acting, and staging.

Chambers, E. K. *The Elizabethan Stage*. 4 vols. New York: Oxford University Press, 1945. A major reference work on theaters, theatrical companies, and staging at court.

Cook, Ann Jennalie. *The Privileged Playgoers of Shakespeare's London, 1576–1642*. Princeton, N.J.: Princeton University Press, 1981. Sees Shakespeare's audience as more middle-class and more intellectual than Harbage (below) does.

Gurr, Andrew. *The Shakespearean Stage: 1579–1642*. 2d edition. Cambridge: Cambridge University Press, 1980. On the acting companies, the actors, the playhouses, the stages, and the audiences.

Harbage, Alfred. *Shakespeare's Audience*. New York: Columbia University Press, 1941. A study of the size and nature of the theatrical public, emphasizing its representativeness.

Hodges, C. Walter. *The Globe Restored*. London: Ernest Benn, 1953. A well-illustrated and readable attempt to reconstruct the Globe Theatre.

Hosley, Richard. "The Playhouses." In *The Revels History of Drama in English*, general editors Clifford Leech and T. W. Craik. Vol. III. London: Methuen, 1975. An essay of one hundred pages on the physical aspects of the playhouses.

Kernodle, George R. *From Art to Theatre: Form and Convention in the Renaissance*. Chicago: University of Chicago Press, 1944. Pioneering and stimulating work on the symbolic and cultural meanings of theater construction.

Nagler, A. M. *Shakespeare's Stage*. Trans. Ralph Manheim. New Haven, Conn.: Yale University Press, 1958. A very brief introduction to the physical aspects of the playhouse.

Slater, Ann Pasternak. *Shakespeare the Director*. Totowa, N.J.: Barnes & Noble, 1982. An analysis of theatrical ef-

fects (e.g., kissing, kneeling) in stage directions and dialogue.

Thomson, Peter. *Shakespeare's Theatre*. London: Routledge
and Kegan Paul, 1983. A discussion of how plays were
staged in Shakespeare's time.

4. Miscellaneous Reference Works

Abbott, E. A. *A Shakespearean Grammar*. New Edition. New
York: Macmillan, 1877. An examination of differences between Elizabethan and modern grammar.

Bevington, David. *Shakespeare*. Arlington Heights, Ill.: A. H.
M. Publishing, 1978. A short guide to hundreds of important writings on the works.

Bullough, Geoffrey. *Narrative and Dramatic Sources of
Shakespeare*. 8 vols. New York: Columbia University
Press, 1957–75. A collection of many of the books Shake-
speare drew upon, with judicious comments.

Campbell, Oscar James, and Edward G. Quinn. *The Reader's
Encyclopedia of Shakespeare*. New York: Crowell, 1966.
More than 2,600 entries, from a few sentences to a few
pages, on everything related to Shakespeare.

Greg, W. W. *The Shakespeare First Folio*. New York: Oxford
University Press, 1955. A detailed yet readable history of
the first collection (1623) of Shakespeare's plays.

Kökeritz, Helge. *Shakespeare's Names*. New Haven, Conn.:
Yale University Press, 1959. A guide to the pronunciation
of some 1,800 names appearing in Shakespeare.

———. *Shakespeare's Pronunciation*. New Haven, Conn.:
Yale University Press, 1953. Contains much information
about puns and rhymes.

Muir, Kenneth. *The Sources of Shakespeare's Plays*. New
Haven, Conn.: Yale University Press, 1978. An account of
Shakespeare's use of his reading.

The Norton Facsimile: The First Folio of Shakespeare. Prepared by Charlton Hinman. New York: Norton, 1968. A
handsome and accurate facsimile of the first collection
(1623) of Shakespeare's plays.

Onions, C. T. *A Shakespeare Glossary*. 2d ed., rev., with en-
larged addenda. London: Oxford University Press, 1953.
Definitions of words (or senses of words) now obsolete.

Partridge, Eric. *Shakespeare's Bawdy*. Rev. ed. New York:
Dutton, 1955. A glossary of bawdy words and phrases.

Shakespeare Quarterly. See headnote to Suggested References.

Shakespeare Survey. See headnote to Suggested References.

Shakespeare's Plays in Quarto. A Facsimile Edition. Ed. Michael J. B. Allen and Kenneth Muir. Berkeley, Calif.: University of California Press, 1981. A book of nine hundred pages, containing facsimiles of twenty-two of the quarto editions of Shakespeare's plays. An invaluable complement to *The Norton Facsimile: The First Folio of Shakespeare* (see above).

Smith, Gordon Ross. *A Classified Shakespeare Bibliography 1936–1958.* University Park, Pa.: Pennsylvania State University Press, 1963. A list of some twenty thousand items on Shakespeare.

Spevack, Marvin. *The Harvard Concordance to Shakespeare.* Cambridge, Mass.: Harvard University Press, 1973. An index to Shakespeare's words.

Wells, Stanley, ed. *Shakespeare: Select Bibliographies.* London: Oxford University Press, 1973. Seventeen essays surveying scholarship and criticism of Shakespeare's life, work, and theater.

5. *Richard III*

Boyer, Clarence Valentine. *The Villain as Hero in Elizabethan Tragedy.* New York: E. P. Dutton; London: George Routledge and Sons, 1914.

Churchill, George B. *Richard the Third up to Shakespeare.* (*Palaestra,* X) Berlin: Mayer and Müller, 1900.

Clemen, Wolfgang. *A Commentary on Shakespeare's "Richard III,"* trans. Jean Bonheim. London: Methuen, 1968.

Driver, Tom F. *The Sense of History in Greek and Shakespearean Drama.* New York: Columbia University Press, 1960.

Kendall, Paul Murray. *Richard the Third.* London: George Allen & Unwin Ltd., 1955; New York: W. W. Norton & Company, Inc., 1956. (The best biography and defense of Richard.)

Krieger, Murray. "The Dark Generations of *Richard III,*" *Criticism,* I (1959), 32–48.

More, Sir Thomas. *The History of King Richard III,* ed. Richard S. Sylvester. New Haven: Yale University Press, 1963.

Moulton, Richard G. *Shakespeare as a Dramatic Artist.* 3rd ed. London: Oxford University Press, 1901.

Ornstein, Robert. *A Kingdom for a Stage*. Cambridge, Mass.: Harvard University Press, 1972.

Palmer, John. *Political Characters of Shakespeare*. London and New York: The Macmillan Company, 1945, 1946.

Ribner, Irving. *The English History Play in the Age of Shakespeare*, rev. ed. London: Methuen, 1965; New York: Barnes & Noble, Inc., 1967.

Rossiter, A. P. "The Structure of *Richard III*," *Durham University Journal*, XXXI (1938), 44–75.

Tillyard, E. M. W. *Shakespeare's History Plays*. London: Chatto & Windus Ltd., 1944; New York: The Macmillan Company, 1946.

Wilson, John Dover (ed.). *Richard III*. New York and London: Cambridge University Press, 1954.

Wood, Alice I. Perry. *The Stage History of Shakespeare's "King Richard the Third."* New York: Columbia University Press, 1909.